A BLAZE OF SUN

A Shade of Vampire, Book 5

Bella Forrest

ALSO BY BELLA FORREST:

A SHADE OF VAMPIRE SERIES:

Derek & Sofia's story:

A Shade of Vampire (Book 1)
A Shade of Blood (Book 2)
A Castle of Sand (Book 3)
A Shadow of Light (Book 4)
A Blaze of Sun (Book 5)
A Gate of Night (Book 6)
A Break of Day (Book 7)

Rose & Caleb's story:

A Shade of Novak (Book 8)
A Bond of Blood (Book 9)
A Spell of Time (Book 10)
A Chase of Prey (Book 11)
A Shade of Doubt (Book 12)
A Turn of Tides (Book 13)
A Dawn of Strength (Book 14)
A Fall of Secrets (Book 15)
An End of Night (Book 16)

The Shade lives on...

A Wind of Change (Book 17)
A Trail of Echoes (Book 18)
A Soldier of Shadows (Book 19)

A SHADE OF KIEV TRILOGY:

A Shade of Kiev 1
A Shade of Kiev 2
A Shade of Kiev 3

BEAUTIFUL MONSTER DUOLOGY:

Beautiful Monster 1
Beautiful Monster 2

For an updated list of Bella's books,
please visit www.bellaforrest.net

DEDICATION

Dear Shaddict, thank you for your loyalty to Derek and Sofia, and for sticking with them this far on their journey.

Contents

PROLOGUE: EMILIA

I pulled the thick fur-lined coat over my body as I took the final step on the winding stairway that led up to the Elder's castle—The Blood Keep, he liked to call it. I shuddered at the thought of entering the castle, carrying upon my shoulders the weight of my failure.

Before I could reach out and open the steel doors, they swung open and I found myself face to face with my older brother, Kiev. He had a triumphant smirk on his face as he eyed me from head to foot.

"You reek of failure, little sis." He tilted his head to the side. "Aren't you supposed to be here with Sofia Claremont?"

Annoyed, I tried to side-step him and rush to my chambers. I wanted to recuperate before having to face the wrath of our master, our father, the one who had sired me—the very first vampire this world had known. Of course, I should've expected that my sibling wasn't going to make it that easy for me.

"Get out of my way, Kiev," I snapped at him, "or I swear I'm going to cast a spell on you."

"Really, now?" He narrowed his eyes at me. "Do you remember the last time you tried that, Emilia?"

I shuddered at the memory of the punishment I'd had to endure under my father's hands, but I stared Kiev down. "It will be worth the pain... to see you croaking around the castle like the frog that you are."

At that, Kiev backed down. I might've been the youngest among those the Elder had sired, but that didn't mean that I couldn't intimidate my other siblings.

I walked past him and headed for my bedroom only to bump into my sister, Clara, just before I reached my door. The beautiful brunette chuckled at the sight of me, her purple eyes sparkling.

"You are in so much trouble."

I grunted, hating the fact that they were finding so much entertainment at my expense. All six of us were always fighting one another to get into our father's good graces. I thought the Elder liked it that way.

This time, I wasn't about to get any favors from him. He had sent me to The Shade, an island occupied by one of the most powerful covens on earth, led by the man the Elder had promised would become mine—Derek Novak. My mission had been to steal Sofia Claremont away from him.

Sofia Claremont was an immune, a young woman who had somehow conquered the vampire curse. Several vampires had already tried to turn her—Derek Novak included—but she hadn't turned. The Elder was obsessed with gathering all immunes and holding them in his Keep. In fact, I wasn't sure if there was a single human in his territory who wasn't immune.

Upon reaching my bedroom, I found one of the human slaves inside, tidying the place up for my arrival. The moment I laid eyes on him, I attacked, pushing him toward the four-poster bed in the middle of the room and biting into his neck. I grinned even as the immune's sweet blood coursed through my body, giving me an immense sense of power as I preyed on the weakling beneath me.

Images of Sofia Claremont and how she'd clung to Derek flashed through my mind. I anticipated the day she would take the place of the young man beneath me, the day when I could treat her as what she really was—sustenance for my kind.

The boy beneath me was growing pale and if I didn't stop soon, I would end his life. I didn't care. I wanted his blood and the power that came with it. I didn't want to feel powerless when I came face to face with the Elder. I simply couldn't afford that. I drank deep and by the time I was done, all life had seeped away from the human slave.

Finally satiated, I sat up and got off the corpse. I rolled it off my bed and onto the floor before heaving a deep sigh. I stretched my neck and headed for the closet to change my clothes.

I had just stripped to my underwear when a cold breeze swept through the room. I shuddered as I felt a sense of fear. That fear always crept into my bones whenever I was in the presence of darkness.

"Emilia, Emilia, Emilia." The familiar deep voice spoke from behind me.

I swallowed hard. It was never a good sign when he said my name three times in a row.

"I was expecting you in the Grand Hall to present Sofia

Claremont—dead or alive. And yet here you are, feeding on one of my humans and hiding out in your room."

"I apologize, Master." He never wanted us to address him as our father, even though he referred to us as his children. He was our lord and we were to refer to him with reverence. "I merely wanted to prepare before presenting myself before you."

His cold hand gripped the back of my neck. With it came that strange and familiar feeling—as if I was absorbing his very essence, his wicked darkness.

"What happened, Emilia? Why did you fail?"

It was Borys Maslen's fault. We should've just gone in there, taken Sofia and left, but no... He was a weakling who died at the hands of two women. I still couldn't believe that Sofia and Derek's sister Vivienne had ended Borys' life even after the Elder had given him all that newfound power. But I knew full well that the Elder would not like it if I started playing the blame game.

"I didn't realize what a powerful force we were up against, Master." I once again recalled Sofia and the way Derek looked at her. What I would've given to have him look at me that way. "She glows with light and she's gotten to him."

"Would he have been able to kill you?"

"I think he was powerful enough, yes. When it comes to brute strength, even I don't stand a chance against him."

"You don't stand a chance against him, not because of brute strength, Emilia, and we both know it." The Elder ran his hand over my hair, his breath cold against the back of my neck. I was shaking. His closeness always terrified me. "You don't stand a chance against Derek Novak because you can't stand the idea of seeing him die. He was and will always be your greatest weakness."

I couldn't respond, because it was true. I was deeply in love with the vampire, something he didn't seem to give a damn about, and yet I hung on to my unrequited love. I ground my teeth. *That's about to change.*

"Did he see you, Emilia?"

Despite the terror the Elder's presence brought about, I couldn't help but steal a smile at the recollection of how Derek's deep blue eyes had flickered with attraction and interest when he'd first laid eyes on me back in The Shade. "Yes, Master. He did."

"Did he like what he saw?"

I bowed my head as the Elder's hand fell to my waist. "How could he not?" The Elder had made me everything that Derek found physically attractive in a woman. I no longer looked the way I had when Derek had broken my heart so long ago. I was irresistible to him now, and I intended to play up that advantage as much as I could.

I was still mulling over my obsession with the king of The Shade when the Elder grabbed a fistful of my hair. I gasped, shocked by the agony.

"I don't like failure, Emilia," he hissed. "Next time, you mustn't fail."

"Of course, Master," I rasped out. "I won't fail."

"You are to return to The Shade, Emilia. I don't want you staying up here, stinking up my castle with your failure. This little spitfire of a human has Derek Novak wrapped around her pretty little finger. We can't have that. He is too powerful a force to let the light have him. We have you to thank for that, don't we, Emilia? Well, you need to fix this. We need to pull him back into the dark. You're going to do that."

"What exactly do you want me to do, Master?"

His fist tightened against my hairline. "Bring on the attack of the covens. Lead it."

The Elder had managed to get all of the other vampire covens to ally against Derek and The Shade. They had no idea the Elder was behind all of it, of course, working behind the scenes, pulling the strings. They'd long been threatening to attack the island and destroy it—something Derek had been desperate to prevent.

The idea of destroying The Shade wasn't one I was fond of, but there was no defying the Elder. "Consider this victory ours, Master. We *will* win."

"No, Emilia. You won't. I want you to lose this battle and I want you to be taken prisoner by Derek Novak."

His plan took form in my mind and I nodded as I grasped what he was attempting to do. "I understand. And Sofia Claremont?"

He finally let go of my hair. "We will end her."

With that, his presence swept out of the room like a wind, the same way he'd arrived.

Once he was gone, I fell to my knees. I was a fool to try to convince myself that he was gone. I'd given myself to him a long time ago and he was a part of me that I could never escape.

The Elder was always with me.

The original vampire. My Master. My father. A creature I had never once laid eyes on.

Chapter 1: Sofia

The moment I opened my eyes to the dim candlelight of my bedroom, I couldn't help but groan. I turned to my side to check if Derek was beside me. He wasn't. He hadn't come to my room or called me into his for the past week. Another reason to groan.

I thought about the day ahead of me and felt like staying in bed forever. But I knew that I didn't have a choice. I dragged myself out of bed and started getting ready. Finally satisfied with my appearance, I stepped out of my bedroom and found breakfast already on the dining table.

I smiled wryly. *Breakfast. Only here in The Shade could you have breakfast in the dark of the night.* I popped a handful of vitamin pills into my mouth and took a seat at the table. I made a mental note to thank Rosa and Lily for the lovely breakfast they had prepared.

I was sharing my quarters with Rosa, Lily and her children—

seventeen-year-old Gavin, seven-year-old Robb, and five-year-old Madeline—and Ian and Anna. None of them were at home; they were hard at work already. Idleness wasn't a welcome trait in The Shade—in The Catacombs, even less so.

Derek had recently assigned me my own team focused on keeping order among the human population of the island. This team walked into my quarters just as I was about to have my first bite of toast. Ian and Gavin stepped into the room, followed by one of Derek's guards, Kyle. They all took a seat around the table.

"Looks like we've got lots to discuss," Gavin announced as he leaned back in his chair and ran a hand through his red hair.

Ian glared at Kyle before looking at me. "What is he doing here?" He pointed at the vampire.

"Kyle has expressed interest in helping us here at The Catacombs and Derek gave him permission." I put down my food, despite the fact that my stomach was growling. "Shall we start?"

The men nodded at me.

"We can't afford to still be fighting amongst ourselves once the covens attack. The riots have got to stop." There'd been a lot of dissent within The Catacombs over the past weeks. The humans had become restless after the vampires' blood supply had been blown up. What I couldn't wrap my mind around was why they were at each other's throats over this matter while the vampires were the ones attempting to find a solution. "When was the last time a vampire attacked one of The Catacombs' citizens?"

Gavin and Ian exchanged glances.

Ian shrugged, scratching his black hair. "There have been attempts... but I can't remember when one was actually attacked."

"So why are the Naturals still going crazy?"

Ian shifted uncomfortably in his seat. "You have to understand,

Sofia, that it's always been this way. There never was order here in The Catacombs. Every day was a fight to survive—if not against the vampires, against your fellow humans. The law of The Shade has always been survival of the fittest until you came along."

"Well, that's a problem we have to solve. We need human cooperation during the war."

"We can't even get the Naturals to work together amongst themselves. How on earth are we going to get them to work with the vampires?" Ian frowned.

"We could just draft all the male population by force," Kyle suggested with a shrug. "Derek did that to the vampires."

"Sending humans off to battle with vampires is sending them to their deaths," Ian snapped. "Are you mad?"

"Well, it's not like we're expecting the humans to face vampires. No matter what they're assigned to do, they're still going to need to know how to defend themselves."

"I don't think getting the humans to do anything by force is a good idea." I shook my head. "It will only create more trouble in the long run."

"Well, then, it's not looking good, Sofia." Gavin spoke up. "Most of the humans are seeing this as a chance to escape The Shade and finally be free."

I was surprised by that notion. "That's foolish. They're either going to end up dead or as slaves of the other covens. I doubt the other covens will be as benevolent as Derek has been."

Ian scoffed. Knowing him as someone who always spoke his mind, I wasn't surprised by the words that came out of his mouth: "As much as I know you love him, Sofia, benevolent isn't exactly how most of the people at The Catacombs would describe Derek."

It was my turn to scoff. "I've known more vampires outside of

The Shade than most humans here at The Catacombs. Believe me when I say that Derek is as benevolent as it gets for vampires. Take it or leave it."

To that, no one could object. I was beginning to find the silence awkward, so I was thankful when Kyle broke it.

"Before we can even talk to the humans about joining a war, I think we first need to find a way to establish some sort of order here at The Catacombs, because let's face it, it's been anarchy. Derek tried to figure out what the humans wanted by calling the general assembly at The Vale, but with the vampire rebellion, that didn't push through."

I nodded, remembering how the vampires had split into two factions—one loyal to Derek, the other to his father, Gregor. Since Gregor's mysterious and untimely death, the vampire rebellion—as Kyle called it—had been quelled.

"Well, there's no rebellion now," I said. "I guess it's time we call another general assembly and figure out what the people at The Catacombs want. I'm putting you three in charge of that. If you come across any problems, let me know."

All three of them grinned.

"What?" I asked.

"Is it just me or is Derek Novak's bossiness rubbing off on you?" Gavin squinted an eye at me. Ian and Kyle were chuckling.

"It's not just you, man." Kyle shook his head. "She wasn't this bossy when she first arrived here. She's definitely getting a lot of Derek into her personality."

I rolled my eyes. "Whatever," I mumbled before finally digging in to my breakfast. They bade me goodbye and left me to eat in peace.

I enjoyed the silence and the solitude, but it also made me sense

Derek's absence a lot more keenly. We hadn't been spending much time together and I couldn't help but miss him. I kept telling myself that he had a lot on his plate, that he was the king of the island, responsible for keeping the whole place together. *That's a good excuse to not spend time with his fiancée, is it not?* Still, I wanted to be with him, but knowing that there wasn't anything I could do about it, I finished my breakfast and hoped that I could spend some time alone with him later that day.

After I put away the dishes, I headed to The Cells, where my father was still being kept captive. Aiden was famous in the vampire world as Reuben, one of the most ruthless and notorious hunters alive.

To say that my father was unhappy about me being in love with a vampire was a huge understatement, but then so was he... After all, my mother was now Ingrid Maslen.

Aiden was doing push-ups when I stepped into his cell. For a man well into his forties, he was still extremely fit and worked at remaining so. I waited for him to finish his set before clearing my throat.

He didn't even bother looking up to see who his visitor was. "How long are they going to keep me here, Sofia?"

"I don't know. I haven't talked to Derek about you yet."

Aiden had ended up in The Shade after he'd fooled me into believing that the hunters had found a cure to turn vampires back into humans. I'd been disappointed to find out that it was all a ruse. When he'd been forced to reveal that there was no cure, he'd ended up in prison.

"The hunters will come for me, Sofia. I'm too important to the organization for them to just forget about my disappearance. The longer you keep me here, the longer you're putting the island in danger."

I knew he was bluffing, so I just stared at him. "They won't know how to get here, Aiden. Your tracker was disabled by Corrine's spell the moment you came within the boundaries of The Shade. You know that. Besides, isn't it hunter protocol to consider anyone caught by vampires dead?"

A muscle in his face twitched. He heaved a deep sigh and sat on the edge of his couch, tapping the space beside him to encourage me to sit.

Despite my apprehensions, I took a seat beside him and we sat in silence for a while before he broke it.

"I'm sorry, Sofia."

I hadn't been expecting an apology. Not from him. I'd been putting off seeing him for days because I felt betrayed. Right after I'd thought we were becoming closer to each other and forming a bond as father and daughter, he'd betrayed me. He knew that I wanted to find a cure to turn vampires back into humans and he'd used that desire against me. I had no idea how to even begin forgiving him for that, and yet I found myself nodding and saying, "I understand why you did it."

"I was doing what I thought I needed to do to get this idea out of your system. You have to accept there is no cure."

I shook my head, refusing to accept what he was saying as truth. "No. There is a cure. I'm going to find it."

His face turned grim. "Stubborn," he muttered. "Just like your mother."

I remembered the last time I saw Ingrid. She'd been looking at me with so much hatred. I had just killed the man who'd turned her into a vampire—Borys Maslen. She was loyal to him above all—a loyalty that transcended even her love for her husband and her daughter.

I shook my head as I stood up and motioned to leave. Before the guard could open the door for me, I turned back to my father. "I am nothing like Ingrid."

I left his cell with a heaviness in my heart. I wasn't sure why, but I felt an overwhelming sense of loss. Perhaps it was just the recent events catching up with me—all the deaths that The Shade had suffered, losing not just my foes, but also people I cared about. Whatever the reason, I couldn't just sit around sulking, so I picked myself up and moved on with my tasks for the day. I headed to meet with two of the most intelligent people in The Shade—the island's resident genius, Eli Lazaroff, and Corrine, The Shade's witch.

The challenge that Derek had placed upon me when we last spoke of the cure weighed heavily on my shoulders. He was prophesied to be the man who would bring the vampires to "true sanctuary." I, on the other hand, was believed to be the woman who would help him do it.

I believed with all my heart that the cure was "true sanctuary." Derek had already lost hope that the cure could even be possible. His words still rang in my ears.

"Don't ask me what true sanctuary is, Sofia. I fought for it for an entire century, practically gave up my soul for it. I thought I already had sanctuary after establishing The Shade, only to find out that I didn't... I just don't understand the prophecy. What I do know is that war is brewing. That's what's going to happen."

"So that's it? More bloodshed?"

"Did you think there was ever any other way?"

Eli and Corrine were supposed to help me discover if a cure could even be possible. Our meeting proved fruitless, with Eli and

Corrine scouring what resources they had to find any indication of the possibility of a cure and the existence of immunes like me. Immunes were humans who couldn't be turned into vampires—for reasons no one knew about. In The Shade, aside from me, there was one other immune. Anna.

I made a mental note to speak with Ian and Kyle about her. The two men had taken it upon themselves to look after the young woman's well-being. Hence the tension between them.

The cure was still on my mind, along with everything else going on in The Shade, when I returned to The Catacombs to have my midday meal. Over the past days, I'd found myself looking forward to spending this time with Rosa and Ashley.

Rosa and Ashley had been abducted and taken to The Shade the same time I was. Along with two other girls, Gwen and Paige, who had met their demise on the island, we'd been given to Derek as his harem when he had just woken up from a four-hundred-year sleep. Because of this history, we'd formed a strong bond.

"I am so exhausted," Ashley complained as she leaned back in her seat and laid down her glass of animal blood. "Derek has been putting us through hell in military training." She shot me a look. "Can you talk him into being a bit more lax? Every bone in my body hurts."

I grinned. "I am not going to interfere with that," I said, throwing my hands up in surrender.

"What good is it that the ruler of this island is in love with you if you don't use your connection to help your friends out?"

I rolled my eyes at her and directed my attention toward the more soft-spoken Rosa. "What have you been busy with today, Rosa?"

"The usual." She shrugged. "Lily and I have been doing our

rounds here at The Catacombs. We really need to do something about those who are sick, Sofia. Also, there are a lot of orphans who need care. Isn't it about time that we get both a hospital and an orphanage here in The Shade?"

"*That* is something we ought to mention at the general assembly." I wasn't blind to all that had to be done at The Catacombs, but due to the incoming war, thinking about all of it at once felt overwhelming. "Gavin, Ian and Kyle are working it out right now."

"Kyle?" Ashley narrowed her eyes at me. Kyle was the one who had turned her into a vampire, so technically, she was part of his clan. "Why Kyle? Isn't he supposed to be preparing for the war?"

"Derek allowed him to focus on the humans upon his request."

Ashley scowled. "Looks like he's enamored with Anna."

"You have a problem with that?" I asked, surprised.

"I don't know. I guess I have to support whatever makes Kyle happy, but Anna... I don't know. She's kind of messed up."

I was hurt by that. Ashley had every reason to make the comment, considering how Anna had lost her mind from trauma and acted like a child, but my heart went out to the girl. Perhaps I held Anna close to my heart because she was the only other immune I knew.

I didn't go into that with Ashley though. For some reason, I didn't like talking to them about the cure or being an immune. Those topics were too heavy, too close to heart, and the time I spent with Ashley and Rosa were times in my day when I could just relax, chat and laugh with them.

With them I could still feel like an eighteen-year-old. Lunch with Ashley and Rosa gave me a sense of normalcy, a rare commodity in a place like The Shade.

I hated that lunch had to end. "Lunch was lovely, Rosa. You really are a great cook."

Rosa smiled. "Thanks, Sofia."

Ashley wrinkled her nose as she stared at the animal blood she'd just finished drinking. "I miss eating food. Pizza in particular. Don't get me wrong, mozzarella and pepperoni don't satisfy me as much as human blood, but considering that we're on a strict animal blood diet, I keep craving." She grinned as she eyed both my and Rosa's necks.

"I don't think Derek would be happy sharing my blood with you," I told her with a grin.

Ashley turned her eyes toward Rosa, who just smiled sweetly in response. "You could never do that to me, Ash."

"That I believe." I nodded. Ashley had the tendency to be protective of Rosa, perhaps because we were all aware what a beauty Rosa was starting to become and it was obvious that more than just one man—human and vampire—found her attractive. I blew out a sigh. "I have to go now. Derek called a Council meeting."

Ashley's eyes lit up with excitement. "Does that mean there won't be any training this afternoon?"

I chuckled. "I doubt it. I'm pretty sure he's going to send either Xavier or Cameron to take over."

I rose to my feet as Ashley's face fell in disappointment. She mumbled that Xavier and Cameron were just as harsh as Derek when it came to training. I tuned out the complaints as I began to feel excitement at the prospect of seeing Derek.

At the Council meeting, Derek sat at the head of the table. I took my seat on his right side, his twin sister, Vivienne, sitting across from me. Derek merely glanced my way before clearing his throat and calling the meeting to order.

I swallowed back the disappointment as we began to discuss the war and all the other issues that seemed to be mounting in The Shade. I reported on the situation at The Catacombs and what we were doing about it. The meeting lasted several hours and by the time it was over, I felt exhausted. I couldn't help but sigh with relief when Derek finally dismissed us all.

I waited for everyone to leave, patiently standing by as the others had their final words with Derek, before approaching him.

When our eyes met, he gave me a tired smile.

"Exhausted?" I asked him.

"More than I can explain."

"I miss you."

His bright blue eyes softened as he brushed his fingers through my hair. I stared up at him, admiring him. The dark hair, the blue eyes, the pale skin and tall, lean, muscled physique... I never quite got used to how attractive he was or how small I felt whenever I was standing next to him.

His large hands engulfed my waist as he pulled me closer. His lips pressed against my forehead. "I'm sorry it has to be this way, Sofia. I hate that we can't spend as much time together as we did before."

I wanted to assure him that it was all right, that I understood that he was under a lot of pressure, but at that moment, I felt a possessiveness toward him that I had never felt before. *Since when were you so selfish with Derek, Sofia?*

I was so sick of all the tension and all the drama. Normal eighteen-year-olds were busy filling out college applications, moving into their dormitories, falling in and out of love. I was trying to figure out how to support a monarch in running his kingdom. And he wasn't just any monarch. He was a vampire. Of course, I couldn't blame anyone but myself for the mess I'd gotten myself entangled in. *It's not like anybody forced you to fall in love with a five-hundred-year-old king in an eighteen-year-old's body.*

"What's going through your mind, Sofia?" he asked.

"A lot," I admitted. "I've been finding it hard to cope."

He tensed at my admission. "It's unfair, the pressure I'm putting on you with all the responsibilities that shouldn't be yours in the first place."

I frowned. "I'm not complaining, Derek. I can handle it all. I just… I miss laughing with you. I miss seeing you smile. I miss trying to teach you to use a phone or how to drive." I chuckled at the fond memories. "I miss us."

The sadness on his face broke my heart. "I know. I miss us too," he admitted.

I was waiting for him to promise that things would change, but no. It dawned on me how unsure Derek was about the future. He no longer had the confidence that inspired him to fulfill his prophecy. I saw behind his eyes anxiety and self-doubt.

I grabbed his arm, my brows furrowing, as I studied the expression on his face. *Something's wrong…* He looked away. Had I not been so tired, I would've pried, but I wasn't sure I wanted to know. "We're both obviously tired." I smiled bitterly. "Maybe it's best we retire to our quarters and have a good night's rest."

"I love you, Sofia."

His proclamation didn't move me the way it used to and that bothered me. I couldn't bear to look at him even as I nodded. "I know. I love you too."

I felt empty as I returned to The Catacombs, escorted by Ashley and her boyfriend, Sam, whom Derek had asked to get me home safely. I hated that he didn't do it himself. There was a time when he would've done it no matter how tired he was.

My two companions were both bantering all the way to the caves, but I remained silent, lost in thought.

A deep sense of loneliness and abandonment took over me. I shivered against the cold night breeze and tasted the scent of the pine trees. I was so consumed, I barely gave Sam and Ashley a response when they bade me goodbye.

I dragged myself through the routine of getting myself ready for bed. Everything about The Shade had begun to feel exactly like that—routine—and I was weary of it all. I had just climbed into my bed wearing a silk nightgown when the door creaked open. I lifted my head and drew a breath when Derek closed the door behind him.

"Derek?" I said, wondering what could've brought him to my chambers. Despite my surprise, my heart leapt. I longed to be in his embrace.

However, when I saw the stare he was giving me, I realized why he'd come. His Adam's apple moved as he gulped at the sight of me. *He's craving.*

I knelt up on the bed and forced a smile as I pulled my long red locks away from my neck. He didn't hesitate. The moment my neck was exposed to him, he sped toward me and sank his teeth into my skin.

I bit my lip at the pain, but I was already so used to it. As I sat there waiting for my fiancé to have his fill of my blood, I couldn't help but wonder.

What has become of us?

Chapter 2: Derek

Her laughter was contagious as she held my hand. Her long, auburn hair was up in a bun, strands falling down her lovely face. We were at a beach and the sun was shining on both of us, our wet bodies glistening as we took a walk along the shore.

Sofia had a huge smile on her face, one that I'd missed.

"Let's make a sandcastle, Derek," she suggested.

"What for?" I asked. "No matter how beautiful a sandcastle is, the ocean swallows it up and ruins it."

She rolled her eyes at me as she wrapped her arms around my waist. "Because beautiful things, even when they are temporary, still leave a part of their beauty with you... even after they're long gone."

I narrowed my eyes at her. "What does that mean?"

"Keep the sandcastle in a memory, Derek, and it will remain with you long after the ocean destroys it." Her green eyes were twinkling with delight. "So? Make a sandcastle with me?"

"How can I resist?" I grinned.

"Perfect!" She skipped all the way to the spot of her choice. My ray of sunshine, a sweet reminder of what it was like to be carefree and full of mirth... We began building the sandcastle, with me stealing glances at her, admiring her beauty, loving it when she peered at me from beneath those long lashes of hers.

It seemed only a couple of minutes before she leaped to her feet and announced, *"We're done!"*

I creased my brows in surprise as I looked at the sandcastle. I gasped. A vortex had formed within the sandcastle, sucking me in until I found myself inside it. I looked around for Sofia and was disappointed when I couldn't find her. My disappointment, however, was short-lived, because I saw her.

I knew I'd seen her before, but I couldn't remember her name. All I knew was that the mere sight of her took my breath away. She was the embodiment of a perfect woman.

Long, wavy hazel brown hair and deep violet eyes... A curvy, slender form... Tall with legs that went on forever... She was stunningly beautiful as she stood in the middle of a lake right outside the sandcastle.

She smiled at me and lifted her hand, coaxing me to go to her. I found myself drawn to her, as if she were a siren.

"Come," she whispered, her voice like music to my ears.

I didn't even hesitate. I just stepped into the lake and began walking through it toward her. I was so focused on getting to her, I barely even thought about the water.

"You belong with me, Derek," she whispered into my ear the moment I reached her.

"No." I shook my head, Sofia's laughter echoing in my ears. *"I belong to someone else."*

"Who?"

I sought for a name and couldn't remember one. "I can't remember just now, but it's not you."

"How are you so sure that it's not me if you can't remember?"

I narrowed my eyes at her, taken by her beauty. "I guess I'm not so sure."

"Yes. You're not. We belong together. You and I."

I nodded, but it didn't feel right. When her lips pressed against mine, my own voice echoed in my mind. What are you doing, Derek? You don't belong with her. You are being an absolute fool.

When my eyes shot open, it took me a while to take in my surroundings. I creased my brows even as my lips still tingled from the kiss I'd shared with the woman in the dream. I turned to my side and the sight that greeted me made me feel even worse. *Your dream is right, Derek. You're an absolute fool.*

Lying next to me was Sofia, sleeping peacefully, unaware of the inner turmoil I was going through. Despite the guilt I felt over betraying her through a dream, I couldn't help but smile at how beautiful she looked. I brushed her auburn hair away from her face so I could take a better look. That was when I noticed the fresh bite mark on her neck and remembered what I'd done to her the night before.

After she expressed how much she missed what we'd had together, I showed up in her chambers demanding her blood. My stomach clenched. *She doesn't deserve this, Novak. What are you doing to her?*

I rolled on my back and stared up at the ceiling, succumbing to some serious self-loathing.

I remembered when I'd cared so much about Sofia that even entertaining the idea of drinking her blood had made me feel sick, but now it'd become a norm between us. There were times when I didn't even bother to ask her anymore. I just took what wasn't mine, taking advantage of the knowledge that she would willingly give what I was asking for.

Lost in my own thoughts, I didn't realize that she'd already woken until her side of the bed shifted as she got up. No words were spoken as she set about rummaging through her closet and picking out an outfit. I knew that she was aware that my eyes were on her, but she ignored me. She made her way to the bathroom and the shower started running.

"Great," I mumbled as I sat on the edge of the bed. "As if there aren't enough wars threatening us, Sofia declares cold war on me."

It felt like forever before she emerged from the bathroom, already dressed. Her eyes widened when she saw me still sitting on her bed.

"You're still here?" she asked. "Don't you have a kingdom to run?"

I didn't miss the ice in her words. "Sofia, about last night... I'm sorry. I was tired and it's been a while since I had your blood and I couldn't get it off my mind..." My excuses sounded lame even to me.

"Yes. I know. I understand." She turned her back on me and stood in front of the vanity mirror, getting ready to fix up her hair and do her makeup.

I knew from her reaction that I had a lot of making up to do.

I thought about everything that I had to do that day, and concluded that spending time with Sofia was far more important. I rose to my feet and approached her. I held her waist and kissed the back of her neck, breathing in her intoxicating scent.

"You love me, Sofia," I reminded her, a smile creeping onto my face. "I've been a fool, but you still love me."

She pouted and rolled her eyes. "Ugh, don't remind me."

I chuckled as I began to rock her from side to side. "I shouldn't have done what I did last night. Let me make it up to you."

"Do you even have time to make it up to me?"

"You're not going to make this easy for me, are you?"

She twisted around and I was surprised when she stood on tiptoes and pressed her lips against mine. It'd been a while since we last kissed and I ached to once again feel her soft, full lips against mine, reveling in the taste of her tongue invading my mouth. Any tingling afterthoughts about the girl in my dream were completely overpowered by Sofia's kiss.

I lifted Sofia up against me as I returned the kiss, my hand finding the back of her head, my fingers entangled in her hair as my arm wrapped around her waist to keep her close.

I was so caught up in that kiss, I couldn't help but gasp when she pulled her mouth away from mine. A smile formed on her face. She pinched my nose.

"We're sooooo serious," she exclaimed, before blowing up her cheeks and crossing her eyes.

I was so taken aback I couldn't even find a valid reaction, but it reminded me of why Sofia was such a breath of fresh air. She had a way of making even the heaviest of situations feel lighter. After everything she'd been through in The Shade and even outside of it, after multiple vampires had threatened to kill her, she still managed to pick herself up and find a reason to smile.

It was like nothing could break her—not completely, at least.

Her face softened when she realized how intently I was studying her. "Smile for me, Derek Novak," she pleaded, as she wrapped her arms around my neck and gave me a quick peck on the lips. "Come on. I know the world is crashing down around you, but this moment is ours. This one moment... I want to see you smile."

I was fascinated by her. "How do you do it, Sofia?"

"Do what?"

"Not hold grudges? It's like you're immune from it. How do you forgive so easily?"

I wished I hadn't asked the question, because a frown marred her beautiful face. She gestured for me to put her back on the ground. I let her slip through my arms, holding her until her feet were planted on the floor.

She wet her lips and forced a smile. "I'm not completely grudge-free, you know. I visited Aiden yesterday. I don't know why it's so hard for me to forgive him, but it is. He's broken my heart so many times, and he's not supposed to. He's my father. Maybe that's why it's so hard." She heaved a sigh and mulled over that thought for a few moments before seeming to decide that she'd had enough of the melancholy. "You, on the other hand... there's something about you, Derek Novak, that makes it easy for me forgive and forget your numerous offenses against me. What is it about you?"

I raised a brow at her, unable to keep the grin from forming on my lips. "I think it's the charm. You can't resist my charm."

She pouted and shook her head. "No." She grabbed the front of my shirt and pulled it upward so she could look at my stomach. "I'm pretty sure it's your abs. Yeah... definitely those abs."

"I knew it. You just want me for my body."

She let go of my shirt and nodded. "I was wondering when you would figure that out. Good thing you're too in love with me to care."

I couldn't keep the smile from my face. "I missed this, Sofia." I couldn't remember the last time I'd exchanged light-hearted banter or even just a laugh with her. I felt like such a fool for being so consumed by the troubles surrounding us.

How could I forget that she's my refuge, that when I'm around her, everything seems to just fade into the background?

She smiled and nodded. "I know. I missed this too, but seriously, Derek…" She drew closer to me and rested her head on my shoulder. "I find it easy to forgive you because from the moment I gave you my heart, you never once broke it."

"And I never will." The words came out instinctively, and I meant every word, but the moment I said

it, an image of the dream I'd just had flashed through my mind. It wasn't the first time I'd dreamed of the beautiful brunette with the stunning violet eyes.

Now I remembered the woman's name. Emilia. She was the original vampire's daughter, and I knew without a doubt that she was trouble. Holding Sofia close, I couldn't help but feel a sense of dread over what the dreams meant. Emilia might be the reason I was distancing myself from Sofia.

I couldn't understand them, but I knew they were lies. Sofia and I belonged together. No dream could ever change that. I wasn't going to allow it.

"I have an idea," I told Sofia. "Let's spend the day together. I'll call everything off."

Delight sparked in her eyes. "Can we do that?"

I shrugged a shoulder. "Why not? I'm the king of The Shade. What could they do to me if I miss a few meetings?"

She was about to respond when someone began pounding on her bedroom door.

"Sofia?" a male voice from behind the door called out. "It's Gavin. Open the door!"

I was annoyed. "Is he always this impatient?"

"Yes." Sofia nodded. "But I think it's mostly because he doesn't know you're here."

Gavin had been like a brother to her since she'd met him in The Shade. There was a time when I'd even been jealous over how close they were. Of course, Sofia had been quick to reassure me that Gavin didn't pose a threat to what we had.

I made my way to the door and pulled it open just as Gavin was about to start banging on it once again. When he saw me, surprise registered in his eyes.

"Oh, it's you. I didn't know you were here." He recovered from his shock and walked right in. "It's good you're here though, because everyone's looking for you."

"What's going on?" Sofia's fists clenched. "What happened?"

"The covens are coming," Gavin said grimly. "It's war."

Chills ran up my spine. This was the moment we'd all been preparing for, and yet now that it had arrived, we were nowhere near prepared.

As I ran off to what felt like death, I forgot to do the most important thing: kiss my fiancée and assure her that everything was going to be all right.

If I hadn't been too busy fearing for the fate of the island, I would've once again heard those familiar words: *You're being an absolute fool, Novak.*

CHAPTER 3: SOFIA

As Derek sped away, my heart ached with disappointment. I wanted to hit myself over the head for being so stupid. We were at war. We could lose our lives any time and I was standing in the middle of that bedroom feeling sorry for myself over missing a date with Derek.

"Sofia." Gavin laid a hand over my shoulder. "Ian, Kyle and I are trying to round up humans from The Catacombs—anyone willing to assist the vampires in defending The Shade. Are you coming with us?"

I was about to nod, but then I caught sight of Vivienne, Derek's twin sister, leaning on my doorpost. I was surprised to see her at a time like this.

Gavin shifted his eyes from me to Vivienne and then back. "I guess that's a no," he said, before rushing out of the room.

My eyes were set on Vivienne. The two of us had come a long

way since the night of my seventeenth birthday when I'd been brought to The Shade. Vivienne had gone from referring to me as Derek's "pawn" to Derek's "queen." There was a time when she had had to transfer some of her memories to me. These memories had been instrumental in reminding her of who she was after the hunters had brainwashed her.

"Vivienne?" I asked, not sure if I was pleased to see her. Vivienne was a seer and she rarely brought good news. "What can I do for you?"

She walked inside my room and sat on the edge of my bed. "I told you that finding the cure is an absolute necessity. Has there been any progress?"

The Shade is falling apart and you came to ask about the cure? "Well, there's no progress whatsoever, Vivienne, but I'm not going to give up..." *What is wrong with you?*

Vivienne took a deep breath. "I am so sick of all this war and bloodshed and revenge. I can't wait until Derek finds true sanctuary. We need that cure."

"Vivienne, you know that The Shade is under attack at this very moment, right?"

She gave me a glance and shrugged a shoulder. "I know."

"Aren't you worried?"

She shook her head. "No, not really."

"Why not?" I asked.

"We're going to win this one."

I knew she was a seer, but I still wasn't able to resist the urge to ask, "How can you be so sure that we're going to win this war?"

She chuckled at my naiveté. "We're going to win this battle, Sofia. Not the war. I'm not sure how the war will end or even if it will end. I do know for certain that the war has just begun, and that the first victory... is ours."

CHAPTER 4: INGRID

I hate her. I hate Sofia.

The image of Borys lying dead on the floor was still fresh in my mind. I had no idea how they'd outsmarted him, but they had and I was to blame. I'd known that Vivienne and Sofia were Borys' greatest weaknesses. He'd been pining for Vivienne for centuries. His obsession with her had only subsided after Sofia had come along.

I'd relied too much on their fear of him and his brute strength. I should've been aware that he would be weak against their manipulations. I should've known.

But it's too late now. He's gone. And while I had my own part in his demise, it's Sofia I ought to blame.

My daughter was a plague I couldn't escape from. She'd taken everything from me and I was determined to make her pay.

I was backed up in a corner of a cot inside their dungeon,

moonlight streaming from the small window above the cell, barred with UV rays. Consumed by my own dark thoughts, I shuddered when a freezing wind began to blow through my cell. The breeze was unlike anything I'd experienced before. I could sense power coming from it and when it hit my skin, it felt as if it were penetrating right through my flesh. I began shivering. *What is going on?*

My eyes darted across the small space surrounding me. I couldn't see anything. Suddenly, I was enveloped by pitch blackness and all the moonlight that had been streaming through the small window disappeared.

"Camilla…"

The hairs on the back of my neck stood up. The voice was Borys', but he'd never called me Camilla. "Who are you?"

"Anybody you want me to be."

I could sense a presence near me, so I began waving my hands in front of me, but I felt nothing. "What do you want? How did you get here?"

"It doesn't matter how I got here, but yes… we must discuss what I want."

Another cold breeze swept through the room and I crashed to the floor, balling up in a fetal position as I sensed the strange presence standing over me. It sank in that I was up against a powerful force. "Please," I begged. "I don't want any trouble."

I didn't know how, but I could sense his dark delight at my surrender.

"Listen to me carefully, Camilla, because I will say this only once. You are never to refer to yourself as Ingrid again. You are to play the part of Camilla Claremont. You will earn back the love of your husband and daughter. You will do everything in your power to get back into their good graces. Do you understand me?"

I wanted to object, but all I could do was nod.

He didn't seem to be convinced, because something hit me on the arm like a whip, burning my skin. I screamed at the pain and began whimpering, afraid that he would hit me once more. "Wh-what are you?"

The response I got was another lash—this time on my thigh, breaking the leather of my pants and burning my skin beneath it. I stifled a scream and bit my lip instead, drawing blood.

"Speak again and there'll be more," he warned, as he watched me shake beneath him.

I could feel his eyes on me, delighting in watching me suffer.

"You have to get it into your head, Camilla, that Borys Maslen is gone, and with him, Ingrid Maslen. You will serve me better as Camilla Claremont than you ever would as Ingrid. You will heed my command and use every feminine and maternal instinct you have to once again be a part of the Claremont family."

I wanted to ask why, but I was afraid to speak. The searing pain in my arm and thigh reminded me that remaining silent was a safer option.

It seemed I didn't need to ask, because he had a ready answer. "You will be my eyes and my ears once you get them to trust you, and when I command you to, I want you to be ready to kill Sofia. Do you understand?"

I nodded as I tried to stifle the smile that formed on my face, surprised by my eagerness to kill my own daughter. *What an evil creature you've become, Camilla.*

"You are vulnerable against Aiden. You're in love with him," the voice scoffed. "Remember that it doesn't matter what you feel for him anymore, Camilla. After everything you did, he could never really love you again."

I'd already told myself the same thing, but hearing someone else say it out loud was like a slap in the face. Despite my desire to remain strong, I began sobbing.

My new master slapped me—a blow so powerful, my head reeled.

"Get a hold of yourself. You're my slave now, Camilla. Do as I say, and your power will increase as your usefulness increases. Of course, cross me and it will be the end of you and everyone you love. We both know that there are only two people you love. Aiden Claremont and yourself. So let's make things simple: you will watch him die a slow and excruciating death. After the man you love dies, I will then kill *you*."

His laughter echoed so loudly I was sure my head would burst.

Even when his presence was long gone and the moonlight once again streamed through the window, his laughter still rang in my ears. There was no mirth or even amusement in his laughter. All I heard was hatred and spite.

I didn't know what I'd just encountered. All I knew was that I was a slave to the dark presence and that whoever or whatever it was, it was pure evil.

Chapter 5: Derek

How is this possible? How are they coming at us without getting detected by the human world?

I stood on top of one of the Crimson Fortress' towers. Over the horizon, I could see the boundary of the spell of darkness. Outside The Shade, the sun hadn't risen yet. *They meant to attack in the wee hours of the morning.* My gut clenched. All the while, we'd been expecting them to attack at night.

I was surrounded by my most powerful warriors, who had spent centuries fighting for The Shade. We were all well aware that we were up against forces far more powerful than anything we had fought before. Helicopters were approaching—five of them—ready to fly over the Fortress and land on the island.

"We're not equipped for this." Xavier, one of The Shade's strongest warriors, stated the obvious.

I frowned, wondering how on earth we could take the

helicopters down before they landed on the island. We had firepower on the island, but none of it could take down a helicopter. I realized the danger we were in. *They brought guns to a swordfight.*

"They most likely have witches working for them. That's how they're avoiding human detection," Cameron said from behind me.

This was still surprising to me. Witches were known to resist vampires. That was why Cora, the original witch who had agreed to protect The Shade four hundred years ago, had been such an exception. Because she'd been in love with me, she'd become the first among the witches to ever side with our kind and all her descendants had followed her lead. It was what made The Shade so unique. *If the other covens had witches under their wing, why didn't they just create sanctuaries of their own that their witches could protect? Why go to all this trouble trying to take over The Shade?*

Of course, I didn't have time to figure out their motivations. Helicopters full of vampires were coming toward The Shade at full speed.

I braced myself for what was ahead and began barking out commands. "We need to assemble squads for every helicopter that's coming our way. We need to be there whenever they land, wherever they land. Xavier! Cameron! Yuri! Claudia! Lead one squad each. I will lead another one. We can't let them take over the Fortress! Liana, make sure Vivienne and Sofia are safe!"

What followed was chaos. We were nowhere near prepared for this. I shuddered at what kind of weapons our opponents had brought with them.

I rounded up my own squad of warriors and began pointing out to each leader which helicopter they were in charge of. I kept my eye on the helicopter assigned to us and began following its direction. It was headed right for an open field. I immediately sped toward that area, trusting that my squad was following right after me.

It landed on the field and dozens of vampires began jumping out of the chopper onto the ground below.

One vampire shot a wooden stake at me from a crossbow, while another engaged me in hand-to-hand combat. I caught the wooden stake shooting toward me and threw it right back at the vampire who had aimed it. The wooden stake dug deep into his heart.

The other vampire attempted to rip my heart out. Using my agility, I was able to get a hold of his wrist before he could dig his claws into my chest. I looked right into his eye before I returned the favor and ripped his heart out.

One of the vampires shot one of our warriors with an ultraviolet ray gun, similar to the ones used by hunters. I sped toward the vampire holding the gun and broke his neck, maiming him into unconsciousness.

I could sense something was wrong after my fifth kill. *This is too easy.* I looked around to check if someone else was attacking me and froze when I saw a familiar face. *Emilia.* Her hands were raised in the air in surrender even as one of The Shade's vampires pushed her to her knees.

Pierre, one of our Elite, was about to stab Emilia right through her heart.

"Wait! Don't! She's surrendering!" I yelled at him.

He immediately heeded my command and I could swear that Emilia smirked. I hated how my stomach fluttered at the sight of her. She was even more beautiful in person than she was in my dreams.

Why are you thinking this way, Novak? I grimaced as I

approached her. She raised her eyes to meet mine.

She flashed a smile. "I knew it. You couldn't let me die."

I wanted to wipe that self-confident smirk off her face, but I knew it was true. The idea of watching her die didn't sit well with me. *Why? She's the original vampire's daughter. She's most likely made of pure wickedness. Why wouldn't I want to see her die?* Frustrated by my own thoughts, I held her by the jaw and twisted her neck in one powerful motion. Bone cracked and my gut clutched at the sound. *How could she have this effect on me?*

Her paralyzed body fell to the ground. They would drag her into prison before returning her neck into place. Then she would heal and return to consciousness. It usually took a couple of hours.

I found myself watching as they dragged Emilia away from the field.

"Word is that the other squads are also finding it easy to take down the attackers from the other choppers." Pierre stood beside me, his eyes set on the chopper on the field. "What are we going to do with that?"

I shrugged. "I'm sure we'll figure something out." I glanced at the chopper before turning back to see Emilia's body being dragged away. *There's just something about her. We have a connection and I can't deny it.* I couldn't keep my eyes off Emilia until I saw another breathtaking sight coming toward me.

Sofia.

No matter how many times I'd seen her, Sofia still took my breath away. The realization relieved me. Catching my breath upon seeing Sofia running toward me was enough assurance that the connection I had with my lovely redhead was far greater than the one I had with the intriguing brunette.

Sofia threw herself into my arms and I held on to her tight. "We won, Derek," she whispered into my ear, her breath hot against my skin.

"Yes." I nodded before kissing her on the cheek. "We did. We won."

She pulled away from me and looked up at my face. She narrowed her eyes. "You don't seem happy at all. Why?"

I tried to make sense of what had just happened. "I don't know. I've fought many battles before, Sofia. This win seemed too easy. I might sound crazy, but it's almost as if they wanted us to win."

From the expression on her face, I knew that something was bothering her too. She began to look around the field. We'd barely lost any of our men, but we'd practically annihilated all those who had attacked.

Sofia wet her lips as she once again gazed up at me. "Why on earth would they let us win?"

I shrugged, but I couldn't help but look in the direction where they had dragged Emilia. *I have a feeling it has something to do with her.*

Chapter 6: Sofia

The romantic setting of the top floor of the Lighthouse was dangerous and I knew it. Surrounded by candlelight and having Derek all to myself, feeling his passionate kisses on my lips and his hands on my body, I knew we were in danger of once again going too far. I couldn't allow that, because I knew Derek well enough to know that he wouldn't be able to forgive himself.

So when things were getting heated, I was the one who pulled away. When he gave me a questioning look, I simply smiled and said, "You know why."

He understood immediately and nodded before stealing another peck on the lips.

After making sure that everything was in order after the battle, Derek had suggested that we both spend the night at the Lighthouse, something I'd eagerly agreed to.

"I wish we could get some sort of musical instrument up here," Derek mused as he leaned back on the couch and motioned for me to snuggle against him, a request I quickly obliged.

I leaned my head on his shoulder, smiling at his love for music and the skill with which he handled any instrument he got his hands on. "Why not? We could have a guitar up here or even a violin..."

"You like it when I play?"

"I love it when you play."

He grinned, knowing I wasn't just trying to flatter him. Of course, he wasn't the kind who needed to be flattered. "Of course you do. How could you not? I'm amazing."

I hit him in the face with one of the pillows. "You're awfully humble."

"I think it's the victory getting to my head."

Questions and doubts began to surface in my mind with Derek's mention of the battle. I wanted to talk about it, but I didn't want to dampen the light mood we were both in.

It seemed Derek didn't want to discuss the battle either, because he heaved a sigh and said, "Since I'm refusing to make out with you any more, what are we going to do now?"

I raised a brow at him and chuckled. "*You're* refusing to make out with me? Really now?"

"Stop insisting, Sofia. It's not very becoming of a lady."

I rolled my eyes, trying to hide how amused I was. Before he could stop me, I jumped to my feet and spun around to face him, taking both his hands in mine. "We should dance."

"Dance?" He raised a brow.

"Yes. Not like the sweet, slow dances we usually have. I want to dance." I began to shake my hips and raise my hands in the air.

He began to laugh. "Who dances like that?"

I threw my hands in the air. "Uh, everyone?"

He was looking at me like I was crazy. It took a moment to register that Derek had lived his teenage years centuries ago. *Of course he has no idea how teenagers today dance.*

"We can't do those silly medieval dances you did in your time. You need to learn how to dance like an eighteen-year-old in a bar."

I coaxed him to stand up.

"We don't have music, Sofia," he reminded me.

"Didn't you tell me once that you always have background music playing in your head?" I began humming an upbeat song. I was surprised when he began mimicking the beat as he caught on to the tune of the song.

A vampire who can beatbox. Who would've thought? I grinned. "That's great. Now we can dance."

For the next half hour, we danced to our own music, laughing at how silly both of us sounded and looked. I loved his laughter. I loved moments when we could just spend time together and have fun. I recalled all those times that had made me fall in love with Derek Novak and realized how much of my heart he held.

At some point, he grabbed me by the hips and pulled me against him and kissed me full on the mouth. I was putty in his hands as I responded to the kiss.

When our lips parted, he said, "Marry me, Sofia."

I laughed as I raised my ring finger. "Uhh... I already said yes to that. Don't you remember?"

He held my raised hand and began thumbing the ring on my finger. "Then let's do it, Sofia. Let's get married."

I frowned, searching his face, wondering if he was serious.

"I'm not joking, Sofia. Let's get married. Let's tie the knot.

Tomorrow, if you want."

I wanted to marry him more than anything, but something about the rush didn't feel right. "I'd love to do that, Derek, but why the rush? We're in the middle of a war. Is it really the best time to toss this into all the chaos?"

His smile widened as he cupped both my cheeks with his large hands. "That's the thing, Sofia. All of this could end soon. I want to live life to the fullest and if this moment is my last with you, then why not, Sofia? Why can't we get married now? We want to be together. Why can't we just give this to ourselves?"

The look in his eyes was my complete undoing. All I could think of was, "Yeah… why not?"

I tried to drift off to sleep, snuggled against him inside the Lighthouse. However, I couldn't help but feel as if something was amiss, as if he was keeping something from me. It wasn't like Derek to jump into a wedding while in the middle of a war. I wasn't sure if I was buying into his reason about living in the moment.

I tried to fend off the thoughts, but it was impossible. I was disturbed by the idea of rushing into marriage. *Is it because you're afraid he might never become mortal? Is it because you fear there might not be a cure after all?*

I shook my head. That wasn't it. I was certain that there was a cure and that we could find it. It was just a matter of time.

I stayed up way into the night, asking myself why I wasn't excited about marrying the love of my life.

It may be because it doesn't feel like the right time or perhaps we don't have the right motives. Either way, getting married now just doesn't feel right.

Chapter 7: Aiden

I stared at my daughter. I was hoping that I hadn't heard her correctly.

"Derek wants to get married as soon as possible," she repeated. "I agreed."

I'd been going through another set or two of push-ups when she'd arrived in my cell, sat on my cot and began talking. I appreciated that she'd come to me to pour her heart out, but I was nowhere near prepared.

"Have you gone mad, Sofia?"

She sealed her lips and looked at me as I stood to my full height, giving her that glare fathers gave their daughters when they were very, very displeased.

"You're a mortal talking about getting married to an immortal. Do you even realize what that means?"

"Well, it's not like you didn't know that he's my fiancé."

I stared at her in disbelief, her green eyes—the same shade as mine—staring up at me in defense of the talk she was giving.

"Why are you even talking to me about this if you've already made up your mind, Sofia?" I leaned against the stone wall across from the cot and crossed my arms over my chest. When she didn't respond, I glared at her. "You're still hanging your hopes on this ridiculous idea of a cure, aren't you?"

She blew out a sigh, her shoulders sagging. "If you'd been listening, you would've heard me say that I do have my doubts. Truth be told, I'm wondering why he's in such a rush. Why now? Why all of a sudden?"

It took a couple of seconds before her words registered. I cocked my head, wondering if she was playing some joke on me, but she really did seem to be considering this. *Maybe she's not as irrational as I think.* I'd been told many times by the people of The Shade that Sofia was a strong and free-spirited young woman. I wanted to see that side of her, but whenever I laid my eyes on her, all I could see was a rebellious teenager lovesick over a vampire, something I could not accept as a hunter.

I wanted to capitalize on her doubts, but for the first time, I gave her the credit she was due and decided to just listen to her. "Why do you think you have these doubts?"

"Well, don't get me wrong, I want nothing more than to marry Derek."

At that, my lips twitched, but I fought my reaction. *Calm down, Aiden. It's not like you haven't seen firsthand how much they are in love with each other.*

"I just feel like something's wrong. Peace has always been my compass, and I don't have any of that when it comes to this. I don't

46

even know why."

"If that is so, why did you agree to the wedding, Sofia?"

"Because I love him. You know that. He seemed so excited it was hard to say no, but now that I'm thinking about it... I feel like we're not strong enough for something like this. Not yet."

"So what are you going to do now? Are you still going to push through with it?" I was testing her, wondering how her mind worked, how she made her decisions. I'd always seen her as impulsive, like a child who followed even the slightest of whims. I was hoping that she would prove me wrong.

"I have to be honest with Derek about this. I can't marry him feeling this way. I need to have clarity for a commitment as huge as marriage. It would be unfair to both of us if I just pushed through with it in spite of my apprehensions."

Every fatherly instinct I had applauded for her. I wanted to pull her into my arms and embrace her for thinking straight for once, but all I did was nod and shrug one shoulder. "Sounds like a plan."

"Aiden..."

I raised a brow at her. "Yeah?"

"When I do get married someday, it would mean the world to me if you walked me down the aisle. You'll do that, right? No matter who I marry?"

"Sofia... I wouldn't miss your wedding for the world."

Later, after she had gone off to do whatever it was that kept her busy in the island of vampires, I realized that I meant it. Even if she married Derek Novak, I could never say no to walking her down that aisle. It would be my deepest honor.

I caught that thought and remembered the last time I'd acknowledged something as my deepest honor. It was the day I'd become a hunter.

Four ugly scars lined the face of my father. Whenever I was in his presence, I would always take a few moments to stare at them, reminding myself that they were one of the reasons I should always hate vampires.

That night, we were at the gardens of his large estate, right beside the koi pond, and he was circling me like he would a vulture.

"This is it, son." He spoke in a gruff voice. "You must avenge the family. You must restore our good name."

Memories of the tragedy that had occurred began to flood back through my mind. Blood streaming over the hardwood floor, lifeless bodies strewn all over the hall—men, women and children alike. Murdered by vampires.

My stomach clenched as I remembered the faces of those who had died that night—all of them familiar, all of them close to me. I belonged to a family of hunters. Every single one of my father's siblings had been hunters and all my cousins had been too. Our grandparents had been hunters and their parents before them had been hunters.

That night, every living member of our family had been killed in a bloody massacre. Only my father and I had survived. My father had risked his life to save me and I owed him everything. I could only repay him by being the greatest and most powerful hunter who had ever lived.

The memories strengthened my resolve to avenge my family.

"I'm going to make the vampires pay, Father. I will."

With the vast fortune we'd inherited from the death of every relative we had, we built a security conglomerate trusted by the entire world. In the underground, I was known simply as Reuben, one of the most well-connected and affluent hunters of the Order. It didn't take long before I rose through the ranks, much to my father's pride.

My father died battling vampires and his death was another reason to take revenge on those vile creatures. *My life revolved around my business and my desire to rid the world of vampires. That was, until I met Camilla.*

I'd always thought that I would have a family who shared my hatred for vampires, but when I married the love of my life, I couldn't stand the thought of dragging her into the violent world of hunters. So she only got to know Aiden, never Reuben.

When Camilla gave birth to Sofia and I held our newborn daughter for the very first time, I took one look at her and knew that I didn't want the cycle of blood and violence to repeat in her generation. I stared into her lovely green eyes and wanted her to never encounter a vampire in her life.

At that, I'd failed, because my precious Sofia had ended up falling in love with a vampire, and not just any vampire—Derek Novak, whose head would be any hunter's prized possession.

I couldn't help but grunt with frustration as I entertained the idea of giving my daughter away in marriage to Derek Novak. The thought made me sick and yet, despite my hunters' instincts telling me that it was wrong, I had been in The Shade long enough to know that what she had with Derek wasn't just a passing flame.

Sofia hadn't been raised to hate vampires like I had. She'd been raised to never know vampires and when she'd encountered one, he'd fought for her and protected her in a way I'd never been able to. Upon seeing firsthand how she interacted with the vampires in The Shade and how much affection they held toward her, I couldn't help but see her through the eyes of the island's citizens. I saw why she was loyal to the vampires, but I also realized that it wasn't even loyalty.

Sofia has simply chosen to take the side of good—to follow where she believes goodness lies. I grimaced. *Hate the idea as much as you will, but your daughter sees good even in vampires.*

I found myself speaking my thoughts out loud in frustration. "How could you be so naïve, Sofia?"

Right then, it dawned on me that I was wrong. It wasn't just naïveté.

She has a strength in her that I've never seen in anyone else. She is strong enough to trust and forgive and to risk getting hurt again, no matter how much she's been betrayed. She doesn't put up walls to protect herself from those who could hurt her. She is strong enough to allow herself to be vulnerable. How does she do it?

Right then, I couldn't help but contrast her with her mother. The irony of a fierce hunter like me ending up with a wife who was a vampire, and a daughter who was madly in love with a vampire, didn't escape me and I grimaced.

Camilla and Sofia had many similarities between them, but I knew then what set them apart.

No matter how powerful a creature Ingrid has become, she has always been weak on the inside in a way Sofia has never been.

CHAPTER 8: DEREK

I couldn't get her off my mind. From the moment Emilia arrived at the island, she invaded my every waking moment and my every dream. The only time I could distract myself from thinking of her was when I was with Sofia, and even then I had to consciously keep my focus on Sofia instead of daydreaming of the lovely brunette.

What is wrong with you, Novak? It's like you've never seen an attractive vampire before. I knew, however, that something was different about Emilia. Physically, she was my perfect woman. The fact that she kept talking about a connection between us, one that I couldn't deny I felt too, made it even more difficult for me to forget her.

At some point, I couldn't take it anymore, and though it was against my better judgment, I walked through the door of The Cells and headed for the jail we were keeping her in.

A smile lit up her face when she saw me—something that I

found unsettling.

"What have you done to me?" I asked her, before she could even mouth a greeting. "Why can't I get you off my mind?"

She laughed. "You're blaming me for that?" She raised a dark brow at me. "How am I supposed to know why you're thinking about me all of the time? I think I'm the one who ought to be worried that a man keeping me prisoner can't get me off his mind."

I gritted my teeth. "Don't play games with me, Emilia."

She rose from her cot as the smile on her face widened. "You remember my name."

"I also remember who you are and why you shouldn't be trusted, so whatever you're doing, stop. I don't want to play games with you."

"Who's playing games? I've been locked up in your prison. How on earth am I playing games with you?"

She began walking toward me and I suddenly felt vulnerable as she got closer.

"Stay there," I commanded.

She stopped in her tracks and studied me. "You really are quite a man, Derek Novak. What a team we'd make together."

What am I doing here? She was danger, and yet I was standing on the precipice, very close to taking a leap. Eager to get away from that place, as far from temptation as possible, I asked her what I needed to ask. "Did you or did you not come here to lose a battle?"

Her face turned serious and she creased her brows. "That doesn't make sense. Why would I purposefully lose a battle—especially against you? Do you have any idea what my father could do to me for this failure?"

The strangest thing happened when I realized that she could get into trouble. I felt sorry for her, worried even. I couldn't understand why, but much as I tried to fight it, I was at ease around her—almost as if she were a kindred soul I'd known all my life.

"What's he going to do to you?" I found myself asking, even though it was a step closer to danger.

"I don't want to talk about that. How long do you intend to keep me here?"

I shrugged. "For as long as this war lasts." I could swear that she sighed with relief. I narrowed my eyes at her. "You want to stay?"

"If I go back, I'll have to face the Elder, my father. And my siblings."

"So there are others like you who belong to the Elder's family."

"Family," she scoffed. "I don't know if I could call it that." She sat back on the cot and stared in front of her, sadness marring her beautiful face.

I fought the urge to draw closer to her, but I lost. I took a couple of steps forward and held her by the chin, lifting her face up so that I could look at her loveliness. "We vampires are very loyal creatures. Betraying your clan is unforgivable. If you really are the original vampire's daughter, you don't seem very fond of your father or your clan, Emilia. Why is that?"

She didn't respond. Instead, she bit her lip and blushed the moment our eyes met. I looked away, bothered by the flutter in my stomach. *This girl is dangerous.* I backed a couple of steps away from her, letting go of her chin as if the feel of her burned. "I have to go." I spun around and I was about to call the guard when she spoke.

"Don't deny it, Derek. I know you feel it too. We have a connection. You can keep fighting it, but eventually, I hope you realize that we belong together."

I shook my head. "I belong with Sofia. She's the woman I'm in love with, the one I will marry soon. I can't deny my attraction to you and yes, maybe there's some sort of mysterious connection between us, but it's Sofia who holds my heart. No other connection can break what I have with her."

I was saying the words more to myself than to Emilia and even with my back turned to her, I could sense her anger like a wave rushing over me. She was no fragile creature, trembling at the thought of what her father would do to her. I saw Emilia in a different light the moment I let my love for Sofia call the shots. What I saw in her was someone I couldn't trust.

I turned toward her. "I'm giving orders that they let you off the island as soon as possible."

"No," she gasped. "You can't do that! Derek, please… You have no idea what my father will do to me!"

"Then don't go to him, Emilia. Run. I don't care what you do, but I can't have you here." *What I have with Sofia is too precious for you to threaten it.*

To my surprise, she stopped begging and gave me a dark glare. "You want to play it that way? Then so be it." A smirk formed on her face. "You'll find you can't get rid of me that easily, Derek."

Chills ran up and down my spine when I realized that she was right. Something was telling me that Emilia would soon find her way back. Strangely, at that moment I didn't feel threatened.

I clenched my fists and smirked right back at her.

Bring it on.

Chapter 9: Emilia

Things weren't going as planned. I was supposed to capitalize on the connection we had to gain Derek's sympathy and yet there I was, left hanging as he walked out of the cell, leaving orders with the guards that I was to be sent off the island as soon as possible.

Now what am I going to do? The plan hinges on me staying here in The Shade. I can't accomplish my task if I'm not here.

I had to find a way to reach The Sanctuary, the place in the island that housed the witch of The Shade. I was trying to figure out a plan when a small, cold breeze began to blow in my ear, carrying with it a message.

"What are you still doing in this dungeon, Emilia? You're wasting time."

My father's chilling voice.

"Forgive me, Master." My voice cracked. "He is more in love with Sofia than I initially thought..."

"Find a way to gain their trust so that you can roam the island freely, Emilia. Don't you dare return here unless you have Derek Novak with you."

I nodded, afraid to speak in case he made it a reason to cause me pain. I backed up on my cot until I hit the corner where the stone walls met. I gathered my knees against my chest and shut my eyes. I felt like I was being enveloped in pitch blackness, shivering against the cold that came with my father's presence.

Seemingly satisfied, he disappeared as quickly as he'd come. I sighed with relief, but found even relief to be momentary. Keys began to unlock my cell door. I was about to be escorted off the island.

I thought about fighting back. I could take down these guards if I wanted to. But if I wanted Derek's love, if I wanted his trust, I couldn't afford to take the risk. I needed to make him see me as a victim, someone he could feel compassion for. I couldn't do that with a display of power.

So I gave in. I followed the guards to the Port and played along with the whole charade. By the time the guards left me at a far-off shore, away from the island, I already had a plan to get back.

You're going to be mine, Derek Novak. I am willing to turn the world upside down until you realize that I am the girl who will help you bring our kind to true sanctuary. Me. Not Sofia Claremont.

Chapter 10: Ingrid

I sensed it when Derek walked past my cell. I knew I had to make a move, a plea, anything to move forward in the task given to me by the fearsome presence that had visited me in my cell.

So I called out the young man's name. I was relieved when he appeared by the door of my cell.

"What do you want?" His words were dripping with spite, and I couldn't blame him.

"I want to see my husband."

He narrowed his eyes, looking straight at me past the bars that kept us apart. "And who exactly is your husband? Is it not Borys? The one Sofia killed?"

The words stung, but I had to keep it together. The thought of having another visit from the dark creature was too terrifying. *You have to learn to be Camilla. You have to earn their trust.* "You know who my husband is, Derek. Please let me see him."

"Why on earth would I allow that? You might end up killing him. Sofia already lost a mother. I can't risk her losing a father."

"I'm her mother. She hasn't lost me yet."

"Sofia's mother is Camilla Claremont. She died the moment she turned into Ingrid Maslen. That's you."

"Sofia would let me see her father and you know it. Ask her. I'll do anything... I want to see my husband and child."

Derek squared his shoulders and began studying me, perhaps wondering if I was sincere. "What makes you think that Aiden would want to see you? Or Sofia, for that matter? After everything you've done..."

"You of all people should know what it feels like to want to be given another chance, Derek. You've had your share of regrets, your own dance with the dark side. Sofia forgave you. Why wouldn't she forgive me? I'm still her mother. And Aiden... I still have hope that he could find it in his heart to love me."

Even as I said the words, I was swallowing back the urge to vomit. I hated Sofia for what she'd done to Borys. And Aiden... as much as I loved him, I had no delusions that he could ever love me back. He loved Sofia too much to ever even entertain it and the idea of going to the lowest lengths in order to woo him back as Camilla made me sick to my stomach.

"What game are you playing, Ingrid?" Derek seemed unconvinced.

"I'm not playing games, Derek. Just please... ask Sofia. She'll understand. She'll listen..."

"If you do anything to hurt Sofia or even Aiden, I swear, Ingrid..."

"Save the threats, Derek. What else can you do to me? I have nothing left for you to take, except maybe my life, and that's something I would willingly lose. After all, what do I have to live for? After losing Borys, the only family I have left is Aiden and Sofia. If they don't take me back, then perhaps you're right. It's better for me to die."

Derek gave me a long glare and nodded. "Fine. I'll let Sofia know. Don't make me regret this, Ingrid."

I hated to make the request, but it was necessary in order for me to completely let go of who I was. "Please," I said, my voice breaking. "I'd like to be called Camilla from now on."

At that, Derek scoffed and mumbled, "Sure you do," before walking away.

I felt emptiness unlike anything I'd ever felt before. I asked myself why I was even doing this and was startled to find that there was still a hint of nobility left in me. I realized that I would rather lose Ingrid Maslen than allow the Elder to end Aiden's life.

No matter how I tried, I still couldn't stop loving Aiden Claremont.

Chapter 11: Sofia

"Why the heck not?" Ashley asked, a playful pout forming on her lips. "You and Derek are practically married already."

We were having lunch at The Catacombs and I'd just asked the girls what they thought about Derek and me getting married. As expected, unlike my father, both of them were ecstatic, squealing with delight like the teenagers that we were.

"What do you think, Rosa?" I asked.

Rosa smiled, her cheeks taking on a pink blush. "It's bound to happen, Sofia. Why not now?"

I bit my lip before confessing, "I'm hesitant, to be honest…"

Ashley's eyes widened with surprise. "Why?"

"Our relationship has been struggling lately. I mean, yes, we have our good times, but… I don't know if it's just me, but there's this gap between us that I can't quite figure out. It's almost like

Derek is distancing himself from me and... I just... I don't understand why I feel this way. Perhaps it's just the familiarity?"

Ashley rolled her eyes and smiled at me. "Well, what did I just say? Didn't I tell you? You're like a married couple already... You're talking like you've been married to him for five years and you're looking for that spark you used to have..."

"Sofia," Rosa interrupted. "Whatever your choice is, you do know that we're going to support you, right? Go for what you feel is right."

Truth be told, after my conversation with my father, I'd already made up my mind. I was just having trouble figuring out how I was going to tell Derek. To my surprise, I saw him taking several strides toward me. A huge smile was on his handsome face.

"You look like you just won the lottery, Novak," Ashley piped up.

"Maybe I just did," Derek quipped before leaning forward and kissing me passionately.

I was so shocked by the gesture, my mouth hung open when our lips finally parted.

This seemed to amuse him, his bright blue eyes twinkling. "Have I told you lately how much I adore you, Sofia Claremont?"

"So, this is you lacking intimacy?" Ashley eyed me and I found myself blushing.

Derek took the seat next to mine and placed his arm over my shoulder. "You told her we were lacking intimacy?"

I bit my lip. "Well, not really... I was just..."

I was expecting him to be offended, but it seemed he was in too light a mood to care. Instead, he gave me a naughty look and said, "I can fix that." He kissed me once again, leaving me breathless, but totally aware of my friends' hoots and cheers. Derek still had that wide grin on his face as my cheeks reddened. "I can't wait for you to become Mrs. Sofia Novak."

I was speechless. *What is going on with him?* The way he was acting was making me feel even guiltier about having second thoughts about pushing through with our wedding. "Are you feeling sick, Derek?" I eventually managed to say as I laid the back of my hand over his forehead to check his temperature. *Chilly as usual.*

"I'm fine." He took hold of my hand and squeezed tight. "I cleared out the rest of the day. Vivienne is on top of everything. Come with me."

I glanced at my half-finished plate of food and then at my two girlfriends. Both seemed eager to see me leave with Derek. I honestly couldn't wait to spend time with him, so I nodded. That was all he needed before he held me by the waist and told me to hold on to him tight. He sped out of The Catacombs until we reached the Pavilion.

Of all the Elite's penthouses, there were four that occupied twenty redwood trees, home to the Novaks, The Shade's royalty. Since Gregor and Lucas Novak's deaths, their penthouses had been given to Cameron and Liana Hendry and Eli and Yuri Lazaroff as a reward for their loyal service to the Novaks and The Shade throughout the centuries.

The wide veranda of Derek's penthouse was home to a view that never failed to take my breath away. As we stared at the magnificent view of the island, illuminated by the moon's soft light, Derek pulled my back against his chest, his hands rubbing against my waist and my hips.

"I love your warmth," he whispered, his voice husky with emotion. "I love you, Sofia."

I wondered what was going through his mind and what could've brought about this mood of his. I didn't want to ask, afraid that it might spoil the moment, but I couldn't shake the feeling that something was amiss.

"I love you too. You know that, don't you?"

I could feel him nod, his lips pressing against the back of my head.

I couldn't help but smile as a wave of nostalgia came over me. "We've been through a lot, haven't we?" One memory in particular came to the forefront. *The Sun Room.* The memory of the first time he'd seen it was still fresh on my mind. It was the first time he'd tried to kiss me, and I had pulled away.

Derek could have demanded that kiss from me, but he'd waited—the same way he'd waited for me to be ready to get engaged to him, the same way he was waiting to marry me before we could make love again, the same way he'd waited for me to agree to turn into a vampire. He never forced me into anything until I was ready. I wondered then if he could wait a little bit more before we could get married.

"Do you really think we should go ahead and get married, Derek?" I felt guilty just asking the question.

"Don't you? You said so yourself so many times… we belong together."

At that, I couldn't help but give in. It was hard not to with him being so loving and tender and sweet. *Why resist it? Why not now?* Still, I couldn't deny that I felt a sense of foreboding.

I tried to shake it off as we spent more time together that night, but I just couldn't. When we ended up in his couch and he began to tug at my shirt to expose my neck, my heart sank when I realized what he was doing. He didn't ask for my consent. He just bit into my neck and began feeding on my blood.

As I sat there, his body pressed against mine, his teeth sinking into my skin, I couldn't help but wonder: *If he never becomes mortal, is this how it's going to be?*

For the first time in a long time, I saw him as a predator and I his willing prey.

Chapter 12: Ian

Screams were common within The Catacombs. They were as familiar to the Naturals as an ambulance's siren would be to people outside of The Shade—or so the books said. While someone screaming with terror was normally a cause for alarm, a Natural never ran to the rescue unless the person screaming was one of their loved ones.

So for me, orphaned at fourteen and without any loved ones to worry about, screams never became a source of alarm.

One night I realized that things were different, because when I heard a piercing scream, I immediately found myself sitting up on my mat, blood pounding and heart racing. One name began echoing in my head. Anna.

Ever since Sofia had led the rebellion against Derek's father Gregor's plan for another culling in The Shade, things had been very different around The Catacombs. I was already leading a group of rebels—mostly teenagers like me—against cullings ever being done again. Once was enough and the horror was still fresh in our minds. During a culling, all the humans of The Catacombs deemed to be useless were killed, their blood harvested and preserved for future consumption by the vampires.

Sofia, whom I hadn't been much of a fan of in the beginning, had been instrumental in getting Derek Novak, then prince of The Shade, to stand with the humans against the culling. Of course, where Derek stood, a whole bunch of the vampire Elite followed.

Since then, the humans had gotten more of a voice in The Shade, and thanks to Sofia, mine was one of them. For the first time in a long time, I allowed myself to hope that things could turn around on the island. More than that, I hoped that perhaps I could have the old, joyful Anna back.

This hope was sparked further one night when Anna found her way to my quarters with a rose. She knelt on the ground and shook me awake. At first, I was annoyed, but when I saw that it was her, my breath caught.

"Anna? What is it?"

She laid the white rose in front of me and smiled. "You don't have to cry anymore, Ian. Everything's going to be all right. I promise."

I wondered where she'd gotten the rose, but I thought better of asking. I was too busy choking back the tears as I remembered her being the adored beauty of The Catacombs, back before Felix broke her.

"Thank you, Anna."

She lay on the stone ground beside me, rolling to her side to face me. "Can I sleep here, Ian? I don't think Felix will mind as long as we don't touch. I'm afraid to sleep alone tonight."

I nodded, careful not to touch her, knowing how erratic her moods were. I liked this docile version of her. "You can sleep here, Anna, but not on the ground." I got up and retrieved another mat—the one my mother had used before—and set it on the space beside me. "You can lie down here."

She seemed grateful as she took her place on the mat. I gave her my pillow and she seemed to hesitate taking it, but I insisted. "A pillow for the rose, Anna."

She understood, smiled, and nodded, before laying her head on the pillow and drifting off to sleep.

She slept in my quarters three straight nights before she stopped. I sought her out that fourth night and found her sleeping like a baby in her own quarters. After another three nights, she once again requested to sleep in mine, something I readily allowed. I got used to her requesting to sleep in my quarters, but I found myself craving her presence more and more.

So when I heard that piercing scream during that night, I found myself worried because I had begun to care about someone other than myself.

The scream was followed by another and then another. I rushed towards the sound of the scream. By the time I got to her quarters, I found three men—all older than me—inside her chambers. One of them had her pinned to the wall, his hand clamped over her mouth.

There'd already been rumors that some men were taking advantage of her, but I'd thought they were just the mutterings of a crazy woman. After all, who would ever want to hurt Anna?

That night, I found out.

"Get your hands off her!"

One of the men glared at me. "What? You're not willing to share? We all know she's been sleeping in your quarters."

The thought that he was accusing me of what they were about to do—or perhaps even what they'd already been doing—caused me to see red. I attacked. While I was able to take one man down in a wild fit of fury, I didn't stand a chance against the two other men.

One was already holding me by the arms while the other was poised to hit me when someone showed up. Kyle. A vampire guard.

What on earth is he doing here?

Anna ran to him, seeking safety behind him.

"Everything's going to be okay, Anna," he assured her, before casting a glare at the two men holding me back. "Let go of him," he commanded and the two men readily obliged, lifting their hands in surrender.

Even they were smart enough not to mess with a vampire.

"Did you ever touch her before this night?" Kyle asked them.

The men shook their heads while one shook as he swore, "We never did. Not until tonight."

I knew without a doubt that they were lying. I brushed a hand over Anna's bare arm and was relieved when she looked my way without flinching. "Have you ever seen these men before, Anna? Did they come to hurt you before?"

She nodded. "They always come. I'm afraid Felix might find out. He won't want me anymore if they touch me. I try to tell them, but they won't listen."

I wanted to kill them then and there, but Kyle beat me to it. "Get her out of here," he ordered. "I don't want her to see this."

The men began begging for their lives even as I led Anna away. I didn't even hear them scream.

I wondered if they had children and wives. I wondered if Kyle had created widows and orphans by killing them. I wanted to feel a sense of loss, but I couldn't. It was the way of The Shade. Life was fragile. We were all used to that.

It didn't take long before Kyle caught up with me and Anna.

"Where are you taking her?" he asked.

"*To my quarters. She'll be safer there.*"

He looked at me suspiciously before turning his eyes toward the young woman who was staring blankly ahead of us. "Did he ever touch you, Anna?"

I gritted my teeth at what he was implying, but I couldn't blame him. I would've suspected myself too.

To my relief, Anna shook her head. "No. He never did. Ian is my friend. He's just sad. Sometimes I wish he could be happier."

I drew a breath at what she said. I loved her. I loved Anna. How could I not? I returned my gaze to the vampire whom we owed her rescue to.

Kyle's eyes softened as he gazed at her. He turned his attention toward me. He was about to say something, but it was my turn to scrutinize him. He seemed to get the implication of my glare. "I assure you I could never do anything to harm her."

I believed him. Anna wouldn't be so comfortable around him if she didn't feel safe with him.

Kyle shifted his weight. "I think she'd be better off staying in one of the spare rooms at Sofia's quarters."

Sofia was still gone. The latest we'd heard was that she and Derek were being held captive at hunter territory. I nodded. "Fine. Knowing Sofia, I'm sure she wouldn't mind."

We brought her to the quarters, where Rosa, Lily and her kids were already staying. We both stayed to look after her that night, glaring at each other every once in a while.

It took some time before we were able to trust each other alone with Anna, but we never quite got past the tension. I knew why.

We never said it out loud, but both of us were hoping that Anna would pick one of us over the other.

I had just tucked Anna into the queen-sized bed in one of the guest rooms of Sofia's quarters. She was already sleeping soundly when the unwelcome visitor spoke up.

"How is she doing?"

I turned around. Kyle leaned against the doorpost, eyes fixed on Anna. I'd never understood his fixation with her. I hated that he had been instrumental in Anna's rescue from the men taking advantage of her. I detested the idea of Anna owing him anything.

"She's all right." I shrugged. "Better than before. Old sparks of who she was before have been coming back. What are you doing here? It's my night to look after her."

He nodded. "I know. I just wanted to see her."

A sense of possessiveness came over me. She was my girl. What business did he have checking on her?

"Did you know that Derek and Corrine suspect she might be an immune just like Sofia?"

I was surprised by that piece of information. Especially considering that Corrine, The Shade's witch, was involved. I couldn't ignore the possibility that it could be true. "Why would they think that?"

"We all saw how Felix was with her. He was madly in love with her. I couldn't understand how he could get rid of her so suddenly. Derek is assuming that he was serious about turning her into a vampire. He tried, but she didn't turn."

I looked up at Kyle, wondering why he was giving me that information. It was the first real conversation I could remember ever having with him. "So Felix just threw her away because she didn't turn?"

"I guess he was faced with her mortality. She probably wasn't able to handle the effects of the attempt to turn her. She may have gone insane because of this."

I swallowed hard before casting a concerned look at Anna. "What do you mean?"

"Borys Maslen tried to turn Sofia into a vampire when she was nine years old."

I squared my shoulders in surprise. I knew Sofia was an immune—everyone did—but I'd had no idea he had tried to turn her at such a young age.

"Ever since then, she's had heightened senses. She was diagnosed with several disorders because of this. Even Corrine mistook her symptoms for a disorder known as LLI, low latent inhibition, but now Corrine suspects that perhaps it's because, though Sofia didn't turn into a vampire, her senses still got heightened. Maybe that's why Anna went insane. Corrine told me that only people with above average IQs could handle that many sensations coming at them all at once."

"Why are you telling me all this?"

"We've been looking after Anna over the past weeks. I wanted to know how you would feel if Anna saw Corrine. Perhaps the witch can help her cope with the heightened senses and hopefully get the Anna we remember back to us."

I stared at him, wondering what he had shared with Anna that made her so dear to him. I didn't want to ask—I didn't want to know what I was competing with—but my view of Kyle changed that night. We could always be annoyed with each other, but we also shared the same feeling toward each other: Respect.

Should Anna ever choose Kyle over me, it would break my heart, but I would also be at peace knowing that he would take care of her.

Kyle was another reason for me to believe that goodness still existed in The Shade.

Every day of my teenage life in The Shade had been a battle to stay alive. I'd lost my father and my sister to a cave-in at The Catacombs when I was nine. My dad had gone in to save my sister. He was my hero and I'd always felt a sense of pride over his bravery.

For five years, it was just my mother and me. I looked after her like I'd promised my father, but in a place like The Shade, life was too fragile. My mother was late in coming home one night, after working as a hairdresser at The Baths. It was the winter season and though it never snowed in The Shade, that night was particularly cold. She contracted a cough that she never recovered from. Her lungs were weak and none of us had any clue how to overcome the sickness.

My mother was unable to go to work for months. Because of this, she was killed at The Shade's culling. I was fourteen years old when I lost her and it felt like I had nobody left. Then I met Anna.

She was a year older than me and the moment I saw her, I knew that she was the most beautiful woman I'd ever laid eyes on. It'd been a week since my mother's death and I was still in mourning.

Anna stood by the door of my quarters and gave me a sad smile. She was holding a white rose in her hand, as white as the dress she was wearing. I remember wondering if she was an angel. She was so beautiful.

I actually flinched when she approached. I could almost swear that she was radiating light. She knelt on the ground beside me and laid the rose in front of me. She kissed me on the top of my head—a gesture of affection that no one in The Shade, not even my mother, had ever given me before.

I was so thankful that she was there, I began to sob. I was embarrassed at first, kneeling in front of a beautiful woman, crying like a baby. My embarrassment quickly faded when she began to cry with me.

The look in her moss-green eyes as they glistened with tears was forever etched in my memory. Anna was a complete stranger, but that day she chose to mourn with me, to join me in my sorrow. She had owned my heart ever since, but then she owned the hearts of many men in The Shade.

It was hard not to fall in love with a girl like Anna. She was one of a kind. Aside from her beauty, she was fun-loving and good-hearted. She always had a smile on her face. And it was easy to catch her humming a tune or dancing to the beat of her own drum. She was joy and laughter in a place that only knew sadness and tears.

We should've known that it wouldn't take long before she would catch the eye of one of the vampires in The Shade. Felix. He wooed her. He didn't abduct her or feed on her. He wanted her light just as much as we did. He was always in The Shade, showering her with gifts, giving her special favors.

I couldn't blame Anna for falling for him. None of us men at The Catacombs could match the way Felix relentlessly pursued her.

Anna broke many hearts when she professed her love for Felix, and yet we were happy for her. We all thought that he was madly in love with her. He had us all fooled.

After a year of keeping Anna in his penthouse, he returned her to her chambers at The Catacombs, but she was no longer her former self. She was child-like, afraid of everything and everyone. She was an empty shell, devoid of life, laughter and light.

Felix had broken her.

When I saw what happened to Anna, I lost all hope that goodness could still be found in The Shade.

Then came Sofia Claremont, and the rest, as they say, was history.

Chapter 13: Kyle

Brigitte was the mayor's daughter. She was kind, beautiful, sweet and down-to-earth. I was in love with her, but then so was every bachelor in our town. I had an advantage though. I was her best friend. My father was her father's bodyguard. For this reason, our family had our own cottage within the mayor's estate.

I grew up the envy of all the other boys in school. We were such close friends, everyone thought that we were sweethearts. We weren't. In fact, all throughout our days in school, she told me about every boy she liked—none of them me. I hated hearing how much she liked them, but I loved listening to her talk, so I bore the heaviness of heart her every story brought me.

As we grew up, she left the estate to go to nursing school and I stayed behind to be my father's apprentice, since we couldn't afford university. We wrote letters to each other frequently. Again, she told me about the young men she fancied and also those who fancied her. I found myself happy whenever she rejected one of them, and though I was hurt on her behalf when she was heartbroken, I was also relieved. I always believed that we belonged together.

By the time she returned, she was a woman in full bloom and I was even more struck by her. I also became her bodyguard, something that pleased me at first. However, I soon realized that it was cruel and unusual punishment, because I had to stand in the sidelines as she fell in love.

I will never forget the night he broke her heart. I wanted to kill him. I wanted to punish him for making her feel like trash. I couldn't imagine how he couldn't have seen how beautiful a person she was.

She was so heartbroken, she was bed-ridden for three days, so sick that I wasn't even allowed to visit her. After the end of the third day, she finally allowed me to come to her chambers.

"Brigitte... Are you feeling better now?"

She shook her head. "I don't think my heart will ever stop aching," she sobbed.

I couldn't help but notice how pale she looked as she gulped at the sight of me. I edged on the bed closer to her. "He's not worth all these tears, Brigitte. He doesn't deserve you." I pulled her into my arms and whispered reassurances in her ears.

"Thank you, Kyle. You're such a great guy. If only I could see you as more than just my best friend... If only I could fall in love with you..."

Her words were a stab in the heart.

"I'm sorry for what I'm about to do, Kyle, but I can't stand the thought of being alone in this."

Fangs bit into my neck.

After breaking my heart, Brigitte turned me into a vampire so she wouldn't ever be alone. I loved her, but she did not deserve my love. When she was killed by the hunters, a part of me was relieved, because

I was finally free.

After escaping the hunters that night, I found The Shade. I also found Anna, and once again found myself on the losing end of an unrequited love.

"Where are we going?" Anna asked, her body trembling, her eyes wide with fear as Ian and I led her out of The Catacombs.

"It's all right, Anna," I tried to soothe her. "You're just going to spend a little time with Corrine so that she can figure out if we can get you back to who you were."

Clearly, from the blank stare she was shooting my way, she didn't quite understand.

"Everything's going to be fine, Anna." Ian began rubbing her back. "We can go to the gardens after. Maybe you can go get some roses."

A smile lit up Anna's face. "Roses!" She nodded with enthusiasm. "I like roses!"

I swallowed back the jealousy. Anna and Ian had some sort of connection. I couldn't deny it no matter how much it bothered me. And whatever that connection was, it had something to do with roses.

We eventually made our way to The Sanctuary, where Corrine was already waiting. Before she had been brought to The Shade to become its witch, Corrine had been in college as a psychology major. I always felt like she was evaluating me. I had no idea if anyone else felt the same way.

"Hello, Anna," Corrine greeted her in a rather formal manner. "How are you?"

"I'm well." Anna nodded, looking like a deer in headlights. "We're going to get roses later. Ian promised."

I wasn't sure if it was just my imagination, but I could swear Ian smirked. My gut clenched. *Is this forever my story? Will I forever be in love with a woman who will never love me back?*

I tried to push the thoughts away as Corrine led the beautiful young woman to a room, leaving Ian and me instructions to do as we pleased while we waited, but to make sure we were around when they were done.

Any time I was alone with Ian, I was unsure what to do. The only thing we had in common was Anna. I was pleased to find out that Ian wasn't up for conversation.

I found myself taking a trip down memory lane... to the day I first saw Anna in The Shade...

Sam and I were guarding the southeast area of the Crimson Fortress. As with any guard duty in The Shade, the whole thing was routine—there really wasn't much else to do. Sam and I were mostly just whiling the time away until the end of our guard duty.

We'd been at it for a couple of hours when we heard rustling behind a nearby bush.

"I'll check it out," I told Sam and approached the area where the sound came from.

Behind the bushes was an opening that led to a large lake. I peered toward the lake and drew a breath when I saw her. I didn't know her name, but her beauty took my breath away. Long, silky, jet-black hair, big moss-green eyes... A lovely feminine form, immersed in the shimmering water...

I was dumbfounded. The last time I remembered feeling that way was with Brigitte. I stared as she bathed in the lake water, humming a tune as she did. I was so stunned by the sight of her, I lost balance and stumbled forward.

She spun around at the sound of me falling, breaking twigs and rustling leaves as I did. Her eyes grew wide with horror at the sight of me.

"I'm so sorry," she gasped. "I had no idea someone was here... I just... the water... I wanted to get clean..."

I shook my head and lifted my hand. "It's fine. I was just surprised that a lovely young woman like you would be out here bathing."

She blushed. "I like going for swims. It relaxes me. Besides, compared to the showers we have at The Catacombs, a bath at the lake seemed luxurious..."

There was a certain ease about her that most of the Naturals in The Shade didn't possess. Whenever I interacted with any of the humans, they cowered as if they were fearful that I would suddenly bite into their necks—something that was known to happen.

She was different, however. She seemed wary of me seeing her bare, but that was more because I was a man and she was a woman, not because I was a vampire she was afraid of.

She stared at the spot where she'd left her dress, signaling that she wanted to get out of the water.

I turned around to give her the privacy she needed.

"Thank you," she said and my heart leapt at her gratefulness.

"What's your name?" I asked, my back still turned to her.

"Anna."

"Anna," I repeated, as the water rippled as she got out of the lake. "You live at The Catacombs?"

"Yes."

"All your life?"

A chuckle could be heard in her reply. "Yes."

"Do you have family left?"

"No. My parents were killed a couple of years back."

"I'm sorry to hear that."

She paused, and I wondered if I'd said something wrong. "Thank you."

I creased my brows, wondering what she was thanking me for. "Thank me? For what?"

"For being sorry... Most of us have lost someone, you know. Most of us Naturals." I could hear the sadness in her voice. "Most of the vampires think that it's normal. It's the first time I heard a vampire sympathize."

I had no idea what to say to that, so I just remained silent, moved by the sweetness of her voice.

"It's okay to turn around now."

I turned to face her and found her tying the knot of her halter dress behind her neck. When she finished, she dropped her arms to her side and smiled at me.

I narrowed my eyes at her. "Why are you not afraid of me?" I couldn't help but ask.

She seemed taken aback. I felt as if she were scrutinizing me, checking if she could trust me. To my relief, she gave me a shrug.

"My parents were always afraid. They would've had a heart attack if they found out that I'd been bathing at the lake and that a vampire"—she pointed at me—"found me doing it. When they died, I decided that I wasn't going to be afraid anymore." She looked around, a bitter smile on her face, tears moistening her eyes. "This is my life. My parents hoped that we would someday escape The Shade, but I don't want to wait until I'm free of The Shade to start living my life. I could tremble in fear of you, sir, but if you wanted to take advantage of me or drink my blood, then you would've already done so. You are doing nothing of that sort, so..." She tilted her head to the side, her eyes set on me. "Should I be afraid of you?"

I shook my head. "No, Anna. You'll never have anything to fear when it comes to me. You're safe with me."

From then on, I began to cherish those moments when Sam and I would be assigned to guard the part of the wall near the lake, because I knew that I would see Anna. I looked forward to the conversations I had with her. She was smart, funny and eager to learn. She often asked me about what the world was like outside The Shade and she hung on to my every word. I wanted to tell her how I felt about her, how much I adored her. One night, I decided that I would, but then she didn't show up.

My heart broke the next time I saw her again. I was at The Vale. She was in the arms of Felix, a huge smile on her face, her green eyes twinkling with adoration as she stared up at the Elite vampire. He obviously thought the world of her as he brushed his finger over her dark hair and placed a gentle kiss on her cheek.

They seemed to be a couple in love. When news broke out that Felix was going to turn Anna into a vampire so they could be together, I lost all hope of ever being with her. Then all of a sudden, he got tired of her. He left her at The Catacombs and she lost her mind.

The next time I tried to approach Anna, gone was the fearless young woman who felt safe around me at the lake. She took one look at me and screamed in terror before backing up into a corner, whimpering. I never found the guts to approach her again after that... until I had to.

It felt like Corrine had been talking to Anna for hours. When the door finally opened, a radiant Anna stepped out. Ian and I stood up at the sight of her. She raised her eyes and gave Ian a quick glance—almost as if she didn't even recognize him—before shifting her gaze toward me. Her face lit up in a huge smile and to my surprise, she ran to me and wrapped her arms around my neck.

I was frozen for a while, not sure what was happening. I looked at Ian, then at Corrine, who smiled and nodded my way.

"Should I be afraid of you?" Anna whispered in my ear.

The familiar question tugged at my heart, reminding me of the first time I'd seen her at the lake. "No, Anna," I responded, my voice choked. "You'll never have anything to fear when it comes to me. You're safe with me."

She nodded into my shoulder. "I always did feel safe with you, Kyle."

Later that day, I asked Corrine what happened and the witch told me that some of Anna's memories had come back—one of which was the time she'd spent with me at the lake.

"She says that she only feels safe with you out of all the vampires here in The Shade."

CHAPTER 14: DEREK

Her laughter echoed. Sofia was in the middle of what looked like a school playground, sitting on one of the swings, rocking as she began blowing bubbles. I hungrily took the sight of her in. She looked my way and flashed me that smile of hers.

She nodded toward me, motioning for me to go to her. I ran. I kept running, but I never seemed to reach her. I could feel the sunlight on my skin, the same light shining on her, shining from her. I ran faster, but it felt like I was running in place and every time I took my eyes off her, the sun began to burn.

Worry began to crease her face when she realized that I was having trouble reaching her. She stood from the swing and began to run too, reaching out toward me. She was about to reach me, our fingers about to touch, then just like that, she was gone.

I found myself standing on a shore just as the dawn was about to break. I was familiar with that scene, but I couldn't remember why. I could see the Lighthouse—my refuge. Right then, I heard a whimper followed by a chilling growl.

With the sun about to rise, I knew I had to find shelter, but I couldn't ignore the sound, especially because I knew that this had happened to me before and that everything was going to be all right.

The name of a woman from my past began to flash through my mind.

I know this scene. I have this memory. This was the morning I met Cora.

I ran toward the whimpers and just as I expected, behind a large rock, I found an unconscious woman about to come to her senses. Something was missing from the scene, but I couldn't put my finger on it.

I called out her name. "Cora?"

She rose to her feet and when I saw who it was, I froze.

It was Emilia. She was trembling and she ran into my arms, clinging tight. I could feel the heat of her tears hitting my skin.

I shuddered at what she said.

"It's me you belong to, Derek. Not her."

As if I was being controlled by a will not my own, I nodded.

"I know, Emilia. I know. I'm over Sofia. My heart belongs to you now."

The moment the words were said, a piercing scream filled the atmosphere.

I jolted up on my bed, my heart racing, my blood pounding. I was desperately trying to catch my breath. I could still hear the scream echoing in my ears. *Sofia's dead. I killed her. It's my fault.*

Guilt and panic overwhelmed me as I began to look around the room. I was relieved to find Sofia's still form on the bed beside me, but I wasn't satisfied with that. I had to know she was still alive. I began shaking her. "Sofia?"

She blinked and began to mumble.

I heaved out a sigh of relief. "You're all right." I scooped her sleepy form up in my arms and held tight.

"What's going on?" she drowsily asked.

"I thought I lost you."

She pulled away from me, this time alert and worried. "What's wrong, Derek? What happened?"

"I had a nightmare." My heart was pounding against my chest. I was breaking into a cold sweat, but I couldn't remember a thing about the dream I'd just had. Not even a single detail. All I knew was that I had this fear inside of me—a fear of Sofia getting hurt. I also had a nagging feeling that Emilia was *a lot* of trouble for Sofia and me. I swallowed hard as I faced Sofia.

"Tell me about it," she coaxed.

I scratched the back of my neck as I searched for the right words. "I don't really remember the dream, but I have to tell you something…"

The confession came out like a flood. I began telling her about the dreams I'd had about Emilia and not being able to remember the details after. Sofia deserved to know what was going on, so despite my fears of how she would take it, I revealed everything.

Sofia listened, taking every word in silently, asking questions where she needed more information.

"I can't deny that I'm attracted to her and that I feel some sort of connection with her, but you have to believe me when I say that she doesn't stand a chance against you. That's why I arranged that she be taken off the island immediately. I don't want anything or anyone to get between us."

Sofia gave me a half smile. "Does she have anything to do with why you want to get married all of a sudden?"

"I can't deny that the dreams had a hand in it. I guess it was my way of saying that it's you I want to be with. It's you I love. You know that, right?"

Her eyes began to moisten. "Of course I do. I adore you, Derek Novak." She cupped my face with her soft hands and pressed her lips against mine. "For the record, I can't wait to become Sofia Novak."

Chapter 15: Sofia

Spending the night at Derek's penthouse, waking up in his bed, and eating breakfast with him reminded me of our first few months together, when I'd still been known as his slave and he'd still been the prince of the island. For the span of a few hours, we were in our own cocoon, away from all the troubles surrounding us.

As I dabbed butter and jam on my piece of toast, I smiled, recalling the time I'd popped a piece of my breakfast into Derek's mouth. I looked at him as he drank a gulp of animal blood from his glass on the table. *I wonder when I'll actually be able to share a meal with him.*

He noticed my eyes on him and a smile formed on his face. "Can't get enough of me, can you?"

I rolled my eyes. "Don't turn the tables on me, Derek. You're the one who's craving me all the time."

His eyes dropped with shame.

I winced. *Bad joke.*

He opened his mouth to say something, then shut it. I wanted to say something to somehow make us forget the elephant in the room—the question we couldn't ignore. *What kind of married life are we going to live if he's craving my blood all the time?*

"It's not right and I know it," he began. "I don't want to give you some lame excuse. You don't deserve that. I'm sorry." He began rubbing the back of his neck.

I was sure that he was recalling what had happened the night before—something that'd been a lot more frequent lately. He just took what he wanted and bit.

I didn't want to talk about it simply because I didn't know how. I didn't want to dwell on the heaviness of the issue. "Let's talk about something else." I pulled a piece from my toast and threw it at him. "Anything other than that."

He seemed a bit more hesitant to move on than I did, but he eventually breathed out the tension and threw the piece of toast right back at me. "You're wasting food."

"It's not a waste if I get a smile out of you because of it." I grinned.

A smile eventually appeared on his chiseled face and despite my familiarity with him, I still blushed.

He seemed pleased, but then he shifted on his seat and I could tell that we weren't about to escape discussing serious matters. To my dismay, he began talking about my mother.

"Ingrid is acting strange. She asked to see Aiden and when I told her that I couldn't risk what she might do to him, she told me to ask you."

I shook my head. "It's too dangerous. We can't trust her." I remembered all the times I'd dared to put my trust in her and sorely regretted it after.

"That's what I said, but she was asking for another chance. She even asked to be called Camilla."

At that, I couldn't help but crease my brows in surprise. "I wonder what game she's playing."

"Whatever it is, it's bothering me," Derek admitted.

"Could you come with me? When I go see her?"

Derek frowned. "I want to, Sofia, but I did leave a lot of my responsibilities to the Council yesterday when I hung out with you. I do need to get back to running The Shade. I can't bail on them again. I can get one of the Elite to escort you. Ingrid won't be powerful enough to go against one of the Elite."

I was disappointed, but I understood. "I think Claudia would be great, if that's all right. She knows Ingrid."

Derek wasn't able to hide his surprise. "You trust Claudia?"

I nodded. "Her relationship with Yuri has been good for her, I think."

"Your ability to forgive and forget amazes me."

Claudia was probably one of the most demented vampires The Shade had ever known. It had taken months of living in The Shade before I'd found out that Ben, my childhood best friend, a guy I'd been deeply infatuated with, had also been abducted and brought to The Shade. He'd been taken by Claudia, who had proven to be a cruel and sadistic mistress. Claudia was the reason Ben hated vampires so much.

Somewhere along the line, however, Claudia had managed to get Ben to forgive her, enough that he'd requested the hunters to spare her life.

"Ben forgave her." I shrugged. "How could I not?"

"Must I remind you that she tried to turn you into a vampire without your consent?"

"She thought she was doing the right thing. She thought it was the only way we could be together."

Our eyes met and the tension—if it had ever left—came right back as we were once again faced by the fact that Derek was immortal and I was not. I was getting tired of the issue, but the urge to find the cure was even more adamant than before. But I had no idea what the cure was.

Troubled, I shook the thoughts away and finished my breakfast. "I think we better go. Long day ahead."

Derek groaned and blew out a sigh. I was expecting him to just shrug, bid me goodbye, and run off. Instead, he reminded me why I was so in love with him when he took my hands and coaxed me to stand up. He held my waist and pulled me close before kissing me on the forehead.

"We're going to find a way to be together, Sofia. I know it." He said it with so much conviction, I found myself wondering if he had doubts. Still, he gave me the hope I needed to get by.

"We're together now," I whispered. "That's what matters."

Derek was still on my mind when I saw Claudia waiting for me at the entrance of The Catacombs. The blonde smiled when she saw me coming. My heart began to race. There had been a time when a smile coming from her had been a reason to get worried, but I had to remind myself that this was a new Claudia.

She raised a brow at me, but there was a twinkle in her eyes. "I was told that I was to be your bodyguard. Why me of all people? Even Yuri was surprised."

"Well, you're the only vampire here who's actually spent time with Ingrid. I was thinking you knew what made her tick. You're not going to do anything crazy, are you?"

"We never know when the dark Claudia might decide to resurrect, but for now, you're good."

"The dark Claudia?" I chuckled.

She smiled as we began to head for the corridors that would lead to Ingrid's cell. "Yes... the one who was stupid enough to value power more than she valued love."

At that, I had to return her smile. I couldn't help but notice that glow about her whenever she smiled—one that could only be found in a person in love. I'd never thought I'd ever see Claudia gush, and yet that was exactly what she was doing right then.

I was about to tease her about Yuri, but then her eyes lit up. Yuri had just caught up with us.

Everyone in The Shade had known that Yuri was in love with Claudia—even Claudia herself—but for some reason, they'd never got together. They'd kept fighting and bickering and making each other miserable. It wasn't until Claudia had betrayed Derek by helping to abduct me and take me to Borys Maslen's territory that she'd realized how in love she was with Yuri. When she'd got back to The Shade, it hadn't taken long before the two of them got together.

"What are you doing here?" Claudia slapped Yuri's shoulder.

"I wanted to trust you, but I also wanted to make sure you don't end up killing Sofia. We all know how crazy you are."

Claudia rolled her eyes. "That's his way of saying that he wants to spend more time with me."

"Stop flattering yourself, Claudia." Yuri scowled. "Why on earth would I want to spend time with you?"

"Because no one else can do this to you." Claudia reached up and kissed him forcefully.

The public display of affection turned Yuri's pale skin a bright pink. Even I blushed as I averted my gaze.

Claudia pulled away and gave Yuri a self-satisfied smile. "No one can do that to you and make your head start reeling."

Yuri bit his lip, but quickly recovered and shot me an embarrassed look. "Aren't you ashamed of what Sofia would think?"

"Ashamed of what *she* would think? Weren't you there all those times she and Derek publicly professed their love for each other? They're the king and queen of public displays of affection."

Yuri chuckled as he shot me a look. I was fighting the urge to blush.

"You got to admit, Sofia," he teased. "She has a point."

To my relief, I found I didn't need to come up with a response, because Ingrid's cell was already in sight. I drew a breath, not quite knowing what to expect. Encounters with my mother weren't ever pleasant.

As if the day didn't have enough surprises, Claudia gently held me by the elbow. "She's just broken, Sofia. Like I was. She'll come around."

Her words tugged at my heart—both moving me and giving me hope. At the same time, I detested the idea that Claudia knew my mother more than I did.

Still, I expressed my gratefulness to Claudia before heading to the cell.

When I entered the cell, Ingrid's eyes lit up. I was disappointed to realize that it wasn't me who caused her delight. It was Claudia.

I found myself standing by the cell door as Ingrid and Claudia embraced and began chatting. They were a picture of the mother-daughter connection that I'd never got the chance to have. I'd known that they'd spent time together, but I couldn't understand how they could've gotten so close so quickly.

"Claudia's been visiting Ingrid," Yuri explained in a low voice behind me. "She says that they're two of a kind. They have this strange connection."

"I can see that," I responded, hoping that my voice wouldn't break. *I just can't help but be jealous. I've never seen Ingrid look at me the way she looks at Claudia.*

Yuri chuckled. "Claudia says that Ingrid is like the mother she never had. It's ironic considering that Claudia is centuries older than Ingrid."

The mother she never had. The mother I never had. I swallowed hard and tried not to think about it. "You really do love Claudia, don't you?"

"From the first moment I ever laid eyes on her… It was a darn long wait, but it was worth every second. Thanks for bringing her back to me."

I was about to respond, but both Ingrid's and Claudia's eyes settled on me. I was unsure what to do.

"I'm sorry." Claudia smiled sheepishly. "This is your time with Camilla, not mine."

My brow rose. *She's calling her Camilla?*

It seemed Ingrid was reading my mind. "I asked her to call me Camilla. I would prefer to be called that from now on."

I just stood there, staring at her. I didn't want to accuse her of playing mind games with me, but I didn't want to be fooled again either.

"I know I haven't given you reason to trust me, Sofia, but I want to make amends. I thought it would be harder to get into your good graces, so I requested to be brought to Aiden instead. At least with him I have a history I can bank on."

"You broke his heart," I said bluntly.

She nodded. "I know. He didn't deserve that." She paused. "I want another chance, Sofia. I have no one left in this world but you and Aiden. Maybe I could still get Camilla back if I tried hard enough."

It felt like she was messing with my mind. I wanted so much for it to be true. It would've been a dream come true for me if both my parents came to my wedding, but this was Ingrid Maslen—the same woman who had allowed the monster Borys Maslen to try to turn me into a vampire when I was nine years old. She was the same woman who'd stood by and watched as he sank his claws into my thighs and fed on me. She was the same woman who'd been obsessed with making me his bride.

"I'll ask Aiden. If he wants to see you, then so be it. If he doesn't, then I guess you'll just have to find another way to convince us that you want to change."

Ingrid gave me a heartbroken smile. "I understand."

Claudia took a step forward and began to speak on behalf of my mother, but I lifted a hand to stop her. "I know you understand my mother more than I ever will, Claudia, but she's not the only one who's broken."

Claudia closed her mouth and eased herself into Yuri's arms. There was an electric sense of sadness as we left Ingrid's cell and began making our way out of The Catacombs.

"I do believe that she's sorry, Sofia." Claudia spoke up.

"I know." As much as I wanted to believe Claudia, memories of the hatred in Ingrid's eyes back in hunter territory made it difficult for me to believe that Ingrid had changed. "If she truly is sorry, Aiden will be able to tell. He knows her more than any of us do."

"I think he still loves her." Yuri nodded with assurance.

My eyes shot toward the vampire. "How would you know that, Yuri?"

"I've been having some talks with Aiden. Whenever Claudia visited Ingrid, I went to see Aiden."

My face contorted with bewilderment. "Why?" The idea of my father hanging out with a vampire seemed absurd.

"Well, aside from your father being a very smart man capable of a good conversation, he loves Ingrid. I figured he'd be the best person to ask for advice on how I'm supposed to keep loving this crazy girl right here." He began messing with Claudia's hair and got a slap on the shoulder from the petite vampire.

"You really shouldn't annoy me too much, Yuri," Claudia warned.

"Oh?" Yuri smirked. "Why's that?"

"I'm a vampire, you know. I could switch off the love I feel for you any time I want."

Yuri began laughing. "No, you can't. If there's one emotion we vampires can't switch off, it's love. Look at Ingrid—no matter how much she tries, she still can't stop loving Aiden. You said so yourself."

"Is that true?" I asked. "You can't switch off love?"

Yuri cast a fond gaze toward Claudia. "Believe me, Sofia. I tried for hundreds of years. I never stopped loving Claudia." Their eyes met and within a few seconds, Yuri made a face. "But I think it's just because Claudia is part witch... a *witchpire*. I'm pretty sure she cast a spell on me or something. Otherwise, why on earth would I love her?"

Something told me that they were going to bicker the whole time they were together, so I bade them goodbye.

Before I left, Yuri grabbed my arm and looked straight into my eyes, his face filled with brotherly concern. "Sofia, I know your story. We all watched it unfold. You know The Shade for what it is—all its darkness, all its light. I'm sure that your experience on this island is of a completely different vein than mine, but I'm hoping you see, just the way that I do, that The Shade is a place of second chances. You gave Derek a lot of chances to redeem himself." Yuri shrugged. "Maybe your parents deserve the same thing."

"I'm working on giving them that chance," I assured him. I was just about to thank him when Xavier arrived, out of breath.

"I think you'll want to see this."

I gulped. The expression on his face was telling me the exact opposite. Whatever it was, it wasn't something that I wanted to see.

What on earth just happened?

Chapter 16: Derek

I couldn't believe my eyes. Emilia was lying face down on the shore in the exact same spot I had found Cora centuries ago. Xavier, Ashley and I had been headed for the Lighthouse so we could prepare my surprise date with Sofia that night when we discovered the young woman.

"Who is she?" Ashley asked, as she approached the motionless body tentatively.

Xavier knelt in front of the girl and brushed her hair away from her face. He lifted his eyes toward me to let me know what I already knew. "It's the original vampire's daughter."

I approached Emilia and gasped.

Xavier's jaw tightened. "She's not looking well."

He was right. Emilia's wet, brown hair was a tangled mess and blood was flowing from her scalp. She was bruised and unconscious, and for some strange reason, I was blaming myself. *Did she not warn you that she would be in trouble if you made her go back to her father?*

My stomach churned. *What kind of a creature is the Elder?* If he was our foe, then we were up against a more powerful creature than we knew how to handle. *How on earth could anyone do this to their own daughter?*

"They must've used one of those serums that keep vampires from healing." Xavier began thinking out loud. "Who would do this to her? Aren't they afraid of her father?"

I scoffed at the question. "Odds are that it's her father who did this to her."

Xavier and Ashley exchanged glances, grimacing.

"What are you going to do with her?" Ashley asked.

I stared at Emilia. I didn't want to touch her. I didn't want anything to do with her, but I knew I couldn't just leave her there. *Don't make the same mistake you did the last time. Don't keep Sofia out of it.*

I decided right then that Sofia and I were a team and that I should stop making decisions without her—especially when the decisions involved young women I was extremely attracted to. "Go get Sofia. I can't decide what to do with Emilia unless Sofia is involved."

Xavier nodded and sped off.

Ashley seemed intrigued. "Since when do you factor Sofia in when it comes to decisions like this?"

"Since I decided to marry her." I looked her directly in the eye. "You do realize that once I marry Sofia, she's going to be your queen."

Ashley just laughed. "I have to remind myself that you're king

100

of The Shade, Derek. Most of the time, I just think of you and Sofia as a regular high-school couple. Only instead of the two of you being prom king and queen, you're running an entire kingdom."

I stared at her, wondering how she could possibly live life like it was a game. I breathed a sigh of relief when Xavier and Sofia arrived. My gut clenched when Sofia's face paled at the sight of Emilia.

"She's back," Sofia croaked.

I was about to approach her and pull her into my arms, but compassion filled her green eyes at the sight of Emilia.

"What happened to her?" Sofia rushed to Emilia's side. "Dear heavens, who would do this to her? I think she needs blood. It will help her heal..."

My eyes widened with shock when Sofia raised her wrist as if she were trying to decide if she should feed Emilia her own blood. *Has she gone mad?* "You are not going to feed her your blood, Sofia." I shot my eyes toward Ashley, eager to rid myself of her peskiness. "Go get some blood for Emilia before Sofia gets any ideas."

Ashley tilted her head to the side. "Animal or human?"

I glared at her and realized that Xavier and Sofia were doing the exact same thing.

"What?" Ashley shrugged. "We've all been skimping on our reserves of human blood. Now we have to feed it to our enemy's daughter?"

Ever since several rebels in The Shade had blown up the chilling chambers, where we stored our reserves of human blood, we'd been living mostly on animal blood—taken from the wildlife of The Shade. We also had reserves of human blood, mostly taken from blood donations by the Naturals, but we made sure to use them sparingly.

"Could you just leave?" I snapped at Ashley.

She ran off and Sofia checked on Emilia. "I think she has a lot of broken bones..." Sofia frowned. "Her body doesn't look right." She gazed up at me and Xavier. "Can't we get her somewhere comfortable?"

"You're seriously considering bringing her onto the island?" I asked Sofia, wondering what she thought about Emilia being back after everything I'd told her.

"All I know right now is that she obviously needs help and that we're the only ones capable of giving it to her."

I couldn't help but admire her. Sofia didn't see a threat. She just saw someone broken and in need of mending.

"Okay then," I finally agreed.

"Where are we going to take her?" Xavier asked.

We all exchanged glances and though my first instinct was to take Emilia to The Cells, I knew that Sofia would object. Someone as wounded as Emilia didn't belong in a prison cell. She needed to be in a hospital. In The Shade, the closest thing we had to a hospital was either The Catacombs—where Emilia definitely did not belong—or The Sanctuary.

I made a decision right there. *At least Corrine can control Emilia in case she tries to do something to harm The Shade.*

"Let's take her to The Sanctuary."

CHAPTER 17: AIDEN

A pack of cigarettes tied to a lighter with a rubber band landed on my bed in front of me. I looked toward the prison cell's bars and found Yuri there smoking a cigarette. I was grateful for the favor and still bothered by the bond I was forming with a vampire. I couldn't help it though. I liked Yuri. He was like the son I'd never had.

"I told you I'd bring you some, didn't I?" Yuri said smugly, before taking another puff from his cigarette.

"Where did you get these?" I asked him, unable to hide my gratefulness. I was infamous in The Shade for my taste for tobacco.

"Claudia has a bunch of them stacked up in her penthouse."

"Have you talked to Sofia about getting me out of here?"

Yuri winced. "Sorry, man. I forgot. It's been crazy around here. I have been putting in a good word or two on your behalf." He

A BLAZE OF SUN

narrowed his eyes at me. "Don't make me regret it, Claremont. I don't ever want Derek or Sofia to have a reason not to trust me."

"Thank you."

"Ingrid is asking to be brought to you…" He paused. "Actually, make that Camilla. She no longer wants to be called Ingrid."

I made a face as I lit my cigarette and took a puff. "What's her game now?"

"She says that she wants her family back."

"Right." I didn't know whether to laugh or get angry. *How dare she play that card after everything she put Sofia through…*

"If she really is willing to change, would you take her back?"

I wanted to say yes. I wanted to trust Camilla again more than anything, but I couldn't. Not as long as she was a threat to Sofia. "I think the only way I can ever trust Camilla again is if she gets back into Sofia's good graces."

Yuri laughed. "Sucks for Camilla then. Sofia says that the only way she can ever trust Camilla again is if she gets back into *your* good graces. Neither of you are willing to take a chance on her."

"Camilla isn't Claudia, Yuri…"

"What's the difference between them?"

Yuri had told me Claudia's tragic story. I could see why he thought that our story was similar to theirs, but it wasn't.

Claudia had been a prostitute, just like her mother. She'd experienced abuse from a cruel man, and was a broken, untrusting creature.

"You know what broke Claudia, Yuri. You understood the depths of her brokenness. You saw why firsthand. You admit yourself that you contributed when you used her that first night."

Yuri's lips twitched at the recollection of the night Claudia had been brought to him in a mask and he'd found out only after

104

sleeping with her that she was the girl he was in love with.

"You can't fix something if you don't know what's broken." Camilla had never let me in. She'd never opened up her past to me. She'd never allowed me to help her heal. "You had to wait hundreds of years before the woman you love came around. I can't wait that long. I will never become immortal like you. I don't ever want to be."

"The way I see it, Aiden"—Yuri smirked knowingly—"you are mortal. You only have this one lifetime, a few decades at best, to be with the woman you love and I think that's what's bothering you. You still love Camilla—even if you don't know what broke her. It doesn't make a difference whether you know the reason, Aiden. We're *all* broken. The question is can you still love her and trust her in spite of that?"

"I did that for a full decade and still she left. Camilla left me. She left her daughter."

"Well, I did it for centuries and still Claudia left. Love doesn't have to be returned in order for it to be true, Aiden. When Claudia came crawling back, don't you think I wanted to make her suffer? I wanted to see her cry upon losing me. I wanted to hurt her like she'd hurt me. But I chose to love her. I made the choice to forgive her and take her back. Part of me is still afraid that she'll go back to the way she was, but at least I'll have this moment in time, this period when I can say that the woman I love shows me that she loves me in return. Don't miss out on that, Aiden."

I stared at Yuri, a man who had been turned into a vampire in his early twenties, half my age. I wondered where all the wisdom was coming from, only to remember that Yuri might look young physically, but he was actually giving me centuries' worth of experience.

I took a long puff from my cigarette, not knowing what to say.

"So what are you going to do?" Yuri asked after a long silence.

I scoffed at the question, "After that long-winded speech of yours, what choice do I have other than to see Camilla?"

Yuri laughed and I realized that as much as I hated to admit it, I considered this vampire my friend.

CHAPTER 18: INGRID

I began to hold my breath the moment Aiden entered my cell. Yuri tossed him a wooden stake as he approached—a safety measure.

The vampire winked at me. "Be careful, Camilla. Word is that he's pretty good with one of those things."

I smirked. "He won't need it unless the only reason he's here is to attempt to kill me, Yuri."

"I don't think he's here for that." Yuri grinned. "Don't get yourself into more trouble than you're already in, Camilla." Yuri nodded at both of us before leaving.

With Yuri gone, I forced myself to look at Aiden. He crossed his arms over his chest and leaned against the stone wall, wooden stake secure in his grip, green eyes glaring at me. "What game are you playing now, Ingrid?" He cocked his head to the side. "Or should I start calling you Camilla like everyone else?"

I had only one chance to get this right, so I asked Aiden the one question I wanted to hear the answer to. "Do you still love me, Aiden?"

A muscle on his jaw twitched. He was quiet for what felt like an eternity as he gave it thought. When he spoke up, I wished he'd just kept his silence. "It doesn't matter whether I love you or not, Ingrid, because you were right. I love our daughter more."

He couldn't have known how much those words stung, but I reeled in my temper. "I guess I deserve that."

"I will never understand how, for nine years, you raised someone as strong-spirited and as kindhearted as Sofia."

I swallowed hard, wondering how many more insults I would have to endure.

"How about you, Ingrid? Do you still love me?"

"If I said yes, would you believe me?"

To my relief, he nodded, "Yes, but you see… that's where we're the same. We love something else more. I love Sofia more than I love you. You love power more than you love me."

The truth was like a splash of cold water and all I could do was hang my head in shame. I couldn't deny it, because for the past decade, I'd been controlled by my thirst for power.

"You found yourself powerless the moment Borys Maslen died. You hate Sofia even more for killing him, don't you?"

Aiden was making me feel vulnerable. I hated that he knew me far too well.

"Sofia did the right thing. Borys Maslen does not deserve to live and with his demise, you became what you always were, Ingrid. A weakling. You have all this power as a vampire, but you're held captive in an island that is not your own by a coven who has vampires centuries older and far more powerful than you. You gave up your husband and your daughter, your whole life, for nothing, Ingrid. I hope you realize that." He scoffed. "It must kill you to think that after everything you gave up, it means nothing to be Ingrid Maslen anymore. You're just as powerless as Ingrid as you were as Camilla. Maybe you're right, maybe I should start calling you Camilla once again... to remind you of everything you've lost."

I couldn't take any more of the truth. "Enough. I don't want to hear any more, Aiden. Shut up or I swear you'll regret it."

He seemed amused by my change of countenance. "There you go. That's it, *Camilla.*" He said my human name as if it was a taunt. "Stop pretending that you want to be a wife to your husband and a mother to your daughter. That's not you. You've been Ingrid Maslen for too long."

He was taunting me. I wouldn't have it. I'd sworn a long time ago that I would never allow a man to treat me that way again. Before I could keep myself from doing it, I attacked Aiden. I pinned him to a wall, ready to bite into his neck, only to find his wooden stake pointed at my heart.

He smiled. "Do it. Take a bite. Drink my blood. Make no mistake about it. I won't hesitate to kill you."

I looked into his green eyes, wondering if he was bluffing, wondering if he could really drive that stake into my heart. Either way, he'd already been stabbing my heart with his words from the moment he arrived at my cell.

Despite all my attempts to keep it from happening, tears began to brim in my eyes and stream down my cheeks. I was still in love with Aiden, and it hurt that we had reached this point—both willing to hurt each other, even kill each other. I still bluffed, poising myself to bite into his neck. I could feel the pointed end of his stake sink into my skin.

I shut my eyes and shook my head. I couldn't do it. I could bluff as much as I wanted to, but I couldn't drink Aiden's blood. I pulled away from him, hating the way my body was trembling as I backed down.

I could feel his stare on me as he heaved one breath after another. "Give me one good reason why I should trust you again, Ingrid. Why should I open my heart to you again? Why should I think that Camilla is still somewhere deep inside your bloodthirsty self?"

One good reason. I tried to hold back the sobs, but I couldn't. Still, despite the way my body was shaking, I managed to answer. "Because you want to, Aiden. You want to trust me. More than that, I *need* you to trust me." *My life and yours hang in the balance.*

He stared at me for what felt like hours, studying me. "Okay, Camilla. I'll play whatever game this is. You really want me to trust you? Oh, wait, not want... you *need* me to trust you. Is that right?"

I didn't respond. Instead, I just lifted my eyes in order to meet his cold glare. I would've given anything at that moment to once again have him look at me the way he had before I became a vampire.

Aiden began to nod slowly. "Fine. I will trust you on one condition, Camilla."

"I will do anything."

"Bare yourself completely to me. Tell me about your past. Tell me why you're so broken. Tell me what you never had the guts to tell me before. Let me in, Camilla. I want to know everything."

I stared at him in horror. He'd asked of me the one thing I could never give. He was asking me to live out my greatest fear— being discovered for what I really was. He was asking me to relive the horrors of my childhood and revisit my brokenness. I shook my head. "I can't do that, Aiden. You're practically asking for my soul."

"That's the price of trust, Camilla. Openness. Vulnerability. The ability to risk getting hurt. And don't think for one second that you can lie to me. I know you well enough to know if you're just giving me some story that you made up. Tell me the truth about who you are. The whole truth. Can you do that?"

"What if I can't?"

"Then I can't trust you, can I?"

"Aiden, please..."

"I've given my condition."

I shook my head and buried my face in my palms. It felt like defeat. I'd never felt weaker than I did at that moment.

When I didn't respond for what felt like an eternity, Aiden nodded and motioned to leave. "Let me know when you're ready to give in, Cam."

Cam... He hasn't called me that in years... Not since... I held my breath when he turned his back on me. He was about to call for Yuri when I did the most courageous thing I'd done in years. "Wait."

Slowly, Aiden turned to face me. His brow rose.

It took hours. It took many tears. I told him everything. He held me. He gave me the comfort that I'd been deprived of through all those years of abuse at my foster parents' hands.

What I was telling him made Claudia's experience seem like child's play. My foster parents had been violent, merciless people and growing up with them had been a living nightmare. They'd helped me through high school and even got me a scholarship for college, but everything had a price and I was often the payment they required. Not money, definitely not gratefulness—me, all of me—my body, my dignity, my very soul.

No man had ever stood up for me before. I knew what it was like to feel helpless and abandoned. Even when I got away from their grasp, I was still haunted by what they put me through. Then came Aiden.

Aiden was the love of my life. I'd never felt like I deserved him. Surely someone as perfect as him didn't deserve someone as broken as me, but he'd come into my life and he'd made me feel like I could be whole again. Still, around him, I was pretending. I was a broken creature, and even his love couldn't fix me.

I told Aiden what it had been like to be married to him, what I'd felt like around him—how unworthy I was.

That night, Aiden listened. He barely even said any words of comfort. He just held me and let me cry into his shoulder as I told him horror story after horror story of all the terrible things I'd gone through as a child and how it had made me the woman I was.

When I finally finished telling him my story, he kissed me on the forehead and told me that he still loved Camilla and that he always would.

"Your past can never change that," he assured me.

I gained his trust that night and in doing so, I had to pay the ultimate price. I had to bare my soul to him and let him see all its emptiness—an emptiness that his love and acceptance was able to fill. I knew what that meant. Becoming vulnerable to Aiden—completely vulnerable to him—would make what I had to do even harder than it already was.

He made love to me—gentle and tender as always, but not lacking in passion.

When I woke up next to him, I was faced with a new dilemma.

Secure in the love Aiden still had for me, I searched myself for any hatred I still harbored toward my daughter and found not a single trace of it left.

I no longer wanted to kill Sofia, but I was still forced to.

Chapter 19: Vivienne

I sensed her presence the moment she was brought within the island. *Emilia.* My heart began to race and my pulse doubled. I dropped my shearing scissors and bolted out of my greenhouse.

"She can't be back," I began to mumble. "She can't be here in The Shade." Following my instincts, I sped towards The Sanctuary and, sure enough, I found Xavier gently laying an unconscious Emilia on the bed inside one of the chambers.

Derek and Sofia stood nearby. Ashley was standing by the bed, holding a packet of blood. Corrine, on the other hand, was seated on an ottoman by the wall, staring suspiciously at Emilia.

"What's going on?" I demanded. All eyes turned toward me as I stepped forward. "What is she doing back at the island? At The Sanctuary of all places?"

"She needs care, Vivienne," Sofia explained.

"Then she should get it from her own people, not from us. I don't trust her."

"Neither do we, Vivienne." Derek spoke up. "But what are we going to do with her? She washed up on the shore beaten to a bloody pulp. We can't just leave her to die..."

That's exactly what we should do. I knew that I was being ruthless, perhaps even dark, but every fiber of my being wanted Emilia off the island. I turned my eyes toward the witch for help, but Corrine just gave me a shrug in response. I stared at Emilia's motionless form. I shook my head. "This doesn't feel right. It's too much of a coincidence..."

Derek creased his brows. "What's too much of a coincidence?"

As twins, Derek and I had always had a strange connection. It'd been there since we were kids. I had a way of knowing his dreams or figuring out what was going through his mind, especially when it was needed.

"You've been dreaming about her. You dreamed about her at the exact same spot you found her, did you not? At the shore near the Lighthouse? You thought she was Cora... The fact that it actually happened, you think it's just coincidence?"

Derek shifted his weight from one foot to another. I sensed from his expression that he didn't remember the dream and it just suddenly became clear to him. "I have to admit that it's strange. But it was just a dream."

Sofia looked at Derek in question. "You've been dreaming about Cora too?"

Derek shook his head. "No... This one... I remember the dream now. It's just as Vivienne said. I saw it exactly like this. That was the same spot I found Cora hundreds of years ago. I dreamed about it earlier. I thought it was Cora who was on the beach, but it turned out to be Emilia."

Sofia nodded, wrinkling her nose in thought. The idea of my brother being able to tell Sofia these things made me feel better about the situation, but I still could not deny the threat I felt just from seeing Emilia there. She was a source of power that we couldn't afford to underestimate.

Xavier, one of my closest friends, stared at me. He knew me well enough to know that I wouldn't be objecting this much if I didn't feel ill at ease around Emilia. "Maybe it's better we leave her this way…" He frowned.

Sofia objected. "We can take her down if she decides to fight against us once she heals. With all four of you vampires and Corrine here, she won't stand a chance no matter how powerful she is, but we can't just leave her like this. It's inhumane."

I grimaced. "She's not human, Sofia."

"Maybe so, but I am, Vivienne, and lest you forget, a part of you is too…"

That silenced me. How could it not? Ever since Sofia became a part of our lives, we seemed to be obsessed with getting our humanity back—humanity that we'd long ago tried to silence.

Ashley looked from one person to the other, still clutching the bag of human blood in her hand. "Are we going to feed the blood to her or not? It's not like she's going to die if we don't. It will just take her longer to heal, right?"

"I don't see why we should prolong her agony." Sofia stood her ground. "It doesn't seem right."

I knew her well enough to know that her greatest weakness was her compassion. She seemed to have a never-ending supply of it and although I respected that about her, there were times when we couldn't afford to let our compassion get us into trouble. That was exactly what that woman was going to bring: trouble.

Still, I was outnumbered and by the look on Derek's face, he wasn't going to abandon Emilia. Not knowing what to do, I stormed out of The Sanctuary.

I couldn't have imagined how big a mistake that was.

I'd barely walked out the large doors that led outside The Sanctuary when Xavier came running after me.

"Vivienne! What's going on?" He held my arm to make me face him. We were already in the gardens outside of the white temple-like structure. "It's unlike you to object to helping anyone—no matter what you feel about the person—and it's not like you to just storm off like that. What's wrong?"

I wasn't being myself and I knew it. I was known in The Shade as the calm and collected one, but after my return from hunter territory, I couldn't find that cool. I was afraid. And I had no idea how to handle it. "You saw how the original vampire killed my father, Xavier."

The memory of my father's body, drained of all blood, impaled on a pole in the middle of The Vale's town square was forever etched in my mind. None of us had any idea how the original vampire had done it, but he'd killed my father even while Gregor was locked up in The Shade. He'd left a message—carved into my father's flesh: *You chose the wrong side.*

I loved my father and I knew that he'd loved me. He'd been willing to start anew, to change. I'd seen it in his eyes the last time I got to spend time with him. The Elder had robbed him of that.

I was still mourning the death of my father and my brother, Lucas. I wasn't about to mourn Derek's. With Emilia on the island, I couldn't shake the feeling that my twin was in grave danger.

"Derek is all I have left, Xavier. I already lost my father and I lost Lucas too... I can't afford to lose Derek. I won't have a reason to live if I lose him. I would rather die."

Xavier was taken aback. "Vivienne, I know you love your family. I admire that about you, but you have to open your eyes and start living for yourself at some point. You have people who care about you and have been loyal to you these past years—not just Derek or Gregor or Lucas. Liana, Sofia, me... We all care what happens to you, but it's not even about that. There's a reason you're alive, a reason *I'm* still alive. You have to keep striving until you've fulfilled that reason. Live for *you*, Vivienne, because damn it... you're worth living for and you're worth dying for."

Xavier gently brushed a loose strand of hair from my face. He leaned over slowly and I was sure he was about to kiss me. I pulled away and shook my head.

"I can't, Xavier." I stepped away from him, watching his eyes moisten at my rejection. "I'm sorry. I just... I need to figure out a way to stop Emilia."

I turned and ran, not exactly certain where to go. I needed space. I needed time to think. Because as much as I hated to admit it, Xavier struck a chord so deep, I had to get away from him to keep myself from crying.

I'd lived the past five centuries for my family, and never for myself. Xavier's words echoed in my head. *Live for you, Vivienne.*

I had no idea how to do that, because I really had no idea who I was anymore.

I ran for hours. I ran until my thighs began to throb. I ran and ran and ran until I ended up back at The Sanctuary, ready to stab Emilia with a wooden stake, only to freeze the moment I lifted the stake in the air.

Emilia's eyes shot open and a manic smile formed on her lips at the sight of me. "It's been a while, Vivienne. It seems like you're going to be a lot more trouble for me now."

I creased my brows, wondering what she was talking about. I tried with all my might to stab her with the stake, but my body wouldn't budge.

"Don't bother, Vivienne. You won't be able to move." Emilia sat up on the bed. "After you left, they didn't give me the blood. They were too alarmed by your reaction, so they figured I could wait another day while they discussed what to do with me. I didn't need the blood to heal. All I needed was The Sanctuary. This is my temple, is it not? My power as a witch comes from this place."

I was so confused by what she was telling me. I tried to speak but I couldn't even move my lips. Panic was beginning to creep into my body. *Corrine, where are you?*

"You may not recognize my face any longer, but you know me." Emilia smiled. "I don't blame you. I'm a far cry from the image you once knew. I was transformed into the woman of Derek's wildest dreams, his ultimate ideal. No matter what your prophecies say, *Seer*, Derek does not belong with Sofia. He belongs with me."

She rose to her feet and began stretching as she walked around the bedroom. Speaking to me wasn't a good sign. If she was confident enough to tell me her deepest secrets, she was planning to get rid of me.

"I waited hundreds of years before my transformation was complete. I waited until the time he would wake up and find that he's supposed to be with me, but then you brought that redheaded spitfire into the island and took everything away from me. You ruined everything, Vivienne. I really should punish you for that."

Suddenly, I understood what Xavier had been trying to tell me earlier. I'd always been willing to lose my life for my family because

I hadn't actually lived it. I didn't have a life of my own, and at that moment I desperately wanted one, but it seemed Emilia wasn't going to make that possible.

If I could move, I would be shivering with terror, but I could only watch her, wondering what she had in mind for me.

"It's a shame I can't kill you, Vivienne. I love Derek and I know that if I ever harm his twin, he'll never be able to forgive me. I can't have that. I can't risk losing his love for me."

Losing his love for you? He doesn't love you, you crazy bitch.

She brushed her fingers over my cheekbone and the moment her skin touched mine, I saw a vision that revealed who Emilia really was. She was no ordinary vampire, and it wasn't just because she was the original vampire's daughter. Terror took over as it sank in how much of a threat she really was to Derek.

"No, I won't end your life, Vivienne. But I can always do the next best thing." She grinned before snapping her fingers.

The sound hadn't even registered in my brain yet when I found myself in my bed. I tried to get out of the bed, but I couldn't. Instead, I found myself battling the urge to fall asleep, a battle I knew I was about to lose. *What has she done to me?*

It didn't take long for me to figure it out. As I drifted off to a deep sleep, I knew that she'd cast the same spell she'd placed on my brother four hundred years ago, and right before I lost consciousness, two thoughts circled in my mind...

First: *Will I ever wake up?*

And second: *Emilia is one of the most powerful witches who ever lived. She is The Shade's original witch.*

She is Cora.

CHAPTER 20: SOFIA

I was snuggled against Derek on his living room couch, my head leaning against his shoulder. We were both exhausted from hours of looking for Vivienne. We had already traveled all over The Shade calling out her name, to receive no response. Nobody else had seen her either.

"I feel so bad about not hearing her out," Derek muttered as he brushed his fingers over my hair. "It's Vivienne. She doesn't freak out like that for no reason."

I didn't voice my thoughts, but Vivienne had been in pretty bad shape back at hunter territory. The hunters had been brainwashing her to try to extract information from her regarding the location of The Shade. She was so loyal and so intent on protecting her family and the kingdom that she had blocked out all information that would compromise The Shade. The hunters had never got anything from her, but she'd been a paranoid mess when she was first brought to me at Hawk Headquarters.

"Don't torture yourself, Derek. We were doing what we thought was right. I'm sure Vivienne is okay. She probably just needs time."

"I just don't understand where she could've gone. Why can't anybody find her?"

"Is there any possibility that she could've left The Shade?"

Derek shook his head. "I doubt it. Vivienne would never risk that. I don't see why she would have any reason to leave. Besides, people at the Port would know. If she didn't pass through the Port to take one of the subs, then she would've been swimming in broad daylight."

Right then, Xavier burst into the room without even bothering to knock. "We've found her," he announced.

Derek and I jumped to our feet.

"Where? Where is she?" Derek asked.

Xavier's jaw clenched. "Inside her bedroom. Fast asleep. She refuses to wake up, Derek."

Derek immediately sped us toward his sister's bedroom. Corrine was standing by Vivienne's bed. She set her eyes on us the moment we arrived.

"What's going on, Corrine?" Derek asked. "What happened to Vivienne?"

"She's under a spell," Corrine explained. "The same spell you asked Cora to place on you. This is definitely her sleeping spell at work. I would know it anywhere."

"Did you do this?" Derek spat at the witch.

Corrine glared at Derek.

I grabbed his arm. "Derek! Corrine is on our side."

"Well, who else would know how to use that spell?" Xavier, who had followed us to Vivienne's bedroom, fueled Derek's suspicions. "There aren't any witches in this island aside from her."

"Why would I do this to Vivienne?" Corrine rolled her eyes. That was when I noticed that she was tense about something.

"What's going on, Corrine?" I let go of Derek's arm and approached the witch who had been a good friend to me throughout my time in The Shade. "What's wrong?"

"I don't think I'm the only witch in this island. Not anymore."

"What are you talking about?" Derek frowned.

"I think Emilia is a witch. I left The Sanctuary a couple of hours after you left. I did my routine visit at The Catacombs, then went to check on Anna and how she was doing. When I returned to The Sanctuary, I couldn't enter anymore." She turned her eyes toward Derek. "I was about to tell you, but Xavier alerted me about having found Vivienne. I think Emilia had something to do with this."

Chills began to run up and down my spine. "What does that mean for us? How much of a threat is she? How could she have healed so quickly?"

"Vivienne was right. We never should've let her on the island." He turned toward Corrine. "Can you break the spell she put on my sister?"

Corrine shrugged. "I can try, but I don't think I have my powers anymore, Derek."

"What? If you don't have your powers anymore then how is the protective spell still over The Shade?"

"Either Emilia is keeping it up or The Shade is no longer protected."

As if The Shade not being protected wasn't enough to contend with, Yuri and Claudia showed up with an alarming announcement.

"The Shade is under attack."

CHAPTER 21: DEREK

I was overwhelmed. I didn't know what to do or where to go. Everyone present was looking to me for either direction or action and I had neither.

I stared at Vivienne's sleeping form, hoping that I could somehow communicate with her. *I never should've second-guessed her.*

Everything that was going on in The Shade crashed down upon me. *The Shade is no longer protected by the spell. That means that the hunters can now detect Aiden's tracker. It also means that we need to finish the battle by sunrise. The battle. The Shade is under attack. My sister is under some sort of spell and Emilia has taken over The Sanctuary. What are you going to do, Novak?*

"I'm going to The Sanctuary," I announced.

Sofia nodded. "I am going with you."

I shook my head at her and was about to tell her why when

Xavier stepped forward, eyes narrowed at me.

"Derek, didn't you hear? The Shade is under attack."

"I know that," I responded through gritted teeth, trying to reel in my temper. "Xavier, you and Cameron think the same way that I do when it comes to battle. Yuri and Claudia are more than capable of helping. Lead the battle. I need to deal with Emilia, because I'm pretty sure that she will refuse to deal with anyone else but me. We can't afford to keep The Shade unprotected. Corrine is coming with me."

Sofia was about to say something, but I shot a glare at her that made her shut her mouth. I could tell that she was trying to be sensitive to the enormous pressure I was under. "Do you trust me, Sofia?"

She nodded. "Of course I do."

"I want you by my side, but right now, I need you to go to your father. Tell the guards there that I've authorized his release. They will believe you. Get him to do everything he can to hold off the hunters. If the protective spell is gone, and I think that it is, I'm pretty sure they have The Shade's location by now."

She gave me a quick nod and assured me that she would be on it. I was about to leave, but I took a step back to assuage my fears. "Make sure you have one of the guards with you, Sofia, okay? At all times. Sam and Kyle... I need to know that you'll be all right..."

Trying to feel secure in the knowledge that I had capable men and women going about the tasks that needed to be done, I grabbed Corrine's hand and sped toward The Sanctuary. The moment we got there, I moved forward toward the door and found an invisible force field blocking my entry.

"She's blocking everyone out," Corrine said, staring at the temple.

"Can't you do anything about this?" I didn't want to lose my nerve in front of the one person who could help us, but the panic was taking hold of me.

Corrine shook her head. "She's more powerful than I am. A lot more powerful. I think she's suppressing my powers."

My fists clenched and every muscle in my body tensed. "Emilia! Emilia!" I began shouting the woman's name out as if my life depended on it. Everything we'd worked to build was gone. With the spell lifted—if it was indeed lifted—I had to find another sanctuary for our coven. *True sanctuary. I don't even know what that means anymore. Where on earth am I going to hide a bloodthirsty vampire coven of this magnitude?*

My breath hitched when Emilia emerged from The Sanctuary's doors, a smile on her face, her eyes fixed on me.

"Hello, Derek," she greeted me.

I hated that even then, I could feel an almost magnetic attraction toward her. Images of what it would feel like to press my lips against hers began to invade my mind. I shook the thoughts away. "What have you done?" I hissed at her. "What do you think you're doing?"

"I know what's going on in your mind, you know." She wet her lips.

I swallowed hard.

"You're wondering if the protective spell over the island is still up. It's not." She directed her gaze toward Corrine. "You did a good job keeping it up this whole time, Corrine." She said the words with fondness, almost as if she were a mother speaking to a child. "But your work is done. It's time for The Shade to have a new witch."

"And you think that's you?" I spat out. Before I could say

anything else, an explosion shook the ground beneath us.

"The Shade is falling apart, Derek." Emilia shrugged one shoulder and pouted like a teenager. "I can put a stop to all of this, you know."

"Then put a stop to it, Emilia." My tone was controlled. I was facing a power far greater than my own and it was capable of destroying everything that mattered to me. "What do you want?"

Her eyes settled on me, blazing with more intensity than I knew how to handle. "You, Derek. I want you."

Another round of explosions began to shake The Shade and I just stood there, not knowing what to say or do until Emilia motioned for me to come to her.

"We need to talk in private. I'm sure Corrine will understand."

I cast a glance at Corrine, who looked perplexed. She was staring at Emilia as if she was some sort of mystical creature that we should be in awe of.

Corrine looked my way. "There's something about her... Something oddly familiar... and utterly horrifying... Be careful, Derek. There's much about her that we don't know."

I scowled. *That doesn't help at all.* I made my way toward Emilia, bracing myself for what was to come. I walked toward The Sanctuary expecting to once again be pushed back by the force field, but then I got through. Corrine stepped forward in an attempt to follow me, but she was blocked.

"It's just you and me now," Emilia said, before gesturing with her finger, directing me to follow her inside.

I took one last look at Corrine, heaved a sigh and followed the young woman.

The moment we were alone in the halls of The Sanctuary, I couldn't help myself. I attacked her, pinning her against a wall, my claws sinking into her skin, right above her heart.

Emilia simply leaned her head back against the wall and smiled at me. "Go ahead. Do it," she challenged. "Let's see if you have what it takes to murder me in cold blood."

I knew without a doubt that she could've held me back, but she didn't. *Why isn't she fighting back?*

"Don't you think I saw the images that flashed through your mind the moment you laid eyes on me?" She smirked before brushing her lower lip against my jaw. "You want me, Derek Novak. I know it and you know it." She pressed her lips against mine and my mind started reeling. "You can have me, you know. Sofia never has to know. I'll be the witch of The Shade and we can all pretend that you're still in love with her, but we'll both know that you belong here with me, at The Sanctuary."

I was losing my senses. All I could think about was how beautiful she was and how much I desired her. When she kissed me full on the mouth, I didn't respond but I didn't resist either. I just savored the taste and feel of her lips and the way her body was pressed against mine.

Still, my consciousness was ringing out in full alarm. *This is wrong, Novak. Stop! Right now!*

At some point, I gathered up enough will to pull away from her. I backed away from her as I wiped the taste of her lips away. "I love Sofia. I belong to her."

Anger flashed in Emilia's eyes. "What has she done to get such loyalty from you?"

"She doesn't need to do anything." I shook my head. "I love her. If you knew what love was, Emilia, you'd know that once you love a person, you remain loyal to them. Get it into your head that I am in love with Sofia and that there's nothing you can do to change that."

"You're wrong, Derek. You thought that she was the one who could help you lead your kind to true sanctuary, but look how that's worked out. Look around you. Look at everything you worked for. It's falling apart. Can she fix this?" Emilia shook her head. "Sofia can't, but I can."

I narrowed my eyes at her, fighting the urge to laugh. "Need I remind you, Emilia, that it is you who contributed to bringing this chaos upon The Shade? You're simply asking me to believe that you can fix the mess you made."

"So what if I created the mess? I merely exposed all the weaknesses of this place. What kind of 'true sanctuary' is it when only a single witch upholds it? You do realize that Corrine is the last of her bloodline? When she dies, who then will protect The Shade? This isn't true sanctuary."

I grimaced. *Tell me something I don't know.* "Get to the point, Emilia. What do you want?"

"I can help you turn The Shade into a true sanctuary, Derek. Just like the prophecy said."

I shifted my weight, unsettled. "What are you talking about?"

"I can put the spell back up, stop my father's vampires from attacking The Shade... make all your troubles disappear. I am even powerful enough to hold back the hunters or distort their lines of communication if I have to. We can defend against the hunters should they try to attack. Better yet, we can work together to destroy the hunters once and for all."

"Then why don't you just do it, Emilia? Why don't you just help without anything in exchange?"

"Why? Because I want something in exchange for it... I love you, Derek. That's why I can't just let you go off with Sofia when I know that it's me you belong to... I need to do this in order to get us both to where we belong."

My jaw tightened as I stared at her. "What exactly do you want in exchange for making all of this go away?" My stomach turned at the notion that she could ask for me or maybe even Sofia in exchange.

I shuddered at the way she smiled. I felt like a piece in a game and she was the game master controlling my every move. Her request, however, I couldn't comprehend.

"Let me prove my love to you, Derek. Give me one week. One week where I can have you all to myself."

"Just one week?"

"Yes. One week with me. At the Blood Keep."

"The Blood Keep?"

"The Elder's castle."

I knew it was a trap, but when another explosion rocked the kingdom, it was a trap I was finding hard to resist. The bait she'd set in front of me was far too good. At that moment, staring at the lovely, but terrifying woman in front of me, all I could think of was, *Don't do anything you will regret, Derek.*

CHAPTER 22: SOFIA

My jaw dropped the moment I stepped into my father's cell. *I'm ruined for life*, was the first thought that came to mind when I saw Aiden making out with Ingrid in one corner of the cell. In the midst of all the chaos going on in The Shade, my parents were busy kissing and making up.

When they realized I was there, my father's cheeks turned red as a beet as he exclaimed, "Sofia!"

If vampires could blush, I was sure that Ingrid would already have been blushing as much as Aiden was.

I stood frozen as I stared at them, trying to remember why I was there in the first place.

Sam, who was standing behind me, cleared his throat, bringing me back to my senses. "Sofia, the hunters..."

I snapped out of my surprise. "Is your tracker on?"

"What's going on?" Aiden creased his brows.

"Just answer my question," I snapped at him.

"It's always on."

"I need you to make a call to the hunters to figure out if they've located The Shade. Try to hold back any attack for now."

"I thought you said that the island's protective spell will keep them from detecting the tracker."

I swallowed hard, wondering if I ought to trust my father with the information I had at hand. I didn't have much of a choice. "The spell is down. The Shade is under attack by the other covens and apparently, the original vampire is also involved. If the hunters attack now, it's the end of The Shade."

I looked at him, searching for any sign that that was exactly what he wanted to hear, but I was surprised when he took one look at my mother and nodded. "I'll make the call."

As if that weren't enough of a surprise, Ingrid approached me. I couldn't help but flinch when she brushed her fingers over my cheek and looked at me with concern. "Are you all right, Sofia?"

No, I'm not all right! The Shade is under attack, Derek is facing off with a crazy witch vampire woman he is deeply attracted to, and you and Aiden are acting like actual parents. A muscle in my jaw twitched as I nodded at Ingrid. "I'm fine. I'm not sure I should be trusting either of you though."

At that, Aiden smiled bitterly. "Can't blame you there, but I won't let you down."

Sam handed him a phone and Aiden dialed a number. I listened as he began talking on the phone.

"Zinnia? It's me, Aiden. I'm fine... Do you know where I am right now? Are you able to track me down?" He paused and waited for a response. "OK, great. I need you to hold off on all plans to attack The Shade. Because I said so… Well, I'm alive and well, and as far as I know, that means I'm still in charge, so do as I say and tell them that all plans to attack the island are on hold…" Aiden's eyes widened with fury before he sealed his lips tight.

I couldn't help but wonder what Zinnia, his right-hand person at hunter territory, could've said to cause such a reaction in him. During the time I'd spent at hunter headquarters, Zinnia had been his little pet. She'd done everything he told her without question. Now it seemed like she was no longer at his beck and call.

When Aiden hung up, I knew immediately that we were in trouble. He shook his head. "Zinnia said she's going to have to ask my superiors. She'll call me back when she hears from them."

So much for not letting me down. I heaved a sigh, hating the idea of going back to Derek with this news. "We can't afford an attack from the hunters, Aiden. Not now."

The earth once again shook after another explosion. The battle raging outside the Black Heights was enough indication of the trouble The Shade was in.

"I know, Sofia, and I'm going to do everything I can to hold the hunters back, but I can only do so much." Aiden shrugged. "They think that I've gone weak, that I'm now siding with the vampires."

"Are you?" I couldn't help but ask, wondering how much sway The Shade now had with Aiden.

"No. I can never side with the vampires, but I'm no longer on the hunters' side either. I'm on yours. I'm siding with my family."

I didn't miss the way his hand sought Ingrid's and the sorrow in Ingrid's eyes when their fingers clasped together. *I don't understand what's going on.* For a moment, I stared at my parents holding hands, wondering what could've happened. I looked at Ingrid, hope surging within me. *Could it really be possible that she wants to change? That she wants to become Camilla again?* I shoved the thoughts away, knowing that I didn't have the luxury of wallowing in my family drama.

I turned toward Sam. "Take me to Derek."

Sam pointed at Aiden and Ingrid. "And them?"

I wanted to see Derek. I wanted desperately to know what was going on at The Sanctuary, but as much as I hated to admit it, I still couldn't trust Aiden. Half of me still believed that he would divulge every secret, every weakness he'd learned about The Shade in order to further compromise it.

"You can trust me, Sofia," he assured me.

It broke my heart to do it, but I shook my head. "I should be with Derek right now or even fighting alongside the citizens of The Shade, but I can't. I want to trust you, but you've said that before and then stabbed me in the back right after."

It wasn't so long ago when Aiden had told me to trust him, to believe that the cure the hunters found was legitimate, only to find out that he had lied to get into The Shade and figure out its weaknesses, perhaps even end Derek.

I could see the hurt in his eyes, but this was his doing, not mine, and he knew that. Aiden just nodded and sat back on the cot, Ingrid sitting beside him, their hands clasped together while Aiden toyed with the phone.

I shifted my weight, unsure what to do. To ease my tension, I tried to make small talk with Sam. "I feel like I have to be out there doing something... anything..."

"You're in here doing what you can, Sofia," Sam assured me. "The vampires can hold their own without your help."

Of course they can, but can Derek really say no to this attraction he feels for Emilia? I was trying not to be paranoid. I'd meant it when

I'd said that I trusted him, but if she was as powerful a witch as she seemed to be, then could she not control him and make him return her affections? *Who knows what she wants?*

I jumped when the phone began to ring. Aiden picked it up and listened, his expression growing grimmer by the second. "This is unbelievable, Zinnia," he muttered in a tone that was more menacing than I'd ever heard him speak before. "After all those years I've given to the order, you turn away from me like that?" Zinnia must've said something that lit his fuse. "Don't give me that crap, Zinnia! I deserve more than that!"

When he hung up, I didn't need him to tell me what was going on. The hunters were coming for us. We had to face the inevitable.

I reached my hand forward, palm up. "Give me the phone."

"Sofia, I tried."

I nodded. It was hard for him to realize that he wasn't indispensable. *He gave his entire life to the hunters and they screw him over.* "I know you did, Dad, but right now, we have a lot to deal with. Please give me the phone."

He handed the phone over. I was about to ask Sam to take me to Derek as quickly as possible, but I hesitated, knowing that my father deserved more than what I was giving him. I stopped to kiss him on the cheek and whisper a thank you to him before Sam and I headed off, leaving them at The Cells.

When we arrived at The Sanctuary, Corrine stood alone outside the temple-like structure that'd been Corrine's home since she arrived at the island.

"What's going on?" I asked the witch.

Corrine shrugged. "I don't know. Emilia demanded time alone with Derek and he's been there with her for about a half an hour. I don't know what's going on inside."

"You don't have your powers?"

"Emilia's using some sort of suppression spell on me. I've been trying to fight it, but she's too powerful."

"We're going inside," Sam decided, and I nodded in agreement.

Corrine shook her head. "She has the building protected by a force field. No one can get in unless she allows them to…"

The witch hadn't finished her sentence when Derek emerged from the doors, anger evident on his chiseled face. His face softened when he saw me waiting there.

"The hunters?" he asked with so much hope, it broke my heart to break the news to him.

I shook my head. "They're coming. It seems Aiden's connection with me lost him his position with the hunters."

Derek heaved a sigh before he did the last thing I was expecting him. He grabbed my waist, pulled me against him and kissed me full on the mouth. I returned the kiss—passionate but at the same time confused by why he was kissing me while everything around us was falling apart. When our lips parted, I couldn't help but look at him questioningly.

"You know I love you, right?" he asked.

This can't be good.

He gripped my hands tightly and nodded toward The Sanctuary. "Come. We have a lot to discuss." He began leading me toward the building before turning toward Corrine and Sam, who were about to follow us there. "Just us."

Corrine didn't seem happy about being kept out of her own home, but there wasn't much she could do about it. Sam, on the other hand, just nodded before another explosion racked The Shade.

Worry flashed through Sam's eyes—the same look of

anxiousness I'd been seeing every time we heard an explosion.

Derek nodded toward him. "Go. You're of better use there than here."

Sam didn't need to be told twice. He was out of there in a breath. I gave Corrine a faint smile before Derek led me to the building where Emilia was waiting.

I didn't miss the spite in Emilia's eyes the moment we entered her chambers, but she couldn't touch me—not in front of Derek. When they told me what Emilia was asking for in exchange for the safety of The Shade, I didn't know how to respond other than to turn my eyes toward Derek. "What do *you* want to do?"

Derek shrugged and shook his head. "I think I don't have a choice, Sofia, but I need to know that you're okay with this."

Emilia rolled her eyes and scowled, but she didn't say anything.

"I don't know what to say, Derek," I admitted. "It feels like I don't have a choice either."

"You know the dreams, Sofia. I told you everything. If you're not up for this…"

"I'm scared of losing you."

Derek cupped my face with his large hands and shook his head before kissing me on the forehead. "That's impossible. You will always have me."

At that, Emilia seemed to have had enough of our melodrama. "This is boring. Do I get my demands or not? The way I see it, you're getting the better end of the deal. You get The Shade back and all I get is one week with the man I love. Hardly seems fair…"

Something about what she said rubbed me the wrong way. I had no idea where I got the confidence, but I stared right at her and said, "You are not to harm Derek in any way."

"I love him," she hissed at me. "How could I ever harm him?"

"Sofia isn't to be harmed." Derek spoke up.

Emilia grimaced. "Really? More demands?"

"Do you want that week or not?"

We were about to find out just how desperate she was to have time alone with Derek.

"You're pushing me." She glared at him so intensely I wondered how she could possibly love him. Her glare darted toward me and I was almost sure she was going to attack me.

Derek, however, was unmoving in his resolve. He took a step forward, pushing me behind him. "Sofia is not to be harmed. Corrine gets her powers back. Vivienne wakes up from the spell. Not only are you going to put the original protective spell back on the island, you're also going to secure it with the same force field you're using to protect The Sanctuary right now—and *I* get to control who gets to go in and who gets to go out."

Emilia was clearly not happy. She began to stretch her neck and her arms as she approached, eyeing me from head to foot.

I felt so young and so unattractive compared to her. She had this sophistication about her. She was elegant. Gorgeous. Self-assured. Things I wasn't. It wasn't difficult to understand why Derek was so taken by her.

She smirked at me, perhaps noticing my admiration. "Very well then. I agree to all those terms."

My stomach turned. I'd been hoping she wouldn't agree. I'd been hoping that Derek wouldn't have to spend a week or even a single second with her. *Who knows what they could do to him there?* One week suddenly felt like an eternity. I was gripping Derek's arm so tightly I didn't even realize it until Derek gave me a look that mirrored my own desperation.

I couldn't even fathom why Emilia would want an entire week

with Derek, but I knew that there was a strong possibility that I could lose him. *Is our love strong enough?* Afraid of what was to come, I stood to my tiptoes, threw my arms around his neck and kissed him, not caring how it would affect Emilia.

It seemed Derek couldn't give a damn about what Emilia felt too, because he picked me up in his strong arms and returned the kiss with equal if not more passion.

By the time our lips parted, Emilia was glaring daggers at us. I could tell that it would give her great pleasure to see me harmed.

An echo from the past began to circle my mind as I realized what was hanging in the balance. Derek and I were strongest together and we were weakest apart. I squeezed Derek's hand. I was reminded of how hard he'd had to fight in order to keep our relationship intact, what with his attraction to Emilia. *How much harder will he have to fight now that we have to be apart?*

I began to tremble and he felt it. He looked my way and whispered into my ear, "Our love is strong enough, Sofia."

I wanted to believe him with all my heart, but looking at the veiled triumph behind Emilia's eyes, I wasn't so certain our love could survive what she was about to put us both through. Still, I mustered up all the conviction and faith I had to nod. "Of course it is, Derek. Of course it is."

CHAPTER 23: KYLE

The Shade was in ruins. The Vale was a pile of ashes and most of the Residences were wiped out. The only structures in The Shade that remained intact were the Black Heights and The Sanctuary. Half of the Crimson Fortress was just a pile of rubble.

We'd been fighting for what felt like hours and the enemy vampires were coming in droves. Just when I thought we had no more fight left in us, someone screamed, "Retreat!" And they all returned to their choppers, flying off and leaving us to pick up the pieces left by their attack.

I didn't know what had caused their retreat, but I was relieved. I had never been more exhausted in my life. I couldn't even count the number of times a stake had almost been driven into my heart. In fact, I still had three stakes buried in my body—one in my back, the other in my shoulder, the other in my leg.

I'd been battling one vampire and another one had been about to come right at me when they called for the retreat.

When they retreated, I just fell to the ground, unwilling to look at the casualties surrounding me. One of the attackers chuckled as he passed by me. "This is what happens to anybody who crosses the Elder," he said.

I wondered what we could've possibly done to cross the original vampire when we weren't even sure that he existed.

I pulled the stake out of my leg, gritting my teeth at the pain. I had just tossed it aside when a familiar voice called out my name.

"Kyle!"

She hadn't even reached me yet, but I already knew it was her. *Anna.* I could sense her presence, smell her sweet scent, practically see in my mind's eye her beauty. She came to me from behind, hugging my neck as she whispered into my ear.

"Are you all right?"

All I could do was groan in response. *As all right as I could be, I guess.*

"You look like crap, man." Another familiar voice. Ian's.

Before I could respond, he pulled out the wooden stake from behind me. I screamed in agony. I could practically see the smirk on his face. I turned around to glare at him and was surprised to find him with an ugly gash right through his upper torso—his shirt torn from the claw marks.

"What?" He grinned. "You're not the only one who wants to fight for The Shade. I mean, I'm not crazy about being a slave to you vamps, but I'm assuming that Derek is a better king to serve than whoever just attacked us."

"Everything is ruined…" Tears were brimming in Anna's eyes as she looked me over with such affection.

I ached seeing the look in her eyes. Since she'd been seeing Corrine, it'd been difficult to figure her moods out. Anna was a pendulum, going from me to Ian, then back to me again. Over the past few days she'd been seeing Corrine, she always seemed to prefer being around either me or him. During the days when she preferred me, it was heaven. She was her old, fun, smart, bubbly self—just like she was during our nights at the lake. Of course, the times she spent with Ian were complete hell. It drove me nuts trying to avoid thinking about what they were doing or talking about.

Does she smile at him like she does me? Do they talk about the same things?

"What just happened?" Ian asked the question that was most likely going through all of the warriors' minds.

"I have no clue." I shook my head before pulling out the stake on my shoulder. Anna winced on my behalf. "I'm fine, Anna," I assured her before looking around.

My breath hitched when I saw Ashley walking towards us. She was the only member of my clan, the only vampire I'd ever sired, and that gave us a connection that made my heart go out to her. She looked so tired and distraught even as the wounds in her body were beginning to heal.

"Have you seen Sam?" she asked me the moment she was within earshot.

I shook my head. I was about to ask her if she was all right, but based on the tears streaming down her face, it was clear that she was not.

"Hey." I tried to soothe her, reaching out. She fell into my embrace and sobbed on my chest as I brushed my fingers through her blonde hair.

"Everything's destroyed," she choked.

I gulped, knowing that the task of rebuilding The Shade was immense. I wanted to reassure her, but I didn't even know how to reassure myself.

Question after question ran through my mind. *What happened? What are we going to do now?* I quickly scoped out our surroundings and found familiar faces sorting through the rubble. Xavier took one look around, tightened his jaw and clenched his fists before rushing off to the direction of the Pavilion—most likely to check on Vivienne. Yuri was kissing Claudia and whispering words of reassurance into her ear. Cameron and Liana were staring at each other from a distance as they both went through the lifeless bodies of vampires—from the enemy's side and ours—and humans. On the far horizon, coming from the direction of The Sanctuary, I caught a glimpse of Sam rushing towards us.

"Hey, Ash," I whispered to the girl who was the closest thing I had to family in The Shade, "It's Sam. He's coming."

Ashley pulled away from me and turned her eyes in the direction I pointed. Within minutes, she was in Sam's arms.

Ian and Anna still stood behind me, looking at the chaos surrounding us.

"I wonder where Sofia is," Ian muttered. "She would have an idea about what just went on."

"She's at The Sanctuary with Derek and Emilia," Sam told us, before filling us in on what he knew. "Corrine doesn't have her powers. She can't even get into The Sanctuary. Emilia has put some sort of force field around it. Vivienne is still asleep and Aiden has lost ground with the hunters. They're gearing up for an attack."

I swallowed hard, letting the implication of everything he'd just said sink in. The horrors of the first years I'd lived as a vampire before finally finding The Shade began to come back to me. Always running, always seeking out a shadow that would keep out the sun… always at the threat of getting murdered or caught by hunters…

"What do you mean Corrine doesn't have her powers?" Ashley said. "What about the spell protecting the island?"

Sam shook his head. "Gone."

"That means that the sun is going to rise?" I asked.

Sam shrugged. "Yes, unless Sofia and Derek find a way to talk Emilia into stopping all this chaos. Perhaps the retreat of the attackers has something to do with…"

Sofia emerged from the woods—coming from the direction of The Sanctuary. It was clear from the glistening in her eyes that she'd been crying. I feared the worst for her and Derek.

All eyes turned toward her. We gathered around her and waited for her to speak up.

Sofia's eyes were downcast, her shoulders trembling. "The protective spell upon The Shade is back up," she announced. Murmurs echoed through the crowd, especially amongst those who hadn't known that it was gone to begin with. "We are safe from further attack for the next week or so. Emilia has placed a force field around The Shade in order to keep us safe."

"Why would she do that?" Yuri couldn't keep himself from asking.

Sofia just gave him a weak smile before looking back down. "Corrine is back in control of The Sanctuary. She has regained her powers."

"Why are you the one telling us this?" a random voice among the crowd asked. "Where is Derek? Where is our king?"

At this, Sofia tried to hold back her tears, but she managed to compose herself like the queen she would eventually be. "Derek will not be on the island for a week. Emilia stopped the war, restored the spell, put up the force field, gave Corrine back her powers and awakened Vivienne in exchange for one week with Derek. He has to spend one week at the original vampire's castle."

"Why?" Cameron and Liana asked in unison, concern on their faces.

Sofia shrugged. "I don't know."

Before anyone else could ask a question, a scream came from the back of the crowd. "The sun! It's rising!"

I spun around and sure enough, the sun was rising for the first time in hundreds of years in The Shade.

"I thought you said the protective spell was back up?" someone cried out at Sofia, who was looking at the horizon with pure shock. She clearly had no idea what was going on.

Panic ensued before Cameron finally got a grip on everything and instructed us all to go to The Catacombs. I rushed toward Anna and Ian, who both coaxed me to rush off to The Catacombs before the rays of the sun could reach me.

I was about to do just that when Sofia collapsed to the ground. I couldn't understand what was happening, but I knew that the battle was far from over. Whoever Emilia was, she still seemed to have control over The Shade.

Chapter 24: Derek

The moment our deal was struck, all it took was a snap of Emilia's fingers before we were both inside what I assumed was her chambers.

She sighed with relief. "Finally. I'm home," she purred even as she fell back into the middle of her four-poster bed. She curled up in the large, soft covers and stared at me, propping her head up with her hand, her elbow on the bed. "And you're here with me."

I grimaced. All I could see was a woman who was as unattractive on the inside as she was attractive on the outside.

She rose from her bed and made her way toward me, exaggerating her every movement, obviously made to seduce. "You're going to fall in love with me, Derek Novak."

Despite the tension, I began laughing. I couldn't hold it back. I found it hilarious that she could even think that I would fall in love with her.

She must've gotten tired of my making a jest out of her, because she threw her arms in my direction and to my shock, I was flung through the air until my back hit the wall, pinned about two feet above the ground. "What the hell are you laughing at?" she screamed at me.

Is she really so naïve? "Is that why you brought me here, Emilia? You thought that I could fall in love with you in the span of one week?"

She wrinkled her nose at me, disgusted that I was finding her profession of love entertaining.

I didn't know what it was about this place, but something about it seemed to bring out the darkness in her. I noted how she'd never acted this way in The Shade. She'd always seemed so cool and collected, but in her father's castle, the Blood Keep, as she referred to it, she was like a volcano waiting to explode.

"I'm glad you're entertained by my words, Derek, but not for long... You'll see. All I have to do is get you to remember, Derek. You'll remember what we had. You'll realize that we've had far more than just one week. You'll realize that you've been falling in love with me for years."

"You're delusional." I practically spat the words.

She smirked and shook her head before pointing one finger at my head. Suddenly, images began to flood into my mind. Dreams buried in my subconscious. Dreams of her and me enveloped in some sort of mist. Then the scenes changed. The dreams turned into memories—those of me and various milestones of my life in The Shade before I went to sleep—each and every one of them a memory I'd shared with one person alone: Cora.

By the time Emilia was done with me, I couldn't look her in the eye. She slowly lowered me to the ground. "I know you, Derek. I saw you give in to the darkness. I saw you for who you were back then when you were at your worst and I loved you. I've always loved you."

I stared at her, still trying to make sense of the visions I'd seen. I steadied myself and stood to my full height, aware that the woman before me could easily break me in half should she wish it. I flexed my jaw before looking her in the eye. "You're Cora?"

She just smiled and said, "I'm the girl prophesied to help you find true sanctuary. Not Sofia."

At that, I smirked, my heart swelling with pride as I recalled the woman I loved. *Sofia.* Her beautiful face, her green eyes, her smile, her touch… I shook my head. "It makes no difference. She has my heart."

Emilia snapped her fingers, and all of a sudden, I couldn't remember what Sofia looked like. Panic took hold of me as my eyes shot toward Emilia.

It was her turn to smirk. "Trust me, Derek. I can take every memory you have of Sofia and replace her presence with mine. You're in my territory now. Sofia Claremont may have your heart today, but believe me when I say that the week won't end without me taking it from her."

Emilia's words hadn't completely registered when a chill began to sweep throughout the room. Emilia shuddered, her eyes betraying her fear. It was the strangest sensation I'd ever felt—one that I hated to admit wasn't completely foreign to me. The cold penetrated through my skin to the very core of my bones. I was aware of a presence, dark and foreboding. Fear began to envelop me and suddenly I couldn't see anything but pitch blackness. I wasn't even sure if Emilia was still there. The presence overwhelmed my senses and I began to find it hard to breathe.

"Welcome to my castle, Derek Novak," came a chilling voice. "Finally, my daughter does something right for once."

Daughter. I shivered. I was in the presence of the Elder. I opened my mouth to speak but my throat was so dry no words came out.

"Does this boy bring you happiness, Emilia? Does his presence ignite your bones?"

"Yes, Master. I've wanted him for the longest time."

I'd never thought I could be elated to hear Emilia's voice. *At least I'm not alone.*

"You gave yourself to me once."

I felt a caress over my hair, an indication that it was me the Elder was talking to. I began to remember the time I'd given myself over to darkness. I'd done it so I could make a sanctuary out of The Shade. *What sanctuary it turned out to be.*

"I'm glad to finally have you back in my territory, Derek Novak. I used to be able to get to you so easily, but ever since you let that impetuous redhead's light into your life, it's been more and more difficult."

I swallowed back the bile rising from my throat. *This was why Vivienne never wanted me to be apart from Sofia. This is why the Elder cannot destroy Sofia himself despite all the power that he has. It's her light. Darkness cannot have control over light.*

The caress over my head suddenly turned into a chokehold over my throat. I struggled to breathe, not quite able to comprehend what was going on.

"Now you're in my territory, thanks to my daughter's obsession with you. I now have you in my full control."

Evil echoed in his voice. I was in the presence of pure and utter evil.

"I must welcome you to my castle, Derek. My daughter, Emilia—you once knew her as Cora—can attest that I welcome all my guests the same way." He paused, relishing the way I struggled as he choked me. "I hit them where it hurts."

He threw me onto the bed and I blacked out.

By the time I came to my senses, I found myself making love to Emilia. She clutched the back of my head and whispered into my ear, "He punished you for turning your back on him. He rewarded me for bringing you back to him. You are my reward, Derek."

At that moment, even as her body bucked and writhed beneath mine, I hated her with every fiber of my being, and yet the words that came out of my mouth were, "I love you, Emilia."

CHAPTER 25: SOFIA

I jolted up on the bed, out of breath, images of Derek kissing Emilia floating in my mind. Tears were streaming down my face and my body was racked with uncontrollable sobs. I looked around and found Vivienne staring at me with concern. I was in my bedroom at The Catacombs and the last thing I remembered was the sun beginning to dawn on the island.

"What happened?" I demanded, panic beginning to take its hold on me.

"After five hundred years of night, the sun has risen on The Shade." Vivienne affirmed my greatest fears.

"She promised. Emilia promised. We had a deal... She could have Derek for a week, but The Shade will remain protected."

"The force field is up. The Shade is protected from any attack or even from being detected by outside forces. To the world, I'm sure we are invisible." Vivienne rose from her seat before sighing. "But I don't think you ever mentioned anything about keeping The Shade enveloped by darkness."

My heart sank. "I just assumed it was part of the protective spell."

Vivienne shook her head. "Cora placed the spell of never-ending night on The Shade during the battle of First Blood. It wasn't until years later after Derek went to sleep that she put the protective spell over the island. And now she has Derek in her grasp. I never would've thought that Cora would ever turn to the dark side."

"I don't understand…"

"Emilia *is* Cora, Sofia."

"How is that possible?"

Vivienne shook her head. "I'm not sure either."

"Can't Corrine do something about it? She's back in control of The Sanctuary, is she not? She has her powers back?"

"Corrine says she's been trying, but the spell was originally done by Cora and she never had to keep that spell running. She doesn't know how Cora originally did it."

I rose from my bed, burying my face in my palms. I had no idea what to do. *You're an eighteen-year-old kid who didn't even hang around long enough to get her high-school diploma, Sofia. Stop fooling yourself. You're no queen. You have no idea how to run things.* "I'm afraid of losing Derek, Vivienne."

She just stared at me. Vivienne Novak was never one to flatter. From the first day I'd met her, she'd been straightforward and honest through and through. "He is more vulnerable now than he ever was before. Our only hope is that what you share together is stronger than what they're putting him through. For the next week, we'll both fare better if we don't think about it. We must concentrate on keeping order here on the island and hopefully finding the cure."

"How do we find the cure, Vivienne? I don't even know where to start."

Before Vivienne could respond, a piercing scream echoed from outside. Our eyes met and we both got up and ran outside my quarters. I leaned into the wooden banister, which allowed me to see The Catacombs below. The first thing that struck my senses was how crowded The Catacombs were. With The Shade surrounded by light, every single vampire was inside The Catacombs, surrounded by humans they craved desperately. *This can't be good.* I swallowed hard.

Ashley appeared beside me. Vivienne was on my other side. "What's going on?"

"I'm not sure." I caught sight of Ian carrying Anna in his arms, heading for my quarters, where she had a bedroom.

"One of the vampires attacked Anna," he explained. "Kyle's fighting him off. He's not Elite, but he's definitely much more powerful than Kyle is."

"Where are they?" Vivienne asked.

Ian pointed toward a level of The Catacombs that was beginning to get crowded with people.

"I'm on it," Vivienne assured me, as she rushed toward the area where the fight was happening.

Ashley rushed after Vivienne, leaving me to fend off my own frustration. Not wanting to be alone, I followed Ian toward Anna's bedroom.

"We have to do something about the living situation, Sofia." Ian frowned. "Having the vampires here every time the sun comes up is complete chaos. A week of this and every human of The Shade will most likely become breakfast. Not all the vampires are as good at controlling their cravings as Vivienne." He began applying some sort of ointment on Anna's bitten neck before putting a bandage on it.

"I have no idea what to do. Where's Gavin? Does he have any idea on what we can do about the situation?"

"He's with Lily and Rosa. They're trying to bring all the orphans and young women together in a safer place. With an attack already happening, the humans are panicking…"

"Well, we can't just send the vampires out into the sun, Ian."

"I know that, but we have to do something. No one will be able to control the vampires if they start blacking out. Derek's not here and he's the only one they respect. You know what happened the last time Derek wasn't here in The Shade to run things."

I shuddered at the thought. While Derek and I had been trapped at hunter territory, The Shade, especially The Catacombs, had descended into rebellions and riots. "I don't know what to do."

"Well then, find someone who does, Sofia. We need a leader."

The Shade had always been ruled by a Novak. But while Vivienne had a voice at the kingdom, she'd never had enough sway to get everyone to listen to her. We were up against far more than we could handle, and the only person I knew who was capable of becoming a strong leader in a situation like ours was my father. I was well aware of the responsibility on my shoulders—I had to step up and take the lead if I was going to be the wife of Derek and the queen of The Shade, but I certainly wasn't going to do it alone. I needed Aiden. "I think I know who to ask," I assured Ian before making my way to The Cells.

I was about to ask Aiden Claremont, the infamous hunter, notorious for killing hundreds of vampires, to help me run The Shade.

Chapter 26: Derek

I was losing my mind and I knew it. I had no control over my actions. The darkness had possessed me and though I did not want to do what I was doing, I still gave into Emilia's every whim. I was a puppet and she was my master.

"Do you love me, Derek?" she whispered into my ear.

No. I love Sofia. "Yes. You know I do," I whispered back into hers.

She smiled and I realized how unattractive she had become to me. She held my hand and led me outside of her room, which she hadn't allowed me to leave ever since the first night I'd had to spend with her.

The corridors we were passing through had high, stone walls, lit by elegant wall lamps. I was expecting to find paintings or even tapestries gracing the walls, but they were bare apart from some heavy burgundy drapery covering the floor-to-ceiling windows.

Our steps echoed through the corridor and I found myself staring at the woman who was holding my hand. *What happened to you, Cora? How did you become Emilia?* Despite my hatred for what she'd become, I could not deny the fact that Cora had been my best friend. She'd been with me through some of the toughest and darkest periods of my life. It hurt to know that this was what she had become.

She smiled when she realized that I was staring at her. She took it as a compliment, I guessed. Anyone would've thought I was in love with her.

"You're staring." She blushed.

I wanted to strangle her. *It's not like I have any control over what I do, you crazy witch.* "I just can't keep my eyes off you. You're so beautiful."

Puppet praise didn't seem to be pleasing to her anymore. "Do you mean that? Or are you just saying it because of my father's control over you?"

Definitely your father's control. "Of course I mean it, Emilia. Any man can look at you and see how beautiful you are."

Someone snickered behind me. We both turned around and I couldn't help but feel amused when Emilia's face fell.

"Hello, Kiev," she said, rolling her eyes. "This, unfortunately, is my older brother."

How many brothers and sisters does she have? How many belong to the Elder's clan? I began studying him just as he began studying me.

He had close-cropped dark hair. His eyes were a chilling blood-red. He also had a beautiful young redhead cradled in his muscular arms.

"So this is him? The man you've been pining for all these years?"

Emilia held her head high and I couldn't help but wonder who the man was. She seemed so eager to prove something—perhaps herself—to him. "If you must know, yes. This is the great Derek Novak."

Kiev continued snickering. "Tell me, Derek Novak. Is Sofia Claremont really as stunning as everyone says? Is she as beautiful as my girl, Vanessa, over here?" He clutched her by the jaw and began shaking her head. Her brown eyes fell on me and I could see desperation in them.

More than that, I could see Sofia in her. My mind was crying out for release, thoughts of the girl I loved filling my brain, yet the words that came through my mouth were, "I have no idea who Sofia Claremont is."

Emilia grinned, but her smile faded when Kiev doubled over in laughter.

"What is wrong with you, Kiev?" she burst out.

"You're fast, little sister. You already have him brainwashed. Let's see how long he can hold up, shall we?" He shoved the girl forward.

"Kiev, no." Emilia frowned, worry creasing her face. From the look on her eyes, I was certain that she wanted to inflict many forms of bodily harm on her brother.

They don't seem to be a very happy family.

"Look at her hair." Kiev held up a clump of the young woman's hair. "Isn't Sofia a redhead? Are you sure you don't remember her?"

Of course I remember her. I love her. I will always love her. I shook my head. "I don't remember."

Kiev grinned and fisted Vanessa's hair, pulling painfully at her scalp until she began whimpering. He pulled her head back and exposed her neck to me. From the fresh bite marks on her neck, it was clear that he had been drinking from her.

"Have a taste of her blood, Derek, and I'm pretty sure you'll remember your dear Sofia."

"Derek, no," Emilia objected. "Don't. You love me, remember? If you love me, you won't do this."

Apparently, my vampire cravings were more powerful than even the control Emilia had over me. The invitation to do anything that would remind me of Sofia was too precious to let go of. I gently pulled Vanessa closer to me and pried Kiev's fingers loose. When she was finally free of his grip, I bit into her neck.

The moment I got a taste of her blood, my eyes shot wide open. Her blood tasted the same as Sofia's. It had the exact same effect on me. The power pounding in my blood, the ecstasy that came with every drop of her blood coursing through me—it was all there. I drank deep until Kiev pulled the girl away from me.

"That's enough." He glared at me. "You're enjoying too much of what is mine. Now tell me, Derek... do you really love my sister?"

Emilia looked at me expectantly and I couldn't help but smirk when I was able to shake my head and say, "No. I'm in love with Sofia."

A scream from the depths of Emilia filled the corridors as she attacked Vanessa. I'd seen many humans die before, but I'd never been more shaken than when Vanessa burned at Emilia's mere touch and crumbled into ashes.

The moment Vanessa's life force disappeared from the room, the back of Kiev's hand connected sharply with Emilia's face and she got thrown into the ground.

I backed up into a wall, wanting to get as far away from the fight as possible.

Emilia pointed her finger at Kiev and I was sure that she was about to use her witchy powers against him, but all he did was smirk, stepping forward to challenge her. "Go ahead, Emilia. Cast a spell on me. Let's see what our father will do to you should you disobey his order never to use a spell on his own children again... especially now that you only have one week to make Derek Novak yours."

Emilia once again screamed at the top of her lungs. It seemed all she could really do against her older brother was throw a tantrum, until she lunged forward and clawed right across his face. He was so angered, he tackled her much smaller frame to the ground.

A brunette with stunning purple eyes emerged from a nearby door, possibly to find out what the commotion was all about. Her eyes lit up with wicked delight when she saw the two vampires wrestling with each other. She stepped forward and stood beside me. "You must be my little sister's pet. I'm Clara."

"I'm no pet. And I'm definitely not hers."

"My brother made you drink an immune's blood, didn't he?"

I raised my brow. *Vanessa was an immune. That's why her blood tasted just like Sofia's.* I nodded. "Yes. Emilia killed the girl right after I drank."

"Really now?" Clara's eyes lit up. "Was it Vanessa?"

"Yes."

"No wonder he's so peeved. He's been obsessed with Vanessa ever since he found out your Sofia is a redhead."

Nothing about that news sat well with me. *Another man who could possibly be obsessed with Sofia.* I stared at Kiev, who was pounding his fists against Emilia's face, and saw him for the threat that he was.

"He's gonna get over it." Clara cocked her head as she watched her siblings fight, unaffected by the gory mess they were creating out of each other. "So will Emilia. The effect of the immune's blood on you will wear off soon enough and you'll be back in Emilia's control in no time."

My gut clenched. I wondered if there was anything I could do in order to keep in control. Only one thing came to mind. *I have to find another immune.* "Vanessa was immune?" I asked Clara.

She smiled at me. "All humans at the castle are immune." She seemed pleased with herself that she was able to give me that particular tidbit of information. Clearly, the Elder's "family" was insanely dysfunctional.

Clara began clapping her hands. "Enough! Much as I would love to watch you two kill each other, I can't allow that."

Emilia gave her brother one last claw right through his upper torso before she stood to her feet. She had barely taken a couple of steps forward before she completely healed. Kiev, too, had just risen to his feet and not a scar was in sight. Still, the two glared murder at each other.

I couldn't have cared less about either one of them. The goal was to find another immune before I once again lost control.

Emilia must've read my mind, because she slapped me in the face so strongly my head began to spin.

Her siblings chuckled. Something told me that though they were apparently willing to kill one another, they weren't about to allow anyone else to hurt them.

Emilia pressed her lips against mine before clutching the back of my head with both her hands and whispering into my ear, "Don't even think of drinking another immune's blood again, Derek. If you do, once this week is over and my vow to you that Sofia won't be harmed is over, I *will* make her pay for every time you've displeased me while you're here."

At that, I chuckled. "You can't harm Sofia. Even your father can't harm her. She has too much light in her for darkness to take hold."

Emilia laughed. "Maybe I can't, Derek, but I know someone who can... someone who will." She relished my short intake of breath before revealing who she had in mind. "Her own mother is going to kill her, Derek. Camilla Claremont is going to kill your Sofia."

CHAPTER 27: AIDEN

"Do you think she'll ever be able to accept me?" Camilla asked me, her voice quivering.

Every time I let my gaze linger upon her, I found myself wishing that the cure was for real, that Ingrid could actually turn back into a human, turn back into my Camilla. I brushed my hand over the back of hers. "I think she wants to, but you'll find it hard to convince her that your intentions are genuine. Can you blame her?"

She leaned her head on my shoulder. "I guess not."

Right then, the door to the cell opened and Sofia appeared. Something was bothering her, by the expression on her face. She swallowed hard before looking me in the eye. "I need your help."

My heart leapt at the words. For the first time since I could remember, my daughter was asking for my help. "What is it? What can I do for you? Anything..." I was desperate not to disappoint her again.

She told me about what was going on in The Shade and I listened intently. "You've led a multimillion-dollar security conglomerate while you were still one of the head hunters at hawk territory. I know you can help me run The Shade."

"I can definitely help." I nodded, already having a fair idea of what we could do to solve the problem of the vampires and humans all being held at The Catacombs. I knew Sofia also had it in her to handle things, but she seemed overwhelmed by Derek being away from The Shade.

She sighed with relief before nodding my way. "Come with me then."

I stood up, still holding Camilla's hand, pulling at her.

Sofia shook her head. "Not with her."

"Sofia..." I took a step forward. "Please..."

Sofia looked longingly at Camilla. "How can I ever trust you?" she asked, her voice breaking.

"You can't." Camilla shook her head. "Not yet. I haven't earned any of your trust, Sofia, but your father trusts me. That's enough for me right now."

"I'm responsible for her," I assured my daughter.

She shifted her gaze from me to her mother. "I'm sorry. I just can't risk it. I already have enough problems on my plate and I don't want to have to worry about what she might do."

My heart sank, but I couldn't blame Sofia. I let go of Camilla's hand as I moved forward to follow Sofia out of the cell. I knew that Camilla's heart was breaking and my heart broke with her, but I figured there was plenty of time for mother and daughter to make amends with each other.

I was wrong.

CHAPTER 28: SOFIA

I was right to consult with my father regarding what to do. We arranged a meeting with the Elite Council and things were immediately put in place. During the day, The Catacombs belonged to the vampires. During the night, it belonged to the humans.

It wasn't easy to get all the humans to agree to being out in the sunlight—especially the Naturals—but they eventually got used to it. Having a little sun on their skin was better than what the vampires could do to them should they stay at The Catacombs.

By our second sunset, we only had one problem left.

"We have no idea where Kyle is," Vivienne announced. "By the time Ashley and I arrived there, the vampire Rex already brought him somewhere, and none of us know where either of the men are. Ashley, Gavin, Sam and a bunch of other guards are all looking for him as we speak."

"What happened? What caused the fight?" I asked.

"I guess only Anna can tell us." Vivienne shrugged.

"Let's hope all that time she spent with Corrine paid off." I sighed.

Minutes later, Ian and Anna were brought into our presence. She seemed confused at first and I could swear that she was going to go back to her old insane self, but after Ian reassured her, she eventually relaxed and took a seat, her hands clasped together over her lap.

"Tell us what happened to Kyle, Anna."

"The vampire attacked me and he began drinking from my neck and from my wrist, so I screamed. Ian told me to scream whenever someone tried to hurt me. Kyle showed up and they fought. Kyle was in bad shape. Blood was all over his body and then the other vampire hit him so hard, he became unconscious. I thought the other vampire was going to hurt me again, but he left. He was angry. I didn't know what to do to help Kyle. I wanted to help him because he was hurting, so I did what Felix made me do when he was hurting before. I fed Kyle my blood through my wrist. I wasn't done feeding him yet when the vampire returned and he attacked me again. After that, I'm not sure what happened. I woke up and I was in my room. Ian told me that I hit my head somewhere…"

We were about to ask Ian what happened when Gavin showed up. "We found him. Sam and Ashley are bringing him to your quarters as we speak."

"Is he all right?" I asked.

"I'm not sure." Gavin shook his head. He looked baffled. "You're not going to believe this, but we think Kyle just turned back into a human."

Chapter 29: Derek

"I hate them!" Emilia hissed. "I hate Kiev. I hate Clara. I hate all my brothers and sisters."

I sat on a wooden bench at the castle's labyrinth, legs crossed, as Emilia paced back and forth in a fury. The immune's blood had already worn off and though I felt nothing but delight and amusement at seeing how worked up the witch was, I appeared sympathetic towards her plight.

Happiness appeared elusive at the Elder's castle. Nobody seemed to have it at all. *I'm pretty sure that even if they did have it, they'd still be fearful of it slipping through their fingers and disappearing.* Emilia continued her tantrum even as I mulled over the kind of relationship the Elder's children seemed to have.

"Are you happy, Emilia?" I asked. "Do I make you happy?"

Emilia stopped her pacing, twirling the tips of her dark brown hair, before she directed her gaze at me, her eyes softening. She came to me and sat on my lap, facing me, her arms wrapped around my neck. She bit her lip as she stared at me. "I still see her ghost behind your eyes. You don't have me fooled, Derek. You don't love me."

Her response made me feel triumphant, knowing that she was talking about Sofia. *Of course I don't. May she haunt you whenever you look into my eyes.* "I love you, Emilia. How could you ever think that I don't love you?"

She pouted at me before playfully biting my lower lip.

What is wrong with you? I was disgusted, but I responded with a chuckle, pulling her closer to me and kissing her full on the mouth.

We began making out until she got bored with that. Nothing seemed to satisfy Emilia for long. She was always craving something, demanding more.

Yawning, she got off my lap and sat on the bench beside me. She leaned her head on my shoulder and took my hand in hers, our fingers clasping together. Despite my aversion to her, my thumb began rubbing the back of her hand.

I'd been there for three days and it already felt like an eternity. The thought that I had four days left was sickening. I hated to think about it, but I had no assurance that Emilia would make good on her word and return me to The Shade after a week. The thought was killing me. I missed Sofia and everyone in The Shade more than ever before, and the idea of being stuck like this was horrifying.

"I can sometimes read your mind, you know." She broke the long silence. "I know what's going through your thoughts, how much you don't want to be with me."

"That's not true," I said.

"Yes, it is. You want to return to The Shade."

I didn't respond. *If you can read my mind, then you know I don't want to be with you. You know how in love I am with Sofia. And yes, I do want to return to The Shade. Nothing's ever going to change that.*

"Why can't you love me? I gave so much of myself to you, risked everything to help you establish The Shade, and yet you never looked at me the way you looked at her."

Because it's Sofia I belong with, not you. That's just the way it is. I didn't get to choose who I fell in love with the same way I'm sure you never chose to fall in love with me. "I don't know what you're talking about, Emilia. I'm in love with you." *What happened to you, Cora? You were my best friend, and now you're just a crazy half-vampire, half-witch.*

"I fell in love with you. That's what's wrong with me."

It should've bothered me that she was able to read my thoughts, but I wasn't bothered. At least she knew that she was fooling herself to believe that I was in love with her. At least she knew that even when I touched her, even when I professed love to her, it was Sofia I wanted. I liked the idea that Emilia would never get the satisfaction she was looking for—at least not from me.

Before our conversation could go to stranger places, we heard a shriek from nearby. Emilia's eyes lit up with excitement. "Finally! Something's happening." She ran toward the scream, hand still clasping mine as I trailed behind her.

We arrived at the very edge of the Elder's territory—the part where the night stopped and the day began. I could see sunlight past the force field that was keeping the Blood Keep away from any human detection—the same spell Cora had cast on The Shade. I wondered if it was the reason the original vampire had made Emilia a part of his clan to begin with. She was too powerful to let go of. *Something tells me that he's just using her.*

The scream came from a young woman—human and immune. She was in the arms of one of the vampire guards. He was drinking her blood and clearly enjoying it. The woman, on the other hand, was clawing at him with all her might.

I moved forward to help the girl, but Emilia held me back. "No. I think she's new. She's most likely being trained to submit." She gave me a pointed look. "Besides, I don't want you going anywhere near an immune."

So we're just going to stand here and watch? This is sick.

"That's exactly what we're going to do, Derek."

The guard seemed to like that Emilia was watching, so he lifted the girl in his arms, wrapping his large arms around her waist as he continued to drink from her neck. She was writhing to free herself from him, but we all knew it was pointless.

I wanted to stop it, but I was powerless. I was under Emilia's control.

For crying out loud, Emilia. Do something. Enough of this.

I wasn't expecting her to do anything, but if she was still reading my mind, then I figured I could annoy her by thinking something that would displease her.

I began thinking of Sofia, of my most treasured memories of her—the way she'd clung tightly to me when I'd first made the hundred-foot leap from the top of the Crimson Fortress to the ground to take her to the Lighthouse, all the times she'd smiled sweetly while she was updating me about the ways of the modern world, her laughter, the slow dances, the kisses, the night she'd agreed to marry me...

"Enough!" Emilia screamed so loudly, I couldn't help but jump back in surprise. She turned toward me with a glare. "Stop thinking about her!"

I would've been intimidated had I not caught a glimpse of the guard, who was just as stunned by Emilia's outburst as I was. With the squirming young woman in his arms, he lost his balance when he jumped back in surprise. He let go of the girl and crashed outside of the castle's protective covering, into the rays of sunlight. He tried to get back into cover, only to be thrown back by a force field.

Emilia stared in horror at the vampire guard. "No... this can't be happening..."

It felt as if my heart stopped beating as the guard screamed in pain when the sun's rays began to peel away his pale skin. *Emilia, do something. He's going to die.*

I gasped when Emilia let out another scream and slammed the back of her hand against my cheek before she pulled a dagger from a hidden pocket on her dress and threw it at the guard, right through his heart.

"Why did you do that? Couldn't you have just saved him?"

"I did. He wouldn't have wanted the consequences his stupidity would've brought about." She brushed past me and began walking toward the castle.

I gave the trembling young woman a glance. She was clinging to her neck, terror evident in her eyes. I was craving her blood, knowing that a drink could temporarily restore my sanity, but I had no control over my actions. All I could do was send the young immune a sympathetic gaze before following Emilia.

For the first time in a long time, I found myself desperate for someone to save me.

Chapter 30: Kyle

It was after the human rebellion in The Shade that I began to hope that I could have the old Anna back. We'd been successful. Much to the disdain of Gregor Novak, there wasn't going to be another human culling. This relieved me, because Anna would surely have been killed.

I searched her out the moment the rebellion was over. I found her in the arms of Ian. I hated the jealousy that I felt.

"What's going on?" Ashley stood by my side, following my gaze. She raised her brow when she realized who I was staring at. "So you're into Ian?"

I scowled at her. "No. I'm into Anna."

"Oh, okay... Well..." Ashley cocked her head. "Isn't she crazy?"

"You didn't know her before Felix got his hands on her."

"You did?" She looked at me curiously, as if she was surprised that I was involved with any other girl in The Shade aside from the girls in Derek's harem.

"We were able to spend some time together by the lake. She was a lot like Sofia actually in the way she relates to people. Like she's friends with everyone, willing to trust and forgive and just be a light."

"Sounds like Sofia all right, but a lot less intense... Sofia can be so intense when it comes to the things she's passionate about."

"That's how she changed The Shade."

"Too bad Anna wasn't able to handle the pressures of the island like Sofia did."

I swallowed hard as my eyes once again lingered on the beautiful girl. Anna's green eyes caught mine and I could swear that there was a flicker of recognition, only for her to dart her eyes around her in panic as if just looking at me would cause trouble. I heaved a sigh, accepting that she would be as she was at that point and that there was little hope of her ever changing.

I turned my attention back to Ashley. "Let's go."

She glanced at me but then looked at Anna's direction. "Not quite yet."

I followed her gaze and found Anna bounding toward me. The raven-haired beauty stopped a couple of feet away from me and looked me straight in the eye. She smiled. It was the first time I'd seen her smile since Felix had returned her to The Catacombs.

I smiled back. She turned around and ran back to Ian, who gave me a bewildered look. I smirked. His turn to be jealous, I guess.

I couldn't get my mind off Anna for the following days. I kept on returning to the lake, secretly hoping that she would show up and I could have those stolen moments with her again.

One night, I thought that my hopes would finally come true, because as I sat at the edge of the lake, my legs dangling in the cool water, a feminine form approached. I took a short intake of breath.

My face fell when I realized that it was Ashley.

"So this is where all your rendezvous with the pre-crazy Anna happened," she muttered, looking around. "Don't look so disappointed, Kyle. It's obvious that you'd rather see her than me."

I rolled my eyes at Ashley. I was still trying to get used to having her around my home since I'd turned her into a vampire. She was the sister I'd never had and she was constantly bugging me. There were times when I honestly thought that she was doing it on purpose.

"What are you doing here, Ash?"

"Well, ever since that time at The Catacombs after the rebellion, when she just approached, stared at you, smiled and ran off, you've been moping like a sap, Kyle."

"I have not."

"Yes, you have." She placed her hands on her hips and rolled her eyes at me. "Please. It's annoying."

"You came here to tell me that you're annoyed that I'm moping?"

"No." She shook her head before smiling. "I came here to give you a reason to stop moping." She raised her finger for me to wait and ran back in the direction where she'd come from.

I could hear her whispering before emerging with Anna in tow.

My eyes widened. Anna hadn't been out of The Catacombs for the longest time. She was kept in there because she was an easy target for attack by vampires. "Ash, what were you thinking? How do you intend to defend her in case an Elite vampire attacks her?"

The sharpness of my tone made Anna withdraw in fear, backing up a couple of steps away from me.

Ashley cast me a glare. "What is wrong with you?" she mouthed. "She's here safe, isn't she?"

I approached Anna, who recoiled with every step I took. "You're safe with me, Anna," I assured her.

At first, she just whimpered in response, but then as I took slow steps *forward, careful not to scare her, she drew close, held my hand and led me to the dock, where we both sat on the edge. Ashley mumbled something about not being needed anymore, but my focus was on Anna and how beautiful and serene she looked as she stared at the lake.*

I didn't say anything, because I wasn't sure what I was going to say. I simply wanted to enjoy that one moment—that one snapshot of time where I felt like Anna belonged to me and me alone. We sat there in silence, enjoying each other's company, our legs dangling over the water below.

Anna nodded before breaking the silence. Her words meant the world to me. "Yes. I'm safe with you."

All eyes were on me as I sat across from Sofia at the dining table inside her quarters. I felt overwhelmed by the stare Sofia was throwing at me, her fascination showing on her face.

Corrine and Vivienne sat on either side of her, while Aiden sat at the head of the table. They were making me feel uncomfortable, staring at me like I had somehow committed a crime.

The elephant in the room, of course, was that I was once again a normal, mortal man, and no longer a vampire. They'd already done every test possible to check if I had indeed turned back into a human, and it was evident that I had.

"How is it possible?" Aiden muttered beneath his breath.

Sofia leaned forward. "What happened, Kyle?" There was a sense of hope and excitement in her voice.

I tried to recall what had occurred. After the ordeal I'd gone through in the pit Rex had trapped me in, everything was a blur. I began to recount exactly what had happened as I remembered it.

Drinking Anna's blood was unlike anything I'd ever experienced before. I didn't want to do it, because I knew that I would crave her every day afterward, but it was pure ecstasy just to taste the red liquid and feel it pounding within me. I felt amazing, powerful, unstoppable. I couldn't even wrap my senses around why I felt that way. My conscience was nagging at me, but once her blood ran down my throat, there was no way I could resist.

She didn't seem to mind. She did it so that I would heal and heal I did—faster than ever before.

Just then, Rex came back and pushed Anna away from me. She screamed as she fell to the ground. Her head hit the stone wall.

I gasped, but before I could go to her, Rex lunged toward me, picking me up before speeding with me into some other part of the cave. I tried to get away from his grasp to check if Anna was all right, but Rex was one of the Elite, the vampire clans that had helped Derek establish The Shade hundreds of years ago. He was far more powerful than I was. Still, I put up a fight until he stopped and pushed me into a cell in The Catacombs that had what looked like a sunroof.

He shut and locked the door. He smirked from the other side of the door. "This is the Pit. Not many know about this room. Only Gregor, Lucas, Felix and a select number of men… We used it to punish vampires before Derek took over and began running The Shade. You can't get out. The sun will rise and you will feel the pain. If you get exposed to more than eight hours of sunlight, you will surely die. That's what sunlight does to a vampire. If I change my mind, I might return before you die, but be warned, boy… Felix's girl is mine."

I grimaced. I'd never spent much time with Rex. He wasn't very important in The Shade and he mostly kept to himself, but he was one of Felix's men—one of those who had surrendered to Derek after the siege at the Port.

When he left, I tried to take down the door, but it didn't work. I figured it might be the same kind of doors they were using at The Cells. I screamed for help, but none came, so I just waited and waited and *waited, dreading the moment when the sun would come up and destroy me.*

When it did, I'd already lost all hope that anyone would come for me, so I braced myself for the agony that was to come. Just as expected, it was excruciating—so much so that after the first hour, I lost consciousness.

When I woke up, Ashley leaned over me, shaking me awake.

"Kyle? Are you all right?"

I felt weak and fragile—like I could break at the slightest touch. "What happened?" I asked.

Standing behind Ashley, Gavin shifted his weight from one foot to the other. "We should be the ones asking you that."

I checked my arm to see if the skin had peeled off and if my flesh had burned. I was wondering if I was numb, because I wasn't experiencing any pain. I was surprised to find my arm intact—with one major difference. It was no longer white. My complexion had returned to the bronzed one I'd had before I was turned.

Ashley swallowed hard as she stared at me before asking a question that I wasn't sure how to answer. "Kyle, are you human?"

"Well, are you?" Ashley butted in after I finished my story. "I'm sorry, but I'm still finding it hard to believe."

"We're *all* finding it hard to believe," Aiden said.

"Have you ever seen someone die under sunlight, Vivienne?" Sofia asked.

Vivienne took a moment to search her thoughts before shaking her head. "No. I don't remember anyone ever dying from sunlight. We always stayed away from it, because getting exposed to it was painful."

I nodded in agreement. "There's no describing the pain. It's torment."

Sofia swallowed hard as she tried to process the information we'd just given her.

Claudia spoke up, her brows furrowed in thought. "Ingrid was once exposed to sunlight. Perhaps we should ask her what that was like."

Sofia narrowed her eyes at the vampire. "Someone please get Ingrid here."

Yuri stood up to fetch Ingrid and returned within a couple of minutes. Ingrid recounted the details of her experience.

"When I escaped hunter territory, I had to spend time running under direct sunlight. It was an awful experience, but I survived it."

"How long were you under sunlight?" Sofia asked.

Ingrid shrugged. "A half hour or so, but it felt a lot longer."

Sofia directed her attention to me. "You must've been under sunlight for over a day…"

Ingrid eyed me. Her eyes widened when she realized what had become of me. "You're human…" She looked horrified, and I wasn't sure if it was because of the recollection of the painful experience or the idea that she could've turned back into a human had she stayed in the sun long enough.

I shrugged when the others looked to me. "There's no way for me to know. I wasn't conscious after the first hour."

"We need to figure this out… What if this is it?" Sofia asked. "What if the sun is the cure?"

"How are we going to test that theory?" Corrine spoke up. "What vampire would want to be exposed to sunlight for more than a day to see if this 'cure' works?"

"The one who doesn't have a choice, because he's been very bad." Xavier spoke up from behind us, pushing into the room the man who'd tried to kill me—Rex.

"No." Rex shook his head, terror filling his eyes. "You can't do this to me. First off, I don't want to turn back into a human. Besides, I've seen vampires die under the sun—isn't that why those UV rays hunters use are so deadly?"

Vivienne raised a brow at him. "You've seen a vampire die under the sun? Who? As far as I know, no vampires were killed in The Shade during the entirety of my father's rule. Besides, The Shade had no sunlight until Emilia took Derek away. How could you have used the cell then?"

Rex grimaced, knowing he was digging himself deeper and deeper. "The Pit is in some corner of the island where sunlight streams through. I don't understand why either, but it seems to be unprotected by the spell. I've never seen anyone die. We always took them out of the Pit before they died. I'd seen them in pain, and I don't want to go through that... It's merciless and none of us are even certain that this could be the cure. Please..."

"So you admit to having tried to kill Kyle by exposing him to sunlight?" Vivienne asked. "And you did this after he tried to stop you from attacking a human, which we all know is prohibited here at The Catacombs?"

Desperation formed on Rex's face. The truth was clear to everyone. We were going to test out Sofia's theory that sunlight could be the cure, and Rex was going to be our very first test subject.

CHAPTER 31: SOFIA

We were headed for the Pit in a rather odd procession. Xavier, Yuri and Claudia were restraining a frantic Rex. He was fighting and clawing with every ounce of his might to avoid what was to come. Vivienne and Corrine were walking right behind them, while I trailed behind. Aiden walked next to me, Ingrid on his other side. I didn't bother to look at whoever else had decided to come to watch the show, because I was torn inside about what we were about to do.

"What if he dies?" I asked. "Is this the right thing to do?"

"If we want to find out if this is the cure, I guess we don't have much of a choice," Aiden explained. "Sofia, when you're leading people, you have to make compromises."

I felt conflicted and sorry for Rex, but it didn't seem like I had a choice. The whole Elite Council agreed that it was the right thing to do to put Rex through the same thing he'd put Kyle through. They all saw it as a fair punishment.

We eventually reached the Pit and it was clear from the dim light inside that the sun was already beginning to rise outside The Shade.

I watched as they threw Rex inside and locked the door from the outside. I cringed when he began to scream. I was about to move forward, but Xavier took one look at me and shook his head.

"It's best for you not to have to sit through this, Sofia," he warned. "Perhaps it's best for you to spend your time elsewhere."

I gulped as it sank in to me how awful it would be. For some reason, the warning only heightened my desire to find out what was going on. Aiden held my arm as I once again moved forward.

"Sofia, no." Aiden shook his head. "Let's just go."

"Your father's right, Sofia," Ingrid agreed. "Believe me when I say that what's ahead isn't going to be pretty."

I stared at her incredulously. I still didn't trust her and by the way she could never look me in the eye, she knew it.

"Perhaps we could take this time to have a talk," Aiden suggested, "as a family."

After everything the three of us had been through, I was finding it hard to believe that we could ever be anything close to a family, but there was such a hopeful tone in his voice that I couldn't ignore it. I nodded.

We returned to my quarters, now abandoned. We made ourselves comfortable on the couches in the living room, aware of how awkward the setting was.

Aiden opened his mouth to say something, but shut his mouth. Ingrid sat beside him, staring into space, looking as if she were about to cry.

"So?" I asked. "What exactly do we talk about?"

"Do you think we could ever be a family again?" He turned toward Ingrid. "How about you? If the cure works, would you be willing to be Camilla again? I know that it's a painful process, but…"

Ingrid nodded, though I could tell that she was torn. "I'll do anything to be completely yours again, Aiden."

I scoffed. I couldn't help it. I shook my head. "I want to believe you, Ingrid. I really do, but how can you have a sudden change of heart? The last time I saw you before you came up with this story about wanting to be Camilla again, you were shouting curses at me and killing me with your eyes because I'd just murdered Borys." I choked on the words. The recollection that my hands had ended a man's life had never sat well with me. Still, I had a score to settle with my mother. "Did you forget that? I killed Borys, Ingrid. I'm supposed to believe you're just going to forgive me for that even after you've made it clear that he means much more to you than we do?"

Ingrid's lips twitched. She didn't seem too happy, but it didn't matter all that much to me. I needed to let my apprehensions out. "I don't know what to say, Sofia." She stood up. "I can't take this. I'm sorry… I need to go out for a walk."

"A walk?" I snapped. "No, you're not, Ingrid. You're not going anywhere. I'm not just going to let you roam the island without…"

Aiden held my arm. "Let her, Sofia."

"It's too much of a risk… I don't trust her."

"But I do," Aiden said firmly. "Trust me instead."

Ingrid took this as a go signal, stood up and headed for the doorway.

When Aiden sat back down on the couch across from mine, I

couldn't help but quip, "You should go after her. You're in charge of her, Aiden. She can't go out, because the sun is up, so who knows what trouble she might end up starting here at The Catacombs?"

I knew I sounded heartless, but two things were predominant in my mind: Derek and the cure. I was used to the issues I had with my father and my mother, so dealing with them didn't feel like a priority to me at that time.

"Do you really think that she's beyond redemption, Sofia?"

"Don't you think I want to believe that this could happen, Aiden? I dreamed of having a family of my own for the past decade. I longed for your embrace. I longed for hers. But neither of you were there. Ben was there for me and when he could no longer be there, Derek filled that place in my life. Now, in the midst of all this, you want me to welcome both you and Camilla with open arms. You want me to forget that you lied to me about finding a cure so you could stab Derek in the back. You want me to forget that Camilla watched without even flinching as Borys abused me."

Aiden's shoulders sagged. He knew he was guilty. He knew she was guilty. I was so overwhelmed, I began to break down in tears. I shook my head and stood, exhausted by the events that had just unfolded.

"I'm going for a nap."

I didn't wait for any response from him. I just went to my bedroom. The moment my head rested on the pillow, I drifted off to sleep and found myself in Derek's arms.

"I love you, Sofia," he whispered into my ear.

He had his hands on my waist and he was rocking me gently as soft music played in the background. We were in some sort of garden and we were both all dressed up. Derek looked dashing in a tux and I felt pretty in the powder-blue pixie dress I had on.

"You believe me, don't you?" he asked. "You know that I will always love you?"

I creased my brows. "Of course I do, Derek. I know you love me."

"I don't want that to change."

I was beginning to get nervous. "Why would that ever change?" I pulled away from him and looked up into those electric-blue eyes that always made me weak in the knees.

"Because we don't have control over everything, Sofia. We never know what life will throw our way."

A cold wind swept through the place.

"No… No… This can't be happening." He shook his head.

"Derek, what's wrong?"

"I don't love you, Sofia. That's what's wrong. I'm so sorry."

"Derek, why are you doing this? What's going on?"

"I don't want to do this, but I have to. I'm sorry, Sofia."

He pulled out a dagger and drove it right through my heart.

I screamed even as I opened my eyes to find myself staring up at my bedroom ceiling. I had broken out into a cold sweat, my breathing heavy, my heartbeat drumming furiously against my chest. I was trying to catch my breath when my father showed up at my door and ran to my bed to check on me.

"Sofia, what happened? I heard you scream from the living room."

I stared at him, unable to speak. I wondered how long I'd been asleep, surprised that he would wait for me in the living room and not just go off and find Ingrid.

"Where's Ingrid?" I asked. "Shouldn't you be with her?"

"When Camilla says that she needs time alone, it's better to give her the space she's asking for. What happened, Sofia?"

I slowly sat up in bed, the dream still running through my head. "I had a dream... How long have I been asleep?"

"A little over an hour. What was the dream about?"

I tried to recall every detail of the dream and when I did, I couldn't help it. Tears began to stream down my cheeks and I broke into a sob.

Aiden didn't seem to know what to do at first. After gathering his wits about him, he pulled me into his arms, cradling me in his lap. "Hey, come on. Everything's going to be all right."

"One minute Derek was professing his love for me and in the very next minute, he was stabbing me in the heart with a dagger."

"It was just a nightmare, Sofia. It doesn't mean anything."

Dreams I'd had before about Derek had served as warnings. I couldn't help but tremble at what this dream could be warning me about. I snuggled into my father's arms. "I can't lose him."

"You know me, Sofia. You know how much I stand against your relationship with Derek, but much as I hate to admit it, the man loves you. I doubt that he'll leave you for anything."

That's because you haven't seen Emilia's effect on him. "What if he does? You don't know Emilia. What if she's right? What if she's actually the girl prophesied to help him bring the vampires to true sanctuary?"

My father's words came as healing balm to my soul. "It won't matter, because it will still be you holding his heart."

I leaned my head against his shoulder and let those words sink in. I couldn't allow myself to be disheartened. For myself and Derek's sake. "Thank you," I whispered to my father before giving him a gentle kiss on the cheek.

We sat there for a while. I relished his company, enjoying the time we got to spend together.

"I love you, Dad. You know that, don't you?"

He smiled and nodded before kissing me on my temple. "I love you too, Sofia."

We walked out of the room minutes later in a much lighter mood, chuckling over who had to prepare snacks for the both of us.

"I want us to be a family," I told him, as we began to prepare our food in the kitchen.

"I want that too. More than anything."

I smiled. "I'll give Ing... Camilla another chance if you want me to."

"That means the world to me, Sofia. I've heard so many stories about you here in The Shade and I know they're true. You're someone who's willing to forgive, forget and trust again."

"Maybe I got that from you." I raised a brow at him, loving that I could feel so light and trusting around him.

"Got what?"

I shrugged as I sliced through a piece of cheese. "The urge to find beauty within people and to create it when it's not there."

"I'm not like that at all."

I chuckled at how little he knew about himself. "You knew that my mother was broken, but you still chose to love her every single day."

His face softened and his eyes began to brim with tears. I was actually eager to see what it would be like to have my father cry in front of me, but I never got the chance to.

Next moment, Ingrid showed up, fangs and claws out, running toward me with determination in her eyes.

My mother was about to kill me.

CHAPTER 32: AIDEN

I'd lost count of the times Camilla had broken my heart. I'd started to get used to it. I'd even been expecting it, but when I saw her with that dagger raised in the air, poised to kill our only daughter, my heart shattered into pieces. I began to see red and every ounce of love that could've held me back from destroying Camilla disappeared. I wasn't about to watch my wife kill my daughter. Not in a million years.

Without any hesitation, I pulled out the one gadget I'd been able to hide from my captors in the Shade. It was a blow dart that would inject a serum into Camilla's system to incapacitate her. I'd kept it for emergency purposes, for when I would need it to save my life. I'd never thought that it would be my daughter's life I would be saving.

With a guttural scream expressing all the anger I felt inside, I blew the dart into Camilla's neck right before she could stab Sofia in the heart.

The effect was immediate. Camilla started screaming in pain. I expected to feel some sort of sympathy for her, but as she dropped the dagger and fell to the ground, screaming and writhing in pain before finally passing out, all I felt was numbness.

I was transfixed by the sight of her motionless body on the ground. For a while, I couldn't move a muscle. I could sense Sofia trembling and I wanted to comfort her, but I didn't know how to give comfort when even I needed it. It took me a while to get back to my senses and approach my daughter.

She was staring at her mother's body, frozen with shock. "Did you kill her? Is she dead?"

"No." I shook my head. "But she will be."

Sofia's eyes widened at the implication. "You mean…"

I lifted my hand in the air, palm up. "I told you to always keep a wooden stake on your person, Sofia. Do you have one?"

"Aiden, we can just imprison her… you don't have to do this."

I shook my head. "I told you that I would be in charge of her. I told you to trust me. I was a fool to trust her." My jaw tightened. "She played me. She promised she wouldn't harm you. She said she wanted to be a family again." My voice choked and a tear ran down my cheek.

"Dad…"

"Give me the stake, Sofia."

"Think this through… this decision could haunt you forever…"

"Give it to me!"

I was expecting Sofia to be intimidated by the strength of my voice. I'd forgotten that she was the fiancée of a vampire much more powerful, menacing and intimidating than I was. Despite the fact that I was consumed by my anger toward Camilla, I was soothed by my daughter's countenance. It reminded me that she'd been through a lot in The Shade... more than I could ever know.

She hiked her dress up and retrieved the stake from a holder wrapped around her thigh. She handed it over to me. "I know you, Dad. You *will* regret this."

I gripped the stake and was about to approach my wife to drive the stake into her heart, but I found myself hesitating. *Is this what Sofia does with Derek?* "How many times have you done something like this to Derek?"

A small smile formed on Sofia's lips. "Many, many times."

"Did he ever push through with doing the wrong thing?"

She shook her head. "Never."

With that, my decision was made. I handed the stake over to her before looking back at my unconscious wife. "What do you want to do with her then?"

Sofia took the stake from me and put it back in place. "That's it? No dramatic struggle? No excuses?"

I shrugged. "If Derek never disappointed you in this area, I don't ever want to either."

She kissed me on the cheek and squeezed my arm. "I have to say though... My boyfriend is much more of a drama king than you are."

I couldn't help but wonder what she meant, but I read between the lines and assumed that he put up a struggle a lot more than I did. I couldn't help but wince at the thought of the price my daughter had to pay, but I didn't want to dwell on it. I trusted that she knew what was and wasn't good for her.

I still loved Camilla, though I hated what she had allowed herself to become. I couldn't understand how she could do what she did, but I had to accept that there was little chance she would ever truly change.

"What are we going to do with her?" I asked once again.

Sofia heaved a deep sigh. "Bring her back to The Cells, I guess... We'll decide what to do to her. For now, we need to deal with finding the cure."

Camilla was brought back to The Cells. I didn't want to think about her so I stayed with Sofia. I was disheartened by Camilla's betrayal, but somehow, what she'd done had helped form a bond between my daughter and me.

For that reason alone, I was secure that everything would be okay.

Sofia and I occupied ourselves checking that everything was running well in The Shade. It wasn't until sunset that we received news on Rex's fate.

Vivienne was the one who gave us the news.

"Rex is dead."

Chapter 33: Ingrid

When I woke up in a cell, Claudia hovered over me with the saddest expression in her eyes. I began to sob.

"Why, Camilla?" Claudia asked. "I thought you said you wanted to change."

To save Aiden's life. If I don't kill Sofia, the Elder will kill Aiden. I couldn't divulge to her the reason in fear of what the Elder could do to her. "I had to, Claudia. I didn't have a choice."

"That's crap, Camilla." Claudia shook her head. "I gave myself that same excuse many times over and it led me to very bad decisions. You have a choice. There is *always* a choice."

"What does it matter?" I ran my hand through my hair, feeling the despair that came with the failure to kill Sofia. "She's alive. Aiden hates me. It's over. What's done is done."

"Are you blind, Camilla? Do you not realize how much those

two love you? You failed them time and time and time again and they were willing to give you one chance after another! How can you turn your back on that kind of love?"

"They want me to become human. If the cure works, they want me to become human again."

"Will you do it for them?"

I shook my head, then nodded, then shrugged. "I don't know. I don't know what I'm going to do." If there was anyone to blame for my misery, it was me and me alone. What Claudia was saying was true. Aiden had given me nothing but true love and Sofia had been willing to forgive and accept despite everything that I'd put her through. I was to blame for the fact that darkness had such control over me now.

I was expecting it to come and take revenge on me, but nothing happened. I feared that Aiden would suffer the brunt of my failure. I feared for his sake and I feared for Sofia's too. At that point, when I was certain that I'd already lost them, I realized how much I wanted them back. The old adage haunted me: *You never know what you've got until it's gone.*

"I will do it. If it's what they ask of me, I'm willing to become human."

Claudia stared at me in surprise. "You're certain?"

"Wouldn't you do it if Yuri asked you to?"

She swallowed hard as she began fidgeting with her blonde curls. "I guess I would... I'm not sure. It's a scary thought. Part of me wants to. For Yuri. Part of me is terrified of the weakness that comes with being human." She sat on the cot beside me before heaving a deep sigh. "I guess it doesn't matter right now. Rex is dead. Their theory didn't work."

I just smirked. "They will find a way. If there's anything I know about my daughter, it's that she will never give up until she finds that cure. She loves Derek Novak too much."

Before she could respond, the cell doors swung open and Aiden appeared. I took a deep breath, gearing up for a fight, for accusations, for pain. Claudia looked at him worriedly, but left, giving us our privacy.

I couldn't look Aiden in the eye.

"Why?" he asked. "Why would you do this? I was going to kill you. If Sofia hadn't convinced me not to…"

I didn't have the answers to his question, not ones that would satisfy him at least.

"Why did you choose this path? Help me understand. I thought you said you wanted us to become a family again."

"I do…"

"Then why?"

"Because I can't afford to lose you." He wasn't going to understand that statement, but it was the only one I could give him.

"Well, you just did, Camilla." He turned back, but before he left, he gave me several last words. "Whatever Sofia decides to do about you, I suggest you just cooperate. Don't fight back."

"What do you think she's going to do?"

"Next time they need a vampire to test out the cure, I'm going to suggest they use you."

Chapter 34: Sofia

"Rex was burned to a crisp," Xavier said. "There are barely even bones left. He's just ashes now."

What are we missing? You have to figure this out, Sofia. I feared for Derek. I feared for us. Amidst all the chaos, the cure felt like my only ray of hope. Rex's demise was disheartening and I felt somehow responsible for it, but I knew that we couldn't give up on the cure and that Rex had it coming. I swallowed back the bile rising up my throat. *Get it together, Sofia. Rex brought it upon himself. It's not your fault.*

"I don't understand..." I frowned. "What caused Kyle to turn back to a human? What was the difference between him and Rex?"

All I got from Cameron, Liana, Vivienne, Xavier, Eli, Yuri and Claudia were blank stares.

"We're going to have to try again," Vivienne said, "but this time, we need to follow everything according to what exactly happened to Kyle."

"What?" Xavier interjected. "We have to beat up the vampire first and feed them the blood of Anna?"

"No… I think Vivienne is on to something." I began nodding. "I don't think the beating is necessary, but I think the feeding is. Maybe the cure is that the vampire must first feed on blood before being thrown into the sunlight."

"From what I understand," Cameron spoke up, "Rex also had a drink of Anna's blood before Kyle came to her rescue and Rex ended up shoving him into the Pit."

"Yes"—Eli nodded—"but Kyle was thrown into the Pit and exposed to sunlight soon after drinking Anna's blood. Rex was thrown into the Pit more than a day after he had her blood. Maybe it has to be immediate. Drink the blood, expose yourself to sunlight."

"That's a great theory." Yuri nodded in agreement. "But after what happened to Rex, who would want to volunteer to test that theory out?"

"I know someone who we can use." Aiden walked into my quarters, which somehow had become the center of all issues that needed discussing after Derek had left the island with Emilia.

My heart sank. I already knew who he was going to suggest. I licked my lips and gave him a sympathetic glance, wondering if he was sure about what he was going to say. I saw in his eyes how much he wanted to believe that Ingrid's desire to be a family was for real. I could tell how heartbroken and torn he was.

"We can use Ingrid." He shrugged one shoulder.

A collective gasp echoed in the room. I noted how he no longer referred to her as Camilla. *He's given up.*

Claudia hung her head at the suggestion. My mother was her

friend. Claudia was closer to her than I'd ever been.

"Are you sure about this, Aiden?" Yuri grabbed Claudia's hand to comfort her. The gesture made me ache for Derek.

"It's a just punishment for the trouble she's caused everyone." Aiden's jaw tightened.

"What do you think about this, Sofia?" Vivienne shot me a look of concern.

I gave it some thought. We'd given my mother one chance after another and every single time, she'd proved that we'd been fools for putting our trust in her. I wondered how many times she'd broken my father's heart.

I shrugged. "I'm not thrilled about the idea, and I don't think Ingrid will agree to it either without a fight, but what choice do we have?"

"I've already talked to Ingrid," Aiden confessed. "She's going to do it whether she likes it or not."

Xavier shrugged. "Let's do it."

"Wait," Liana interrupted. "There's the matter of whether or not Ian or Kyle—or even Anna—would agree to letting Ingrid drink Anna's blood. We can't just force Anna to let Ingrid drink. She already lost a lot of blood with Kyle drinking from her."

"Ingrid can have my blood," I suggested.

"No." Aiden shook his head. "She is not going to drink your blood. I'm not going to allow it."

"Then whose blood are we going to give her? I don't want it to be Anna's again."

"She can have mine. It's about time I got to experience firsthand what it's like. Besides, if this doesn't work, I'd rather have Ingrid craving my blood instead of craving yours."

I narrowed my eyes at him. "Aiden, do you not realize that if this doesn't work, she's going to die? The sun will kill her."

Aiden shrugged. "Well, there's that. Still, I'd rather she have my blood than yours."

"What if only an immune's blood works?" Claudia asked, not bothering to mask how disturbed she was at the thought of Ingrid being led to her possible death. "Or what if only Anna's blood works? Sofia, think this through. She's your mother. I know she screwed up, but still..."

I wanted to feel something. I wanted to hesitate, but I couldn't bring myself to do it. I was just numb. I straightened in my seat. Even though my heart went out to Claudia, we had to do what we had to do. "We don't want this either, Claudia, but if Ingrid agrees to this, then I think there really is no other choice. We need to find the cure."

That was it. It was set. Ingrid was going to drink Aiden's blood before we threw her into the Pit and waited for the sun to rise and either cure her or kill her.

As my mother drank my father's blood, Vivienne came to my side and squeezed my elbow. Despite my better instincts, I ran toward Ingrid and threw my arms around her neck before she could enter the Pit.

"Do you hate me, Ingrid?" I whispered into her ear.

She shook her head. "No. I don't."

"Do you love me then?"

She paused and it felt like my heart stopped beating. "I don't know."

Her answer was heartbreaking, but it was honest.

"I just hope you know that I wish things were different, Sofia. I wish *I* were different. I never should've left you and your father."

I nodded as I pulled away from her embrace. "That's good

enough."

"Come on, Ingrid," Aiden said, grabbing her and pushing her toward the Pit. "That's enough."

Ingrid looked at him in a way that made me realize how much she too loved him. "Please say my name."

A muscle in Aiden's face twitched as he eyed her with a mixture of affection, loss and contempt. "Go, *Camilla*."

None of us were expecting it, but she threw herself in his arms and kissed him. Aiden stood there, stunned. By the time their lips parted, he was in tears and so was she.

As Camilla entered the Pit, I felt a deep sense of foreboding. I thought we all knew that she was going to die—even she did—but none of us did anything to stop what was about to happen, not even her.

Hours later, we found out that we were right.

Ingrid Maslen, and what was left of Camilla Claremont, was gone.

Chapter 35: Emilia

I rolled over on the bed and stared at Derek's sleeping form. I ran my fingers over his bare torso. A tear ran down my cheek. I was in deep trouble and there was every possibility that the Elder would punish me by taking Derek away.

When the Elder arrived in my bedroom, I felt it immediately. The bone-chilling fear always came with him and I began shuddering.

"You have been a disappointment, Emilia."

"Master?"

A stinging pain whipped my back and I fought the urge to scream in fear of waking Derek. This confrontation with my father was best done without him being aware. Physical assaults from the Elder always meant one thing: I was to be silent as he spoke.

"Must I remind you, Emilia, that you only have control over

him for a week? You only have a couple of days left. Even with him in your control, you still fail to make him fall in love with you."

How am I going to make him fall in love with me? He can't stop thinking about her! Sofia Claremont needs to die.

"You mustn't acknowledge his thoughts, fool. He is attracted to you. He is professing love to you. The more you draw this side of him out, the more he will lose the part of him that loves the redhead, but you keep listening in on his thoughts to check if he is indeed in love with you when you are fully aware that he is not!"

I began to sob, which, of course, irritated my father. I got another stripe on my back for that.

Derek began to stir on the bed, muttering something under his breath. As if I weren't already in enough heartache after what my father had told me, he had to add to the pain by whispering her name.

"You have failed time and again, Emilia. You let your brother feed Derek the blood of an immune. Even worse than that, you almost let Derek discover our secret. Do you have any idea what would have happened if Derek got any idea how to..." He cut his sentence off, hating even the mention of the one thing that could end him.

My father was furious and I knew that if I failed in this mission, I was never going to get back into his good graces. *If Derek doesn't fall in love with me, it will literally be the end of me.*

"Ingrid is dead, and with her passing, I've lost my eyes in The Shade. I do know that they are very close to finding the cure. If they find it, it will be the end of us. I swear, Emilia, even if you are my daughter, if you fail to find a way to stop this, I *will* end you myself."

My gut clenched. Ingrid had failed to kill Sofia.

His going after Ingrid had been an act of desperation. His threat to end Aiden should Ingrid fail to kill Sofia had been the biggest bluff I'd ever heard him speak. He couldn't kill Aiden the way he'd ended Gregor. Aiden hadn't gone over to his darkness—even more so now that he was being influenced by his daughter.

I had no idea what kind of a relationship Aiden had with Sofia, but I couldn't help but be jealous. She had a father.

I blinked, hoping to catch a glimpse of the Elder, supposedly my father. Of course, same as before, I never saw him with my own eyes. He was always just a shadow, a fearsome presence, a cruel master. I couldn't help but wonder why I gave in to his demands, part of a family who threatened punishment at every mistake, brothers and sisters who would betray me and stab me in the back the first chance they got.

Why did I do this to myself? Why did I allow Cora to ever turn into Emilia?

Then I remembered...

I stared at Derek's sleeping form, my heart breaking. He had abandoned me.

I loved him and I'd hoped for so long that he would one day return my love, but he'd given himself to the darkness. Then when all was said and done, he couldn't live with himself, so he'd come to me—the woman who would give anything on his behalf—and asked of me something that he knew would kill me. He'd asked me to end his immortality, to give him an escape from his own conscience.

"Eternal sleep is the equivalent of death, Derek," I told him, hoping that I wouldn't choke on my words.

"I've lived more than a hundred years, Cora. I don't mind dying..."

"Then why don't you just ask me to kill you?"

"Would you?"

I drew a breath as I stared up into his stunning blue eyes, so taken by his handsome face and masculine features. He already knew the answer to his question. I wouldn't be able to do it even if I wanted to.

Despite my reservations, I pulled myself closer to him and craned my neck to put a kiss on his lips. I loved him and he knew this. I wanted him to respond. I wanted him to think about what we could be together. We'd already done so much in The Shade as a duo. We could be great together and I couldn't understand why he didn't see that.

It tore me apart when he broke away from the kiss and shook his head.

"You are too good for me, Cora. There's so much goodness in you and there's so much darkness in me. That's what keeps us apart."

I wanted to object. I wanted to tell him that I saw goodness in him, but all I had to do was remind myself of all the things I'd seen him do under the control of darkness. Even I couldn't understand why I was still so enamored of him. Then it happened. Something clicked in me and I stopped desiring to be good.

If goodness is the only thing that's keeping me away from him, then I might as well go to the dark side.

When he'd told me those words, he couldn't have understood how much he would change me. That night, I gave myself over to the darkness. I wanted to be transformed into the woman who would belong to him.

The Elder was quick to grant my request, but he told me that it would take time. It would take hundreds of years. So I placed the spell upon Derek, but I didn't grant his request that it would be eternal.

In the eyes of The Shade, I was a broken-hearted woman who eventually got married to one of the humans of The Shade, a man I killed with a heart attack shortly after the birth of our son and daughter. He was kind, he was handsome, but he wasn't Derek, and I was bored with him.

I trained my daughter to become the witch of The Shade. When she was ready, I asked Vivienne for permission for me and my son to once again return to the outside world. She didn't withhold this from me.

"You've experienced so much heartbreak here in The Shade, Cora," she told me. "I wouldn't dream of keeping you here against your will. We owe you so much already."

I smiled at her, but I hated that she could ever look at me like an object of pity. I wasn't to be pitied. Not by her. Not by anyone. Still, I gave Vivienne a prophecy about Derek. "Your brother isn't going to sleep forever, Vivienne. He will wake up and rule, but only when the girl who will help him bring your kind to true sanctuary takes her place beside him."

Hope sparked in Vivienne's eyes when I told her that she would have her brother back. I anticipated that day too, but I had to prepare. I raised my son in the outside world, reminding him that at least one woman in every generation must be trained to keep The Shade safe. He was my apprentice. He knew what to do and he promised me that he would do it. When he finally married and had a family of his own, I knew that it was time for my transformation.

Since I'd left The Shade, I'd stopped the spell that was keeping me young and immortal. When I arrived at the Elder's castle, I was an old, decrepit woman, ready to become whatever I needed in order to be Derek's.

The deal was struck. The Elder asked me what kind of woman Derek was attracted to. I described what Derek's ideal was based on my observations.

The Elder smiled.

"I can do that," he said, "but it will take time."

He turned me into Emilia, his daughter, that night. And since then, I'd slowly transformed from the old Cora to the beautiful, young and vibrant Emilia. I looked forward to the day Derek would be mine. In the meantime, I had to follow my father's every beck and call… and with every command that I followed, I lost a part of my soul.

I blinked back the tears as I set my eyes on Derek even as the Elder's presence hovered over me.

"You gave up your goodness in order to match his darkness only to find that you came too late. He woke up and discovered his goodness in the form of Sofia. Bring him back to the darkness, Emilia, or I will make sure that you will never see Derek again. I *will* find a way to destroy him."

Chapter 36: Derek

The night after that encounter with the young woman and the vampire at the labyrinth, I decided to focus all my energies on thinking about Sofia. One memory in particular kept running through my mind. No matter what Emilia's control was making me feel, my mind kept reminding me that I wanted to marry Sofia.

I was so preoccupied reliving the moment Sofia had accepted my proposal, I hadn't even noticed how Emilia was glaring at me from across the table until she slapped my face with the back of her hand.

"I thought you said you loved me, Derek. You're not even listening to me!"

That's the point. I don't love you. "I'm sorry, Emilia."

I got another blow and then another and then another. Every fiber of my being longed to fight back, longed to retaliate, but I could not. What she was doing was a stark reminder that I wasn't in control. I was losing my mind and I knew it. I could access memories of Sofia, but I couldn't even think about anything that was going on at the castle. Everything was confusing. I'd only been there for a few days, but it felt as if I'd been there for centuries. I was beginning to feel differently. I was beginning to feel like I was in love with Emilia.

I was losing the battle and I knew it, but I clung to every last straw of hope that I could still overcome this, that I could get back to Sofia.

"You love me!" Emilia screamed before once again hitting me until I couldn't take it anymore. I didn't know where the strength came from, but I hit her back so hard she went crashing to the ground.

And for some reason, I knew that she had won. She smirked as I lunged forward to attack her. I hit her and clawed at her. I watched her heal, then I did it again. By the time I was done, a sick feeling came over me, because she snickered. I watched her heal before she fisted a clump of my hair and kissed me full on the mouth.

When our lips parted, she smirked. "Welcome to the darkness, Derek."

I realized why she was acting so triumphant. The act of violence was me giving in to my dark side. She had provoked the part of me that would react with violence—a side of me Cora knew very well.

"Sofia doesn't know about this side of you… I'll introduce it to her when I make you kill her, Derek."

Emilia kissed me again and I could feel it happen. Every memory I had of Sofia faded. I couldn't even remember Sofia's face. All that remained was that strong conviction that I was in love with Sofia.

I was under Emilia's full control for the rest of the day and I couldn't even think of anything apart from her, but in the back of my mind that thought remained: *I love Sofia Claremont. Not Emilia. I love Sofia.*

Still, even that thought didn't take long to disappear.

My stay at the Elder's castle felt like an eternity I couldn't escape from. I was falling in love with the woman I'd been deeply attracted to from the moment I first laid eyes on her. Emilia was the girl for me and I had no doubt about it, but I was also consumed by another emotion: fear. Emilia terrified me—even the sweet, doting side of her.

One night, after we made love, I drifted off to sleep. I had no clue how long I'd been sleeping when she once again did something unexpected... and rather agonizing.

I woke up to Emilia's claws raking my torso.

"Say her name again, Derek, and I will kill you!"

I swallowed hard, wondering whose name I'd just said, but I knew better than to ask.

"You're mine, do you understand? Mine!"

The look in her eyes was terrifying. I couldn't suppress a shudder. She must've noticed my fear, because she mellowed and tears began to drop from the corners of her eyes. "I'm sorry... I just... I'm so in love with you, Derek."

I sat up on the bed, beginning to heal from the wounds she had just inflicted on me. "I know that, Emilia. I'm in love with you too. Why do you still doubt this?"

"Because you still say the name of the woman I hate, instead of saying mine."

That tugged at my heartstrings, but I couldn't help but sense that something was different about this woman she was speaking of. Emilia harbored hatred for more people than just one, but I could tell that this woman was high up on her list. "What has she done to you that you would hate her so much, Emilia?"

"She tried to take you away from me."

I sneered. "No one could ever do that, Emilia. We belong together." Anger was beginning to build up inside of me as I contemplated the thought of anyone ever trying to take me away from Emilia. "Who is she?"

Emilia's eyes widened with suspicion. "Why do you want to know?"

"Because I want to know who would bother you in such a way. I want to know how I can help."

"Kill her. I want you to kill her. If you love me, you will end her life."

Knowing how consumed she was by her own darkness, I wondered to myself why I loved her, but I did and I wanted to please her. "If I do this, will that prove my love for you?"

"Yes! Yes, Derek. Kill Sofia Claremont and we will be in love and happy forever."

"Consider it done. The moment I first lay eyes on her, I will rip her heart out for you."

I couldn't help but feel an agonizing void form within me when I thought about killing the stranger who was Sofia Claremont.

Chapter 37: Emilia

I knew he was telling the truth and it was pure delight to see the determination in his blue eyes when he assured me that he would indeed end the life of the young redhead who was the one person who could take him away from me.

I couldn't help but throw my arms around his neck and press my lips against his, reveling in the fact that his thoughts no longer fought against me. He was mine. Derek Novak was finally mine.

"You make me so happy, Derek," I whispered into his ear as I kissed him.

Just like clockwork, he told me that I made him happy too. I bit my lip and smiled, wondering how long the bliss would last, hoping that it would last for eternity.

We made love again and I snuggled into his arms, enjoying every moment I had, knowing that his heart was mine and mine alone.

I longed for the day that I would see him make good on his promise to end Sofia's life. When the familiar, fearsome presence of the Elder swept across my room, my eagerness to tell him what had occurred overpowered the dread I felt whenever he was around.

"He has agreed to kill young Sofia, Master," I blurted out. "Shall I arrange immediate transport to The Shade? It has to be done before the week is over and control over him is lost, although he is so enamored of me right now, I doubt we'll lose control."

I was expecting him to be happy. I wanted him to congratulate me or to express how proud he was that I'd pulled Derek back to the dark side. I'd made Derek fall in love with me like we had planned, but I got a lash right across my chest. *Why?* I asked the Elder, knowing that he knew my thoughts. *What have I done?*

"You fool, Emilia. You're nowhere near done." He hit me again and that was when I realized that never had I seen him happy for me nor for anyone else. Every triumph—whether by me or my siblings—was met with another challenge. We were never enough. We had to do more, be more until we failed so badly, he ended us. That was the Elder's endless and deadly cycle, and I could never get away from it.

"Will you ever be satisfied?" I found myself muttering despite my better judgment.

His reply was as sinister and as dark as his presence. "When your soul is a black hole, it can never be filled." The lashes then came one after the other until I was a bloody mess, whimpering in Derek's arms, but desperate to not wake him.

"Gloat to me once you actually have him in your control, once he is once again mine, because if not for you, Derek Novak would've remained mine hundreds of years ago. Return to The

Shade and have him end the impetuous redhead's life and then come to me with your bright-eyed eagerness. Until then, you've no right to the bliss I have allowed you to have in his arms."

I knew then that as long as I was in league with the Elder, my happiness would always be temporary and never satisfying. It was a counterfeit version of the delight in Derek's eyes whenever he laid eyes on Sofia. I knew that what I shared with him was a fantasy, but I wanted it to be real so badly, I was willing to embrace even the counterfeit pleasure it brought me.

I tried to force back a sob, but it came out anyway. I wished that I hadn't surrendered to the Elder. I wished that I could go back and do things all over again, but it was too late. I'd gone too far into the darkness to ever be rescued.

I miss who I was when I still had goodness in me, when I was still Cora.

The moment the thought planted itself in my head, I saw it—a flash of the Elder's bloody red eyes. "How dare you, Emilia! How dare you think that after everything I've given you."

Without another word, I was taken from Derek's arms into one of my father's chambers where I endured a night of torment in my so-called father's hands. It took hours before he was satisfied with my punishment for ever thinking of going back to the way I was before I'd met him.

When he was done, he whispered, "Go to The Shade and destroy Sofia Claremont like you promised, Emilia. Otherwise, this night will feel like a walk in the park compared to what I'll put you through."

I found it insane that I hadn't seen it before. The Elder had nothing good in him—no joy, no love, no mercy, no peace. He was pure evil. He was darkness itself. And he was determined to drag us all down with him.

And yet, despite the awareness of the darkness I'd given myself over to, I was still willing to be under his control. I told myself that it was the fear, but it was more than that. I had become just like him. I had already become a daughter of the darkness and if I were to be miserable, just like my father, I refused to go through it alone.

Chapter 38: Derek

She was beautiful. The green eyes, the soft auburn locks, the splashes of freckles on her cheeks, the beautiful smile... The sight of Sofia standing by the shore, wearing a stunning white dress, wind blowing her hair, would never fail to draw me in.

As I walked towards her, I knew I was in a dream and when I woke up, I would be in love with someone else.

I approached Sofia with a heavy heart, hoping that she knew that I wasn't betraying her, that I'd tried to fight against the darkness controlling me, but I'd been overpowered by it. I felt like there was nothing I could do to stop its hold over me. When I reached her, however, I couldn't say a thing. We simply held hands and we both cried.

I felt an overwhelming sense of loss as I stood there with her, drawing her close, knowing that our hearts were breaking in unison. We both knew that we loved each other and she made that clear when, *between her sobs, she told me exactly what was going through my mind.*

"I can only hope that our love is strong enough to overcome this."

And then she disappeared and I was left alone, trying to reconnect with myself while I still could, while I still had control. And I stayed that way until the dream was over and I had to go back to the lie that Emilia and her father had painted for me.

I was aware of the truth only in my dreams. From the moment I closed my eyes and drifted off to sleep to the moment I opened them to a new day, I was right where I belonged. I was Derek Novak, king of The Shade, the love of a beautiful and kind redhead's life. And she was mine.

But once I woke up, I would see Emilia snuggled against me and I would feel an overwhelming wave of love for her—a love that wasn't from within, a love that felt unreal, but was nonetheless consuming.

I had an inkling in the back of my mind that I wasn't being who I was, but I had no choice other than to be him: a man stricken with love for Emilia, who would do everything she asked of him without hesitation.

Now, when I woke up, the space in the bed beside me was empty. I creased my brows even as I battled with the immediate sense of relief. *Where's Emilia? Why am I relieved? The woman I love is gone. I should go and look for her.*

I climbed out of bed and got dressed. I was about to bolt out of the door when Emilia arrived. I smiled at the sight of her. She looked stunningly attractive—the woman of my wildest fantasies. She gave me a weary lookover—almost as if she was annoyed by me.

"Get ready. We're leaving in an hour."

"Leaving? Where are we going?"

"You promised me you'd kill her." She looked away from me, opened her armoire and began rummaging through her clothes. "You're about to make good on your promise."

A wave of nausea came over me—a sensation I couldn't quite explain. "Today?"

She halted and turned to face me. "Don't you want to do it anymore?"

Something was different about her. She seemed exhausted, beaten down. I wondered what was wrong. She seemed different than the sweet woman I'd made love to the night before. "Of course I do. If she's the only person standing between us, then I wouldn't hesitate to end her life in a heartbeat."

A small sigh of relief escaped Emilia's lips. I made my way to her, wrapping my arms around her waist and pulling her to me. She buried her face in my chest. "I've always wanted you. From the moment I first laid eyes on you, I've wanted you, Derek."

"I know. I want you too, Emilia. I've always wanted you."

She moved away from me, contempt on her face. "No. That's a lie, Derek. What we have is a lie."

I was confused. Her words rang with so much truth—a truth I couldn't completely fathom, a truth that was echoing in my head even as I attempted to reassure her. "Emilia, what are you saying? What we have is real and beautiful."

A deep sorrow the likes of which I'd never seen before flashed in her eyes. She kissed my lips—her teeth grazing my mouth, causing it to bleed. She pulled away and nodded. "Of course. Real and beautiful—just like it's supposed to be. You're mine now, Derek. That's what matters." She gave me a sharp look. "Now, get ready."

The moment she said the words, a knot formed in my stomach. Every step I took toward The Shade, I felt even worse. I couldn't understand why, but something about the island's name was familiar. I'd been there before and I knew it, but I couldn't remember anything about it.

As we took a ride on the submarine that would lead us to the island, Emilia never left my side. She held on to my hand like her life depended on it. I could sense her anxiety and I wondered what was causing it.

"You love me, right?" she asked me for what felt like the millionth time. "You'll do this for me, won't you, Derek? You *will* kill Sofia?"

Sofia. The name put butterflies in my stomach and I was revolted by the idea that such a sensation could be caused by anyone other than Emilia.

Emilia gasped and bit her lip the moment she said the name, as if she never should've done it.

I squeezed her hand. "This is the last day you will ever have to worry about her, Emilia. I promise."

"You've had her blood, Derek. You will crave her the moment you lay eyes on her. You will want to drink her blood, but you can't. Promise me that you won't. I want you to rip her heart out. I don't want a drop of her blood to ever enter your system again. Do you understand me?"

I narrowed my eyes at Emilia, wondering what kind of powers this young woman possessed that even Emilia trembled at the thought of me being around her.

I soon found out.

After they made us wait at the Port for Sofia's arrival, my senses went into overdrive the moment I laid eyes on the girl, who was surrounded by a group of vampires. Everything about her screamed at me to feed on her. Her long, red hair, her green eyes, her lovely, nubile form… She was a siren begging me to partake of her.

If it weren't for Emilia holding on to my elbow, I would've lunged at her and fed on her the moment she came within sight. Instead, I just stood there and stared at Sofia, wanting her. I wondered why she had such a look of delight on her face.

She broke into a smile the moment she laid eyes on me. "Derek!" she exclaimed. "You're back." Tears began to moisten her eyes. "I missed you so much." She looked at Emilia and back at me, most likely sensing something amiss. "What's the matter?"

The thought of ripping her heart out became sickening. *This is why she is a threat to me and Emilia. Emilia was right. I* must *end her.*

"Remember what I told you, Derek," Emilia hissed. "You can't drink her blood."

Sofia furrowed her brows. "What's going on, Derek?"

Her voice was music to my ears—sweet and intoxicating. I couldn't understand the sensations and emotions coursing through me, but I knew that I had to gain control of myself and end Sofia like I'd promised. *I have to do it or I will lose the woman I love forever.*

I was about to lunge toward Sofia when, to my surprise, she pulled her hair back to expose one side of her neck to me. "Why can't you drink my blood? Did she tell you why?"

I couldn't respond, because my eyes were already fixed on her neck and all I could think of was taking a bite. Despite Emilia's admonitions, I wanted this young stranger's blood coursing through me. Ignoring Emilia's screams for me to stop, I threw Sofia against a wall and took a bite. My claws came out. I wanted to rip her heart out as I drank her blood.

I was expecting her to whimper, to beg for her life, to scream.

Instead, as I drank her blood and threatened to end her life, all Sofia did was hum me the most haunting tune I'd ever heard. She gently took hold of both of my wrists as she whispered, "Remember, Derek."

I don't know who you are. Even as the thought came to me, I knew immediately that it was a lie. I knew this woman. The feel of her blood inside me—the power that came with it, the pleasure that was beginning to pump through my whole system—all of it was too familiar. I was so consumed by Sofia, I lost track of everything else around me.

All that was left in my consciousness was Sofia and my determination to kill her.

Chapter 39: Sofia

I knew from the moment I saw Derek that something was wrong. He had a glazed look in his eyes. He looked at me as if it was the first time he'd ever seen me.

I knew Derek Novak. He was the man of my dreams and the man Emilia returned to The Shade with was nothing but a shadow of the original.

I glared at Emilia. *What have you done to him?* He was looking at me like I was his prey. I could sense the thirst emanating from him. He was craving a drink. At that moment, he wasn't seeing his lover. The predator was seeing his prey.

I was surprised when Emilia told him that he wasn't to drink my blood. *Why? Why doesn't she want my blood coursing through you?*

I was losing him and I knew it. By the look on his face, he was about to do something he was going to regret for the rest of his life.

I went by gut instinct and did what I knew would horrify my father.

I pulled my hair back and offered myself to him as I had done many times before, but this time, I was no longer expecting him to hold back. I wanted him to give in. I wanted him to break free of whatever grasp Emilia had on him.

I succeeded, but I wasn't prepared for what came next. Derek lunged for me, throwing me into the wall stronger than he ever had before. My breath got knocked out of me the moment my back hit the wall. My shock hadn't even worn off yet when his teeth sank into my neck and he began drinking my blood.

"Derek, no!" Emilia began to move toward him, but the Elite Council lunged toward her to stop her.

The pointed end of Derek's claws pressed right over my heart. I drew a breath when I realized what he was about to do. I tried to think of words that would jolt him back to reality. He was about to kill me, the girl he professed to love, the woman he'd sworn to marry.

No words came, so I simply hummed our song—the same one he'd hummed to me time and time again, the same one that I hummed to him whenever he was about to do something he would sorely regret.

Derek Novak was about to rip my heart out and all I could do was breathe out two words.

"Remember, Derek."

I was beginning to get dizzy from the blood loss. He'd never drunk so much of my blood. I couldn't tell anymore who was saying what around me; it was a cacophony of voices.

"Derek, you're going to kill her! Stop it!"

"He's going to kill my daughter! Do something!"

"Hold Emilia back!"

"Kill her before she ruins everything! Do it! Rip her heart out!"

Emilia threw herself at Derek to keep him from drinking more of my blood, but he threw her away with one growl before once again drinking my blood. I was confused. *Why is she trying to help me?*

Derek's eyes were pitch black instead of their normal bright blue. He was completely out of control. The other vampires tried to stop him, but none of them could pry him off of me. I knew the effect my blood had on him. It made him powerful.

I didn't know what to do until I recalled the same thing I'd told him the first time I'd met him, when he'd had me in that same position, about to devour me: "You can control yourself. Don't do this to me."

It was a bare whisper, but the moment the words came out of my lips, he stopped drinking and his claws withdrew.

Relief washed over me when he responded with the exact same words he'd told me that first night. His eyes—black as the darkest night—met mine, my blood dripping from the corners of his lips, his fangs bared. "I can't. You're too beautiful, your blood too enticing, too sweet..."

Tears began to stream down my face—partly because everything that'd been happening came crashing down on me, partly because of how much I ached for my Derek to return to me.

"I know an excuse when I hear one. Don't you dare deceive yourself into believing that you're the victim, Derek Novak."

A gasp escaped his lips the moment I said the words. I couldn't help but sigh with relief when his grip around my waist loosened. His lips remained pressed on my skin. He eased me down so I could stand on my feet again. I felt so small and fragile standing so close to him. The moment my feet hit the ground, my knees buckled and I found myself leaning on him for support.

His eyes were still on me as he spoke. "Tell me your name."

"Sofia... Sofia Claremont."

Just like that, his eyes began to clear—the haze giving way to those clear blue eyes, light twinkling in the darkness' place.

"Sofia," Derek gasped and I knew then that he recognized me.

I managed to smile at him, but the blood loss had finally taken its toll. It felt as if my heart stopped beating and everything surrounding me dimmed into black.

Chapter 40: Derek

The memories came like a flood right after she spoke her name. Starting from that memory of our first encounter, every single moment I'd spent with Sofia Claremont returned to me and haunted me into realizing what I was doing, what I was about to do.

The moment Sofia collapsed in my arms, panic rushed through me as I cradled her close to my chest, kneeling on the ground as she fell.

"No," I gasped, as I held her against me.

Vivienne rushed beside me to check Sofia's pulse. "She's alive," she assured me.

I was about to cut my wrist in order to feed Sofia my blood, but Vivienne shook her head.

"I don't think your blood is going to cure her. That much blood loss is different. Your blood can heal the bite marks and the claw marks over her heart, but you can't replenish her blood with yours."

"Then let's close those wounds first," I responded with resolve before swallowing hard. I force-fed Sofia my blood, hoping that it would revive her, but Vivienne was right. All it did was close her wounds. I stared at my twin desperately. "What are we going to do now?"

Vivienne breathed out a sigh. "We'll need to get her medical care if she's to survive. I'm sure Eli will know what to do. What were you doing, Derek?"

"There's no time for explanations. Get her help. Now!" I had half a mind to stay by Sofia's side, but I had a score to settle. I rose to my feet and turned to face Emilia, who was being restrained by Xavier and Yuri. I wondered why she wasn't fighting back. I knew she had the power.

She stared at me with both defiance and defeat. "You said you would kill her. You *promised*."

Everything that I'd gone through in her hands came flooding back to me. The thought that I'd believed that I was in love with her, that I had actually shared a bed with her, was revolting. I wanted nothing more than to end Emilia's life.

"You're supposed to be in love with me," she screamed, tears streaming from her eyes. "Why didn't you do what you promised?"

"It's over, Emilia. Whatever spell you had on me has been broken. Enough of your delusions."

"You belong with me, Derek." She finally got away from the vampires holding her back. She threw herself into my arms.

I shook my head. "No. I belong with Sofia, and if I lose her... If she dies..." I wanted to threaten revenge, but instead my shoulders just sagged. Sofia would never take the path of vengeance, and neither would I. "If I lose her, Emilia, you might as well kill me. I would rather die than live the rest of my immortality without her."

Emilia stared up at me as if it had dawned on her for the first time that I was truly in love with Sofia. "I can't believe you conquered the lure of the darkness, Derek. For her."

Emilia placed a soft kiss on my jaw. I flinched at the feel of her lips, my fists clenching as I fought hard not to respond with violence.

"I should kill you," I whispered.

"Please do… If I return to the Blood Keep without having accomplished my mission, I might as well be dead. My master will be far less merciful than you."

I couldn't keep myself from asking the question. "Why aren't you fighting back?"

"I lost control of you the moment you remembered. And the spell of night is now back upon The Shade. I can't harm The Shade or Sofia. I'm powerless here where, despite there being an endless night, there is barely any darkness… Darkness is powerless against light."

I found the statement ironic. Sofia was light and she was absolutely powerless against me in my moment of darkness. The thought that her life was hanging by a thread at my own doing was horrifying.

"What is the Elder going to do to you if I don't kill you myself?" I asked Emilia. I wanted to get away from her and back to Sofia as soon as I could.

"Please… Derek, don't…"

"Answer my question, Emilia."

"He's going to turn me back to a human and give me over to

my brother. I will be under his control until the day I die... Derek, you need to understand..."

I'd seen enough of her family to know that the worst fate she could endure was to be amongst them. Without hesitation, I sank my claws into her chest and looked her straight in the eye as I gripped her beating heart. "I show you this mercy as gratefulness for everything that you did in order to make The Shade safe. We owe you that much."

"Thank you," she mouthed to me before I ripped her heart out.

We both knew it was an act of mercy.

"I'm confused," Xavier confessed. "What just happened, Derek? Why did you attack Sofia? What happened to you?"

I stared at Emilia's motionless body. "She and the Elder brainwashed me to believe that I was in love with her and that I wanted to kill Sofia."

Without another word, I turned my back on them and rushed toward Sofia's quarters at The Catacombs. I found her in her bedroom, with Vivienne, Aiden and Eli circling her bed. The others were right outside the room waiting to be told of her condition.

"Is she all right?" I asked.

Eli looked at me pointedly over his black-rimmed glasses. "She lost a lot of blood. We have to do a blood transfusion. Aiden's donating his blood. It's a good thing they're compatible."

Vivienne motioned for me to take a walk with her. When I refused, she insisted. "You're not going to help anyone—least of all Sofia—by staying here and hovering over Eli as he does his work. Come with me so you can tell me what just happened."

I knew she was right, so I obliged. It helped that I couldn't stand looking at Sofia without the guilt eating me up.

I told Vivienne everything that had happened at the Blood Keep and she told me everything that had happened in The Shade. When she mentioned that Kyle was human, hope surged within me.

"How is that possible? What happened? Where's Kyle now? Have you tried it on anyone else?"

Vivienne nodded. "Rex and Ingrid."

My eyes grew wide open. "And?"

She shook her head and my heart dropped. "They're gone."

I swallowed hard. The idea that Sofia had lost her mother while I was gone pierced me. "I should've been here."

"You couldn't have done anything to change that. Besides, if you were here, I doubt Rex would've tortured Kyle."

"You have a point." I paused, hope still lingering inside of me. "So after Ingrid... do you still have a theory on what the cure might be?"

"We didn't know who to test it on next, but the theory is that an immune's blood must first be running through a vampire's system before he's immediately exposed to sunlight. That, we believe, is how Kyle turned back. Or it was all just some sort of fluke."

I recalled the vampire Emilia had killed when he fell into the sunlight. I nodded violently. "No. I think that's it. Let's try that theory out."

Vivienne's eyes grew wide open. "On whom?"

Sofia's blood was still pumping through mine, so the only logical thing that I could respond with was, "Take me to the Pit."

I couldn't think of a better person to test the cure out other than myself. Vivienne stood adamantly against it.

"You can't be serious, Derek. You could die! Do you understand that?"

"Who better to do it than me, Vivienne? I'm the leader of The Shade. I can't just let us test it on someone else… not while I'm around."

"What if the cure doesn't work? Do you really want Sofia to wake up after what you just did to her only to find out that you're dead?"

"But what if the cure works? Why would you assume that I would die?" I told her what had happened in the labyrinth. I was sure Emilia had killed the vampire guard because she hadn't wanted me to see him turn back into a human. "If this *is* the cure, Sofia and I can be together."

"I know that, Derek, but if you're going to try this cure out, you're not going to do it without her consent."

"I'm still king of The Shade, Vivienne. I want to do this."

Vivienne scoffed. "You are our king, Derek, but I would like to think that you're not completely foolish. Sofia is your queen, and to make a step as big as this without even hearing what she thinks about it is your downfall and hers. You two are most powerful when you put your wits and strengths together. Don't do this to her, Derek."

My sister was speaking truth. I gave her a lingering look, realizing what an ally she had become to Sofia. I had to take note of the difference in all of us ever since Sofia had become a part of our lives. *She changed us all… for the better.* I loved Sofia. I just hoped that she wouldn't deny me this.

I gave Vivienne a nod, determined that no matter what Sofia said, I would stand by my decision to be the next person to test the cure out. "This is the cure, Vivienne, and I feel confident about it, but you're right. Sofia deserves to have a say in this."

I honestly thought nothing would shake my decision to test the cure out. That was until I returned to Sofia's bedroom to find her surrounded by her dearest friends, a huge smile on her face. My resolve crumbled the moment she laid eyes on me.

"I'm so sorry," I rasped out. I didn't want to go near her in fear of somehow breaking her. I was once again aware of how fragile she was compared to me. It didn't help that I could feel Aiden's eyes on me, studying my every move. He blamed me for what had happened to Sofia.

I struggled to meet Sofia's gaze. I could never get used to the way she looked at me like I was the most worthy person in the world, like I meant more to her than anything else. *How could she still look at me that way?*

Everyone filed out of the room to give us our privacy, Aiden more hesitant than the others. The moment we were alone, she reached out toward me.

I drew near, still apologizing, but she shook her head, refusing to hear any of it.

"Shut up, Derek. I'm just glad you're back. We're both all right."

She held me close and kissed my lips gently and I knew then that she was right. We'd survived. What my sister had said was true. Sofia was my queen and if I wanted to rule well, I couldn't do things without taking Sofia into consideration.

When I mentioned the cure and that I wanted to be the one to test it out first, she just listened to me, hearing me out before giving me a response.

"I understand why you want to do it, Derek, but you do realize that the cure might not work?"

"I'm ruler of The Shade, Sofia. I can't have another one of my subjects die testing out a cure that I'm not willing to go through myself."

"If it doesn't work, I could lose you."

"We can't just risk some innocent, Sofia. Not after the lives that have already been lost. You know what the prophecy says. It's me who will lead my kind to true sanctuary. That's what I have to do now. Lead."

A long moment of silence followed. "Fine," Sofia said, tears brimming her eyes. "I do have one condition, Derek."

"What's that?"

"I want to marry you first."

That took me by surprise. "Why?"

I never would've imagined that she would give me the response that she did.

"I loved you as a vampire. I want to marry you while you're still one."

I hadn't thought I could love her more, but I did. She made me feel like she accepted me for everything that I was, while still looking forward to what I would become. I was in love with Sofia Claremont and the thought of her being my wife was more than anything I could ever ask for.

"I wouldn't want anything more than to have you become Sofia Novak." I wrapped my arms around her and pressed my lips against hers, looking forward to the endless possibilities that came with us being husband and wife.

CHAPTER 41: SOFIA

I could never wrap my mind around how we pulled it off, but with Vivienne and Ashley at the helm, while Eli kept me under his watch to make sure I would recover in time, we pulled off a wedding in three days.

Those three days felt like an eternity. I couldn't wait to become Derek's wife, so when the evening of our wedding came, I couldn't keep the smile off my face.

My father watched me curiously. He'd been quiet about the whole thing, not once letting me know how he felt about me marrying Derek Novak while we were still so unsure that the cure would work. Though I felt guilty about it, I didn't want to ask him because I was afraid of what he would say. I was afraid that he would change his mind about Derek and decide that we were no good for each other. Aiden's opinion mattered to me. I wondered if he knew that.

When he came to my room to check on me, I was just about to put on the white dress, with Ashley and Rosa bustling around the room—already in their bridesmaids' dresses—assisting me.

Upon seeing him, Ashley rolled her eyes, more at ease with my own father than I ever was.

"Aiden, you're the father of the bride and all... that's wonderful, but this is a bad time for a private father-daughter session. We have to get Sofia ready."

Aiden stared at me, his mouth hanging open. He was making me uncomfortable.

Ashley began laughing. "Yes, yes, I know... She's gorgeous." Ashley nodded. "And she isn't even in her dress yet. Now, go away, Aiden."

I blushed. My father got himself together, stood to his full height, squared his shoulders and shook his head. "No. I'm going to have a talk with my daughter, and I'm going to have it now. Is that all right with you, Sofia?"

Ashley glared at me.

I smiled at her, knowing that I couldn't march down that aisle without having that talk with Aiden. I nodded toward my friends. "We're not going to take long."

Ashley huffed. Rosa just giggled, but they both made their way out of the room, leaving me with my father.

We exchanged glances before he gave me a wry smile. "You look lovely, Sofia."

"Thank you," I told him, conscious of the blush on my cheeks. I took my seat on the edge of the bed and waited for him to say something. I wanted to initiate the conversation, but with all the emotions whirling in my chest, I couldn't. *I'm about to marry Derek! I'm going to be Sofia Novak.* I was utterly thrilled.

My father, on the other hand, wasn't as thrilled. "So you're really going to go through with this, huh?"

I stared lovingly at the dress. "Did you ever really think that I wouldn't?"

"Part of me hoped." He nodded as he sat beside me on the edge of the bed. "I still can't believe that my daughter is about to marry Derek Novak."

"I love him."

"I know... I know that he loves you too. I just didn't think that this would be the kind of life that you would lead, Sofia..." His voice broke and he gave me a bittersweet smile.

I knew that his upbringing and the way he'd lived his life over the past years still made it difficult for him to accept what was to come.

"I don't understand how this is going to work..."

I didn't know how to respond to him. My heart was breaking over the whole matter. I realized then how much I wanted my father's approval. The idea of not getting it was painful to me.

"I don't want to disappoint you, Aiden, but I know that this is what I want. And it feels right. I'm at peace with this."

He smiled as he forced back the tears threatening to spill. He nodded reassuringly. "You can never truly disappoint me, Sofia. You've become far more beautiful, more wonderful than I could've ever hoped... and"—he heaved a deep sigh—"trust me when I say that I know you've thought about this and that this isn't just some teenage whim. I've seen enough of who you are to know that you wouldn't be doing this if you didn't think it was the right thing. I was just hoping that you would wait until the cure is discovered. What if you marry him and he tries out the cure and..." He paused.

I knew what he was thinking. *I'd be a widow.* I grabbed his arm and squeezed tight. "Thank you."

He gave me a quizzical glance. "For what?"

"For being a father to me. For not trying to stop this. For making me feel like I have your blessing."

Aiden wrapped his arm around my shoulder and pulled me closer. "I want you to be happy, Sofia, and I know that no man in this world can make you happy the way Derek does. For that, I am grateful to him." He kissed my temple and then my cheek. "No matter what you decide, I'll be right here to support you. We're family, and if you want Derek to be your husband, then vampire or not, he's my family too."

I couldn't keep the tears from streaming down my face. I had no idea if he realized how much that meant to me. I twisted toward him and kissed his cheek. "Thank you... Dad. It means the world to me to hear you say that."

We pulled away and he chuckled wryly as he looked me over. "You're about to marry a five-hundred-year-old vampire, Sofia—one of the most powerful ones. I would think you'd be a little more nervous."

It was my turn to chuckle. Marrying Derek was a decision I knew I would never regret. "I don't have a reason to be nervous," I told him. "Even if we were born centuries apart, we belong together."

My father's face softened and he kissed me on the forehead. "Derek Novak is a lucky man to have you, Sofia."

I smiled, amazed at the sense of worth I'd been able to build throughout the time I'd spent in The Shade, because I actually believed it when I responded, "Yes. He is. He's just as lucky to have me as I am to have him."

Chapter 42: Derek

The Sanctuary's lush garden was a sight to behold. The moon shone down on the gazebo, its white façade shimmering with an almost ethereal glow. The stone pathway was lined with white roses from Vivienne's greenhouse. Wooden seats cushioned with red pillows were positioned on either side of the pathway.

Everything about The Sanctuary was breathtaking that night. Everyone had been working hard the past three days to make this wedding happen and now it was here.

Sofia Claremont was about to become my wife.

As I stood at the end of the pathway wearing a crisp black tuxedo, images of Sofia walking down the aisle filled my mind. She was about to become mine. My lovely, vibrant, stunning Sofia… The idea that I was about to marry her caused a whirlwind of ecstasy to surface within me.

"It's beautiful, isn't it?" Ashley stepped next to me, a smug smile on her face.

"Breathtaking," I admitted.

She looked me over from head to foot. "I gotta say... you clean up well, Novak."

The compliment fell on deaf ears. I swallowed hard at the idea of Aiden talking Sofia out of the wedding. I cleared my throat.

Ashley knew me well enough to tell when I was anxious about something. "Eh, don't worry your pretty little head about that, Derek. I doubt anything can be said or done to convince that crazy girl not to marry you."

"So you think Aiden is convincing her not to go ahead with this?"

"He's Reuben, one of the most powerful hunters of all time. Aiden wouldn't be himself if he didn't at least try." She heaved a sigh before tapping me on the shoulder. "Don't worry. Everything will be all right. Looks like everything is all set up here. I'm gonna go tidy my hair. Hopefully, by the time I'm done, Aiden and Sofia's father-daughter drama is over."

As Ashley walked away, I wanted to ease my nerves, so I walked over to the grand piano and began playing the first tune that came to mind. Every note brought back memories of Sofia... The first night she'd spent with me in the Music Room of my penthouse, the look on her face when she'd showed me the Sun Room, the surprise in her eyes when I'd asked her to marry me.

"So this is it, huh?" Vivienne leaned against the piano, a smile on her lovely face. "My brother is finally getting hitched." She took the seat on the bench beside me. "Took you long enough."

"You made this possible, Vivienne. You brought Sofia back to me so many times."

"You two were meant to be together. It's funny that it took hundreds of years before you finally found your soulmate, Derek. I just wish Dad and Lucas were here to be a part of it."

I paused and stared at her. Neither my father nor my brother would've wanted me to marry Sofia. But she'd always seen the goodness in them and I wasn't about to ruin that. So I just nodded before grinning at how clueless my sister was. "You're going to find yours too." Out of the corner of my eye, I saw Xavier, looking rather debonair in his gray suit, coming into the venue. I couldn't keep the smirk off my face. "Truth be told, Vivienne, I think you've already found him. You're just too blind to realize it."

Even the Seer of The Shade was far from all-knowing, especially when it came to matters of the heart.

"What do you mean?" she asked me in bewilderment.

I chuckled and shook my head. "You'll realize soon enough, Vivienne."

I knew she was about to pry, but Aiden was approaching us. I should've talked to him during the past three days, but I hadn't wanted him to try to talk me out of marrying Sofia. I didn't want to go into the whole thing with apprehensions. It seemed Sofia felt the same way, but here he was. This was inevitable.

"May I have a word with you, Derek?" he asked before he took the final step toward the piano, drumming his fingers over its surface.

Vivienne, eager to get out of the tense situation, nodded. "I'll leave you two alone to talk."

"Aiden." I bowed my head slightly, having never felt more tense around a human.

"It seems you've been avoiding me."

There was no use in denying the truth. "I have. I meant to ask for your blessing, Aiden, but I was afraid you wouldn't give it. I love Sofia. I will do everything in my power to protect her and to make her happy."

He chuckled wryly. "I fear that I'm not at all confident in your ability to protect my daughter, Derek. Even as the most powerful vampire, you've gotten her in all sorts of trouble. What makes you think you can protect her as a human—assuming that the cure even works?"

I swallowed hard. I had no idea what to say to that. It was true. Sofia's life had been terribly endangered ever since she had met me.

Aiden smacked me on the shoulder. "Get that guilty look off your face, Novak. It doesn't suit the king of the vampires to look that way. I don't think any man can protect her completely—even I failed in that. I do know that no one can make her as happy as you can."

I breathed an audible sigh of relief.

"All I ask is that you be faithful to her, love her… and, as much as you are able, try to protect her. It won't be easy considering all the trouble she seems to entangle herself in."

I nodded even as I tried to chuckle. I couldn't hide my relief. "So I have your blessing?"

The father of my bride nodded. "I want my daughter happy, and I would give the world to always see her face light up when she looks at you. Do well by her."

"Yes, sir." I nodded. And just like that, I had his blessing.

"But don't think this means I trust you or like you, vampire."

I chuckled. "It would be strange to have it otherwise." I realized then that I liked the tension between Aiden and me. He kept me on my toes, always reminding me how precious Sofia was. She deserved that.

The place was beginning to fill up. My breath hitched. This was it. Nothing could explain the joy I felt inside as the ceremony began. It was surreal. I wanted to pinch myself to find out if it was all really happening.

All of it—all those years in battle, all of those years fighting for the survival of those I loved, fighting for the fulfillment of a prophecy that I did not even fully understand—all of it boiled down to this one moment, standing at the end of a pathway beside a magnificently lit gazebo, watching my beautiful bride come to me.

When she showed up, everyone else faded into a blur, dimming against the radiance of her light. Standing at the other end of the aisle, holding her bouquet of lilies, she was breathtaking in her intricately embroidered gown. When she raised her green eyes to meet mine, I was done for. She had me captivated—even more so when that brilliant smile lit up her countenance. She winked at me before beginning her march down the aisle.

It felt like an eternity waiting for her to come to me, but watching every single step was absolutely worth it. I wanted to freeze that moment in eternity. That tantalizing vision of her in that white dress, looking more ethereal than ever, would forever be etched in my mind.

When she took that final step toward me, taking her father's hand so that he could bring her to me, one truth hit the very core of my being. I'd been racking my brain for the past three days wondering how to express myself once we exchanged our vows, but when it came time, I knew exactly what to say.

I could barely look at her as I said the words. Despite all the acclaim and the power I had as Derek Novak, the king of The Shade, in that moment, eighteen-year-old Sofia Claremont made five-hundred-year-old me feel like a boy.

"You saved me, Sofia. You rescued me from myself. You gave me room to feel again, to love again, to once again believe in goodness and kindness and the possibility of light even in the darkest of nights. I've lived under the shadow of the prophecy about bringing my kind to true sanctuary. The cure might be my kind's true sanctuary, but I know now that it's not mine, Sofia. Your smile, your heart, your life, your love… You, Sofia, are my true sanctuary."

CHAPTER 43: SOFIA

Chills ran down my spine as he uttered his vows. I could swear that he was blushing. I wasn't even sure if it was possible for a vampire to blush.

"I will protect you with my life, Sofia," he proceeded to say, clasping my hands.

I was trembling, overwhelmed by the emotions coursing through me. I hadn't known that I could be capable of loving someone this much.

"I will love you and support you and do everything that I can to make sure that I become your sanctuary as surely as you are mine."

When he finally raised his eyes to look directly at me, a lump formed in my throat. Then a tear ran down my cheek. "I love you," he mouthed to me, and I responded in kind.

I smiled at him. "You already are my sanctuary, Derek." He

caught his breath and I couldn't help but do the same as I brushed my thumb against his hand. "You have been since the day I met you. I am who I am because you brought out the best in me. You challenged me to become all that I could possibly be and you continue to challenge me to live life that way. We are our strongest selves together, our weakest apart. I can't imagine a life without you and on this day, I hope you know without doubt that my life, my heart, and my love is yours."

When his brilliant blue eyes began to moisten, I couldn't stop the waterworks. I didn't want to cry anymore, but the emotions were so gripping and strong, so overwhelming. In my attempt not to sob, I laughed nervously, and I guessed he felt the exact same way because he began to laugh too.

"Sunshine," he whispered, as he put the ring on my finger. "You're like sunshine. You light everything up."

My cheeks heated as I clung to his hand, sensing both his strength and his vulnerability at the same time. I felt both powerless and powerful all at the same time. I was vulnerable to him, and I knew it. But I also knew that he was just as vulnerable to me.

That realization spoke to my longing for intimacy. When Corrine finally pronounced the words that sealed my marriage to Derek, I couldn't wait to have his lips press against mine. Corrine hadn't even yet recited the traditional, "You may kiss the bride," before Derek was holding my waist and pulling me against him, his lips covering mine.

I lost myself in the heat of his kiss. When his lips pulled away from mine, I found myself leaning forward, practically begging for more until I saw a huge grin on his face.

Derek winked at me. "I want to kiss you, Sofia, but if we go on like this, I might end up hauling you out of the wedding reception and right to my bedroom."

Right then, I became aware that we weren't alone. Our friends and loved ones were still surrounding us. I practically jumped from where I was standing when they began to applaud us—the newlyweds.

"Sofia Novak," Derek pronounced in his smooth baritone. "Mmm… I love the sound of it."

As much as we tried to keep a show of chastity during the rest of the wedding festivities, we simply couldn't keep our eyes or hands off each other. The idea that I was Sofia Novak was still ringing in my head, emphasized even more when our friends approached us with unadulterated glee.

"You did it!" Ashley exclaimed, as she threw her arms around me. "You married a vampire." She then gave Derek a teasing lookover from head to foot. "*This* vampire at that. Who would've thought? You better take care of her."

Derek grinned. "I'd better. She's my life."

"I didn't think I'd ever see this happen." Gavin nodded. "History is being made right here. Congratulations to you both."

"I guess we're sisters now," Vivienne said, clasping my hands tightly.

"We are," I responded, as I embraced her. "Thank you, Vivienne," I whispered into her ear, recalling the price she'd paid in order to get me back to The Shade not so long ago. "For bringing me back to him."

She chuckled. "Well, that wasn't entirely selfless… we all like him a lot more when he's around you."

Derek feigned being wounded. "I heard that."

Vivienne just laughed. "I love you both."

"Here's to hoping you don't kill each other," Cameron teased, as he lifted a glass of wine toward us. "Welcome to married life."

"Don't scare them, Cam," Liana reprimanded.

Derek's hand tightened against mine and a feeling of heaviness settled on my chest as we greeted more of our guests. It wasn't until Kyle approached that I placed the reason behind my melancholy. Seeing Kyle as human made me remember what had to happen tomorrow. We were going to test the cure and we had no assurance whatsoever that it was going to work on Derek.

Kyle smiled at me as if he could read my mind. "It's going to be okay, Sofia." He cast a longing look at Ian and Anna, who were dancing. He swallowed hard and then looked at Derek. By the reaction on Derek's face, he was thinking what I was thinking.

When Kyle left us with his congratulations, I couldn't help but turn toward Derek and hug him as tightly as I could, clinging to him.

"I don't ever want to lose you," I confessed breathlessly against his ear.

He shook his head. "You won't, Sofia. You can never lose me."

He sounded so sure of it, but the heaviness in my chest remained. Suddenly, I began to feel greedy for him. I wanted to make the most of the time from then until the following day. "Can we go now? Please? I want you all to myself..."

"My thoughts exactly."

We made as gracious an exit as possible and sped to the Lighthouse, another reminder that the moments we were spending together were borrowed. We hadn't even planned a honeymoon because we weren't sure if we were going to have one.

Of course, we still wanted our first night as a married couple to be intimate and special, so when the girls asked where we wanted to spend the night, no place seemed more special and intimate to us than the Lighthouse.

"Sacred space," I said, just before Derek pushed me against the door that led to the octagonal room at the top of the Lighthouse. I responded to his kiss, clinging to his neck.

His lips departed from mine. "What?" he asked.

"Sacred space," I repeated breathlessly, as I twisted the doorknob to show him what we'd done with the room. "That's what Rosa called this place. Ashley says that the room has an energy to it... something that belongs to us. Just us."

He smiled when he saw the room. The sectional couch in the middle of the room had been shoved to one side. In its place was a mattress with linen sheets and a red blanket. White rose petals were scattered all over it. Candles surrounded the room. Derek had them lit within seconds.

"They were right." He nodded. "This is our sacred space."

I began to walk toward him, but halted immediately when, to my surprise, he stepped away from me. His smile faded as he looked at me from head to toe. His breath visibly hitched as his electric-blue eyes rose to my face, causing me to shiver with desire.

I swallowed hard, sensing his tension. His hands balled into fists and his muscles went rigid, as if he were trying to gain control. I didn't have to ask what was going on in his mind. It'd been a long time since we last made love, a long time since he'd sworn that he wouldn't take me to his bed until after he'd married me.

I gave him a soft smile. I reached back and tried to unlace my corset. My eyes were fixed on Derek. I actually enjoyed seeing how nervous he was. I wouldn't be able to finish the task myself so I unlaced it as far as I could before walking toward him and asking for his help.

I couldn't stifle a giggle when he flinched. "Relax, won't you? You're acting like it's the first time you've ever been with a woman."

It didn't help to ease the tense look on his face. I walked toward him, lifting my hair up so that he could undo the laces. His fingers trembled as he went about the task.

Once we were able to remove the corset, I turned to face him. I began to pull his tux off and unbutton his shirt. I was already on the fourth button when he clutched my hand, stopping me from continuing the task.

I raised my eyes to his questioningly. "What's wrong, Derek? Don't you want this?"

"I want this more than you can imagine right now, Sofia, but…" He gulped.

"You're not going to hurt me, Derek," I assured him. "Relax." I laid my hand over his chest and looked into his eyes. "I trust you."

I stood to my toes and planted a soft kiss on his lips. It appeared that was all the approval he needed, because his hands clasped around my waist. He no longer tried to stop me from unbuttoning his shirt.

Keenly aware of how precious each second we had with each other was, we made our first night as husband and wife as memorable and sweet and passionate as we could. I was his and he was mine, and on that night, to us, the Lighthouse truly became our sacred space.

Chapter 44: Derek

She's my wife.

I woke up to find her sleeping form next to mine, our bare forms intertwined on the soft mattress. Waking up next to her, knowing that she was officially mine, that my name was also hers, took my breath away. I couldn't pry my eyes away from her lovely face.

Peaceful. Serene. Beautiful.

All the compliments in the world wouldn't have been able to describe her.

When her eyes opened and her face brightened into a wide smile, it felt like a piece of heaven.

"Good morning, husband," she greeted.

"Good morning, wife," I responded.

Then we both heaved a sigh. I saw despair in her eyes as she ran her fingers against my cheek. I ached under her touch.

We didn't need to say out loud what was bothering us both. It hung over us like a cloud of premonition. I had to test the cure. There was no other option.

"Do we have to do this?" she croaked out.

I didn't respond. We both already knew the answer to that. Instead, I pulled her against me, kissed her on the cheek and whispered into her ear. "Everything's going to be all right, Sofia. I promise."

"You can't promise me that." She shook her head. "You don't know for sure."

"You've always had more faith than I do, Sofia. Don't let it run out now."

It broke my heart when tears started to brim in her eyes. "I won't know what to do if I ever lose you."

"You won't. We have to believe that you won't."

I kissed her and once again took her in my arms, making love to her, assuring her that no one could take away from us what we had. I whispered all the assurances I could think of into her ear, hoping that I could convince her and also myself that all would be well. By the time we both reached our climax, she was sobbing. Each sob cut me to the core.

"Sofia..."

Before I could say anything, her lips were on mine, her hand gripping my hair. Once our lips parted, she gazed up into my eyes and nodded.

"Everything is going to be all right," she said, as if saying it with conviction would make it happen. "We're going to be together."

I rolled over on the mattress beside her, and we both lay breathless. What was to come still weighed heavily on our minds.

"The sun is going to rise soon," I said, knowing that we had to test out the cure and have me enter the Pit before the sun reached its peak.

"Maybe we shouldn't do this. Maybe we can postpone it... Tomorrow maybe... Or let's have our honeymoon first," she begged.

I shook my head. "No. I want to be human, Sofia. I can't be a vampire one day longer." I turned to my side and let my eyes fall over her lovely bare form. My stomach turned at the sight of a few bruises on her thigh and neck.

When she realized what I was looking at, she covered up with the blanket. "It's nothing, Derek."

"Don't tell me it's nothing. I should be able to make love with my wife without worrying about hurting her. You've never made excuses for me, Sofia. Don't start now."

She rolled to her side to face me. She stared at me with those green eyes, her fears and doubts evident on her face. Eventually, she came to an acceptance of what had to be done and my heart leaped and sank when she nodded. "Very well then."

Sofia gave me a soft peck on the cheek before she sat up on the mattress. My breath hitched when she began to pull her auburn mass of hair to one side of her neck. I couldn't help but cringe. She was offering her neck to me.

"You haven't fed for ages," she said.

"You're my wife... I can't... I just... Not anymore."

"You need an immune's blood in your system. I would rather we do it here than in front of everyone else. Besides, this is the last time you'll ever have me this way." She paused and her eyes met mine. "This is the last time you'll ever feel the power of my blood coursing through your veins, the last time you'll feel the ecstasy that it brings."

I sat up as I took in all of her magnificence. She was a feast to my eyes. Feeding on my young wife on the morning after our marriage was a stark reminder of why I wanted to escape what I had become. The battle raging inside me was now full-blown. The moment I dared look at the nook of her neck, generously offered up to me, my senses went on overdrive, my blood pounding within. I wanted her. I wanted her badly, but a part of me hated myself for doing this to her. I was supposed to protect her.

One last time... I shut my eyes as I drew close to her. *One last time and I hope I never have to do this again.* I bit into her neck, not missing that short intake of breath she always took whenever I began to drink from her. *After this, never again will I put you through this, Sofia.* But the thought faded into a blur when the effects of her blood began to consume me.

No matter how much my mind fought against my enjoyment of drinking from her, my nature made it impossible. I drank from her and I drank deep. Guilt took over me and I wondered why. It wasn't like I hadn't done it so many times before. Something about that morning was different. I hated every moment of it, but I couldn't stop until I was satiated. Somehow, my system knew what I was about to put myself through and it was begging for her light inside me, but as I drank, it felt as if darkness was taking hold.

Once I was done, her blood dripping from the corners of my lips, I pulled away from her. My gut clenched when I noticed how pale she looked. She looked my way and smiled. I felt then such overwhelming love for her and undeniable hatred for myself all at the same time.

"I don't deserve you, Sofia..."

She shook her head adamantly. "You do, Derek, but even if you don't, it doesn't matter, because I'm yours." She spun around and faced me and it felt as if I was completely bare before her—like she could see right through me into my very soul. "Don't you dare feel guilty, Derek. Not now. Everything you are—even in all of your weaknesses—made everything I am right now possible."

I frowned, but then with a flicker of insight, I got it. "You're strong where I am weak."

She nodded. "We're both far from perfect, but we're complements. That's why we belong together, so right now, I need you to be strong for me. I need you to survive this cure, because I cannot go through this life without you."

Her words were still swirling in my mind as we made our way to the Pit. A group of people were already waiting there when we arrived—just as had been discussed. The atmosphere was solemn, everyone was silent. Even Aiden couldn't look me in the eye. Instead, he gave me one quick nod. Sofia took her place beside Aiden, holding his hand.

It felt like I was about to walk to my death.

Vivienne approached and opened her mouth to say something, but it seemed she didn't know what to say, so she just hugged me. She whispered into my ear, "True sanctuary. You have her blood in you?"

I nodded. "Yes."

"Are you sure you want to do this?"

An image of walking along the shores of a white sandy beach with Sofia flashed through my mind. A sudden pang of longing hit me. I needed to turn back into a human. It was the only way I could completely get rid of the darkness within me. I needed to step into the light. "More than anything, yes. I want to do this. I want to become human." *I want to become the husband Sofia deserves.*

Vivienne nodded. I knew that she understood. Of all the people there, it was my twin who had seen firsthand how much I had struggled against being a vampire, how much I wanted to be freed from the curse our own father had subjected us to.

We pulled away from each other. I looked into Vivienne's blue-violet eyes, hoping that she would have a prophecy, a vision... anything to let me know that all would be all right. Nothing. Instead, she squeezed my hand and nodded before stepping aside to make way for Sofia to throw her arms around me and kiss me.

"Don't you dare make a widow out of me, Novak," she whispered into my ear.

A lump formed in my throat and I couldn't respond to her. Holding her, I felt like backing out, but it was too late to back down now. I pulled away from her and kissed her forehead.

"I'm gonna be right here the whole time," she promised. "I'll be here when you get out."

I made my way into the Pit and the doors slammed closed behind me. It didn't take long before the first rays of the morning sun began to show. And the moment they hit me, I was blinded by the most excruciating pain I had ever encountered.

Chapter 45: Sofia

Only Aiden, Vivienne and I remained to wait for the first signs of sunlight. It felt like my heart was being torn from me when Derek screamed, a sign that his torment had begun.

"How long is this going to take?" I asked Vivienne.

"We won't be able to check on him until the sun sets," she replied.

Another scream of pain came from inside.

"I want to go in," I announced, as I moved to open the latch that was keeping the door locked and secure.

"No!" two voices said with alarm.

Aiden and Vivienne were by my side immediately.

"You're not going in there." Aiden shook his head. He gave Vivienne a look. "Maybe we should get her out of here."

I could barely make out what he was saying. His voice was being drowned out by Derek's screams. *What if there's no cure? What if we got something wrong?* "No. I promised Derek I'd stay here."

"Sofia, you're torturing yourself."

Vivienne took a step forward. "We don't know what he might end up doing to you, Sofia. We don't know what's going on in there. It's enough that Derek's life is at risk. We're not going to risk your life too."

We'd been thinking of putting surveillance cameras into the Pit in order to observe what was going on. Derek had voted against it for reasons I couldn't understand. The only explanation he'd given was a simple, "I don't want anyone to have to see what I'm going through."

Eli had insisted on it, and Derek had agreed under the condition that it would not be seen by anyone as it happened. It would only be used for study purposes after we found out the results.

The unknown was killing me. I wanted to know what was happening and I didn't even have any idea why. *Do you really want to see your husband in sheer torment, Sofia?*

Another piercing scream came from inside. I grabbed a hold of my father, hoping to somehow fast-forward time and take Derek out of his misery.

"You don't have to be here for this, Sofia. He'll understand."

"No." I pulled away from my father and leaned against the door. *Get a grip, Sofia. Be strong for him.* "I'm here, Derek." I spoke up, hoping that he would somehow hear me. "Survive this. Please. Be strong."

Right then, Yuri and Claudia showed up. From the grim expressions on their faces, something was very wrong.

No matter how difficult it was, I pried my attention off Derek.

"What's going on?"

They hesitated to answer my question. Yuri looked at Vivienne and Aiden instead, motioning for them to follow him so they could speak in private—away from me.

"No." I rose to my feet, Derek's screams pounding in my brain. "What's going on? I'm queen of this island now. Let me know what's happening."

The atmosphere was thick with tension. I could practically feel the static in the air.

Yuri and Claudia exchanged glances before Claudia nodded toward him. He blurted out the problem. "The hunters are coming."

A chill began to settle beneath my skin.

"I need to talk to them before they arrive at the island," Aiden announced.

"Should we be preparing for war?" Yuri asked.

Aiden scoffed. "No. They're not going to risk man-to-man combat. Not against The Shade. I took part in planning the destruction of The Shade, and if they're going for what we planned, they're going to blow the island up."

"Even if you're here?" Vivienne frowned.

"The hawks have no loyalties. Our mission is to destroy all vampires. I am collateral damage."

An adrenaline rush surged through me. "Someone get my dad a phone."

Vivienne nodded. "I'm on it." She sped away.

I continued to list my instructions to Yuri. "Get Corrine in here. Fast. We need to see if she can do something to ward off the attack or even escort Aiden to the hunters before they get here."

Yuri nodded and quickly made his way to The Sanctuary.

I looked straight at Aiden, unable to hide the tension in my voice. "Is there anything you can do to convince them not to attack?"

"I don't know if they'll listen, but I'll try. Perhaps it's best to have Kyle come with me... Our only ace against them is that we've found a possible cure."

I wondered what the hunters would do to Kyle and Derek if we actually found the cure, but I had to shove it out of my mind. "Do everything necessary to make them hold off on the attack. Let the hunters know that the vampires are surrendering. They don't have to kill everyone off."

"Surrendering?" Claudia gasped. "What? Sofia, they're going to kill us!"

"Not if you agree to try out the cure."

"A cure that we're not sure works."

A groan came from within the Pit and my stomach formed into knots. "It's going to work."

"It doesn't matter." Claudia shook her head. "Not all of us want to become human again."

My jaw tightened. "Would you rather die, Claudia? If we don't give them a good enough reason to hold off on their attack, this will be the end of The Shade."

Claudia was about to say something else, but Vivienne came just in time, phone in hand, to listen in on our conversation. She handed the phone to Aiden before addressing the blonde. "Sofia's right, Claudia. We can worry about the consequences later. Right now, we're just wasting time arguing over this."

Claudia scowled, but backed down.

Aiden dialed a number on the phone, putting it on loudspeaker.

"Hello?" Zinnia's familiar voice came from the other side.

"Zinnia, this is Aiden. Don't you dare hang up."

"Our superiors want you to know that we value everything that you've done for the hunters, but you understand the way it works."

"We found a cure. One of the vampires is now a human and the cure is being administered to Derek Novak as we speak. By the end of the day, he will be human again."

I was surprised to hear the conviction in my father's voice. It was as if he was one hundred percent sure that the cure would work on Derek. I tried to listen in on what was happening at the Pit but it seemed Derek had grown silent. I had no idea if that was a good or a bad sign.

"I don't believe you," Zinnia responded.

I could practically imagine the grimace on her face. The petite, raven-eyed hunter had never been a fan of me, but she was important to my father and to my late best friend, Ben. I'd had to deal with her snarkiness a lot while I was at the hunters' headquarters.

"There are thousands of humans here, Zinnia. A good many of them are women and children. Not all of them have to die. You can check the headquarters' database for a man named Kyle Madison. He was a vampire, but now he's human again."

"Get Kyle here," I told Claudia, before speaking to Zinnia over the loudspeaker. "Zinnia, this is Sofia."

"Great... if it isn't the princess of vampires herself."

"Look, we'll send Kyle to you so you can see for yourself. There *is* a cure. This could be the answer we're looking for. Please..."

All I got from her side was silence. I held my breath as I listened to her uneven breathing.

"I'll ask my superiors. I'll call you back."

Just like that, she hung up.

It was the longest five minutes of my entire life waiting for Zinnia to get back in touch with us. When the phone rang and Aiden answered, I held my breath in suspense.

"You'd better not be bluffing."

I heaved a sigh of relief, but then a scream from the Pit reminded me that I was still a far cry away from any semblance of peace.

CHAPTER 46: DEREK

The pain was indescribable and all my senses were in overdrive. I was aware of everything happening within a hundred-mile radius, but I couldn't comprehend any of it, because the agony was making it hard for me to have any coherent thought.

The light of the sun burned my skin and I was certain from the moment it hit me that there was no way I could survive it, but still there was this will to survive. I had no sense of time. The pain seemed endless. My heart would triple its pace and blood would pump at high speed throughout my system, then the pain would subside, giving me a couple of breaths, a momentary reprieve, before escalating once again.

There were voices outside the Pit, but I was only focused on one. Sofia's. She'd told me that she wouldn't leave, which both comforted and tormented me. I knew how compassionate she was.

I knew the effect my pain had on her.

I wanted it to end. I wanted it to end badly. One word and they would open that door to let me out of the Pit, but something kept me from ending my own misery, something more human than beastly. Hope. The hope that the light—no matter how painful it was—was my door to freedom.

The agony went for what felt like days until I reached a tipping point. I'd gotten used to the pain and I was about to surrender to death when I heard Sofia from the other side of the door. She was humming... her sweet, gentle voice hummed our song. It was exactly what I needed to remind myself that I couldn't die. I simply couldn't.

The tune played in the back of my mind and slowly but surely the pain subsided. A strange black substance began to ooze out of my skin, my mouth, even my nostrils.

I tried to make my claws come out. Nothing. I felt my mouth and I couldn't touch my fangs any longer.

The last stings of sunlight crept through the layers of my skin right down to the marrow of my bones. The black substance was replaced by radiant light oozing from my every pore.

I could feel life overtake me where nothing but death used to be. For the first time in five hundred years, I felt alive.

I rose to my feet, basking in the warmth of what I was certain was the afternoon sun. "Sofia!" I called out, my back still turned to the door as I lifted my face, eyes shut, to the sunlight. The ever-present coldness under my skin was gone. I felt warm from the inside out—a sensation I had long forgotten.

I could hear them remove the locks of the door. It swung wide open and without looking, I could sense Sofia nearby.

"Derek?" Her voice broke.

She approached me. I wasn't sure if it was just the high that I was feeling due to the success of the cure, but I was just as keenly aware of my surroundings then as I had been as a vampire.

Must be the adrenaline rush.

My senses came alive when Sofia touched my arm. She circled me in order to look into my face. I opened my eyes to find a mixture of wonderment, delight and apprehension on her beautiful face.

Tears ran down her cheeks as the sweetest sound I'd ever heard came through her lips: her laughter. She threw herself at me. "It worked. I was so scared... Derek... It worked."

I held her close, breathing in her scent, running my warm fingers through her soft, red hair. A vampire's senses were supposed to be far more heightened than those of a human, but holding my Sofia as a man—and not some beast—that sensation was far better than any I had experienced as a vampire.

I put Sofia down on her feet before leaning down to kiss her. It was the first time I'd been able to be around her without having to fight the urge to sink my teeth into her. I could touch her, hold her, be with her without wanting to devour her.

"As touching as this scene is, we have business to take care of." A deep, gruff voice spoke from behind us.

I turned around to find a stranger—an old man with graying hair, but perhaps one of the most intimidating presences I'd ever been around. Aiden was standing beside him.

"This is Arron," Aiden introduced us. "He's one of the hunter elders."

My gut clenched. *Hunters. In The Shade.* It felt like the beginning of the end.

"So this is him? The infamous Derek Novak? The ever-elusive

king of the vampires…" Arron stepped forward and retrieved a dagger from his pocket. "It's a pleasure to meet you."

He grabbed my arm and then ran the dagger down it, cutting deeply. I winced at the pain. I couldn't remember a dagger ever cutting so painfully when I was a vampire. We watched the wound, waiting for it to heal. Nothing happened.

Delight flickered in his dark brown eyes as a manic grin formed on his face. "Wonderful."

That was when I came upon an important conclusion. Vampire or not, I had absolutely no business putting my trust in the hunters. Sofia's face told me that she thought the exact same thing.

CHAPTER 47: SOFIA

It felt like every moment I spent with Derek was just borrowed time.

The hunters insisted that Derek, Kyle, Anna and I be shipped to hunter headquarters immediately. A select number of vampires were also to be taken to headquarters—mostly those who were willing to become human again. The rest were to remain on the island—under hunter surveillance. If we refused to cooperate, they would blow up The Shade.

Derek shook his head. "I'm not going to hunter headquarters to spend my honeymoon getting poked and prodded for your research."

We were at his penthouse, Arron and Zinnia sitting across the dining table from us. Aiden was sitting beside me, while Vivienne was sitting beside Derek.

I clasped Derek's hand tightly, wondering what it was that he had in mind. *Does he not realize the threat that the hunters pose to all of us?*

Arron eyed Derek. "We're not exactly giving you a choice here, Novak. Either you accept our demands or we destroy The Shade."

"Arron, they just got married. If you want people to study, Kyle and Anna are more than willing to take Derek and Sofia's place while the couple have their honeymoon." Aiden was speaking very carefully, as if he was afraid of making a mistake.

I'd never seen him as on edge as he was around Arron. I eyed the imposing old man with a sense of intrigue. *How can he make even my father tremble?*

Arron shifted his beady eyes toward Aiden. "Do you really think I care whether Derek Novak has a peaceful honeymoon? He may be human now, but that doesn't erase the hundreds of years when he was a beast."

Derek slammed his left hand down on the wooden table while tightening his grip on mine. "Let's cut the nonsense, Arron."

Vivienne was staring at her twin in horror. I could practically read what was going through her mind. *Does he not realize that he is no longer as powerful as he was yesterday? Does he not realize how vulnerable The Shade is?*

"Now that we've found a cure, you and I both know that to blow up as valuable an asset as The Shade—and all its citizens— would be complete nonsense. The Shade has existed autonomously for the past four hundred years. We have a strong workforce and our own technologies that have enabled us to thrive independently and without your knowledge. To destroy The Shade—after having found a cure—is stupidity."

"Are you saying that I'm bluffing, Novak?" Arron sat up

straight.

He appeared menacing to me, but a quick glance at my husband took my breath away. Derek was just as intimidating as a human as he was a vampire. Everything about him exuded power.

"Yes. I think you're bluffing. The cure changes everything and you know it. I was a hunter once and I've heard the whispers of what a cure could mean. You and I both know, Arron, that any vampire who would willingly take the cure isn't your enemy anymore."

Arron wetted his lips, giving thought to Derek's words. It seemed to me as if he wasn't used to people standing up to him.

"We are willing to cooperate with you, Arron, because we want this cure just as much as you do, but we're not going to do it as your prisoners or even as your hostages. I may be human now, and no longer the beast that I used to be, but I am still ruler of The Shade, and I will not let you treat my subjects like lab rats. If we're going to find a cure that won't require every single vampire to feed on Anna or my wife, then we're going to do it here in The Shade—*after* I spend time with my wife on our honeymoon."

"If I disagree?"

Derek shrugged. "Well, it's not like there's anything you can do about it, is there? I would think that you'd prefer our cooperation instead of taking us by force, and we both know that you're not going to blow the island up. It's a waste of a valuable resource."

Zinnia chuckled. "I don't believe this. He's talking about a partnership between hunters and the vampires of The Shade."

I could swear that I saw a flicker of respect in the way Arron eyed Derek as he gave thought to what Derek was saying.

He nodded. "Two weeks. I expect your honeymoon to be over in two weeks, and then we can discuss how to proceed. During that time, I expect to have full access to all the people and resources of The Shade, as well as the cooperation of everyone in finding a way to multiply the blood of the immunes. Do we have a deal?"

"No."

"Excuse me?" Clearly, Arron was getting irritated.

"One month. Our honeymoon will last for a month, and during that time, none of you will get in touch with us. You will give us the privacy we deserve. You are not to try to find us. Give my wife and me a chance to enjoy each other's company."

"How do I know you're not just going to run off?" Arron asked, squinting in suspicion.

"We couldn't do that even if we wanted to." I spoke up. "We've both fought and bled for the people of The Shade. We wouldn't abandon them. We couldn't."

Arron's gaze settled on me. He seemed to want to say something but thought better of it, but the way he was looking at me sent shivers down my spine. I could almost feel the hatred.

I had no idea who Arron was or what he was capable of, but I knew that he couldn't be trusted. I made a mental note to ask Aiden about him at some point, but for now, I found solace that even in his human form, Derek was still a force to be reckoned with.

Arron rose to his feet. "Very well. One month," he conceded.

I searched Derek's face for some sign of relief, but found none. He kept his poker face as he stood up to shake Arron's hand. "One month."

"Don't try anything foolish, Novak. There is value to The Shade, but our patience can only last so long."

Derek's grip on the older man's hand tightened. "I am a man of my word. I *will* see you in a month, and hopefully, no sooner than that."

Arron smirked. "I share the sentiment. Your presence grates at my every nerve, Novak. Make no mistake about it."

"In our absence, my sister Vivienne and Sofia's father Aiden will be in charge. I trust that they will see to what's best for The Shade."

I was surprised that Derek would trust my father, but whatever surprise I felt was overshadowed by Vivienne's face. Fear, uncertainty, apprehension—qualities that I rarely saw in the Seer's cool and confident countenance.

***

Her face was etched in my mind the first day Derek and I spent on the sandy beaches of Tahiti. I felt guilty that I was worrying over Vivienne and The Shade. I had every right to enjoy my honeymoon, but I couldn't help it.

"How do you think they're doing back in The Shade?" I asked. We were a few feet away from the water, bright orange beach towels spread on the ground, a picnic basket and our clothes sprawled around us. We were both seated enjoying the sun's rays.

"It's our first day here, Sofia. You're already worried about what's happening back home?"

Home. The word struck a chord. Derek was right. The Shade, with all its craziness, had become our home. I still couldn't wrap my mind around the idea that I was married to the ruler of The Shade.

"I can't help it. It feels selfish that we're having a great time, while having no idea what's going on in there. I mean, do you really trust that Arron will keep his word and..."

"Trust me on this, Sofia. The cure changes everything. Arron would be a fool to go against us. With the cure in play, The Shade has become a sanctuary to all vampires. I have my reasons for believing that he won't do anything he'll regret, but I don't want to discuss it right now." Derek sat up and began running his hands through my hair. "Be here with me, Sofia. Let's enjoy this. Let's be that normal young couple for once. After everything we had to go through to get here, I think we deserve that... don't you?"

He gently brushed his fingers over my cheek, tucking loose strands of my hair behind my ear. I smiled. "Of course I do." I took a deep breath and forced myself to enjoy this moment with my husband. *My husband.* I'd never dreamed that I would get married at eighteen, but I had no regrets. Derek was more than I could ever have hoped for.

We both set our sights on our surroundings, enjoying the scenery and the sound of the waves. I couldn't remember ever seeing Derek as happy. He seemed light and carefree. If I didn't know better, I would've pegged him for just another teenager, enjoying a vacation with his lover.

I loved how much he was enjoying the sunlight. His skin was white as a sheet in broad daylight, but even though I warned him that he might end up looking like a tomato by the end of the day, he didn't care. He hadn't had the privilege of basking in sunlight for hundreds of years.

"Don't you know that it's rude to stare?" he quipped without even bothering to look at me. "I can't believe you, Sofia... You're shamelessly checking me out in public." This time, he looked my way and winked. "Don't make it so obvious that you think I'm hot."

"I married the most humble man on earth," I muttered. He playfully threw a fistful of sand my way. "Hey!" I squealed, jumping up from my beach towel. I began patting off the sand from my bare legs before scowling at him.

"Come on, Sofia... Admit it. You think I'm hot." He stretched out on his towel, his hands tucked behind his head.

I rolled my eyes. "I think"—I paused and narrowed my eyes at him—"that"—I leaned forward toward him, while fisting a clump of sand with the hand I was using to support my weight—"you're going to get sunburn if you don't let me massage some more sun block on you." I grinned before throwing the fistful of sand onto his bare chest. "I also think that you can be an arrogant pain in the neck sometimes." I winked. "No pun intended."

He didn't seem to mind the sand on his chest at all. He grabbed me by the waist and pulled me on top of him. He ran his hands through my hair, lowering my head so he could kiss me. Both of us had yet to explore all the changes that we were dealing with since he turned back into a human, but one thing I knew for sure: he was just as good a kisser as a human as he was a vampire.

By the time our lips parted, I was out of breath and flushed red. I could feel the heat climb from the tips of my toes right up to the freckles on my cheekbones. I drew a breath before looking at him. He had a smirk on his face. "See? Hot." He raised his dark brows at me, obviously proud of his performance.

I could barely think straight, so coming up with a good comeback was close to impossible. I was surprised by how ridiculously attractive I found him at that moment. *I can't believe he still has this effect on me. He is fully aware of it too...*

"That's a first. I don't think I remember ever rendering Sofia Novak speechless." He grinned before once again uttering my name. "Sofia Novak." His hands tightened around my waist, his thumbs gently caressing my skin.

I placed both hands over his chest as I propped myself up to look him straight in the eyes. "We did it, Derek. We made it."

He smiled. "Didn't I tell you that I was going to marry you? You should believe me more often."

"What is it about you turning back into human that has made you so arrogant?" I teased, though I had to admit that I was greatly amused by this playful side of him.

He was about to respond when we heard a grumbling. His eyes widened and his arms clasped around me protectively. "What was that?"

I listened and there it was again.

"Did you hear that?" he asked, looking alarmed.

I burst out laughing. "That was your stomach, dummy."

He frowned. "Mine? Are you sure it wasn't yours?"

"Poor baby... You've forgotten what it's like when a human gets hungry. Your fangs—not that you still have them anyway—won't begin to ache and your blood won't begin to pound. Not anymore. When you're hungry, your stomach growls." I reached for our picnic basket and grabbed half a cheese sandwich. I shoved the whole thing into his mouth before he could even respond to what I had just said. Whatever it was he was going to say got muffled by the sound of his own chewing.

I snickered as he chewed and swallowed the food. "I never thought I would find the sight of a man eating food sexy."

"You admit it finally!" He raised his arms in the air in triumph. "You're so into me."

"Well, I married you..." I shoved a chocolate-covered strawberry into his mouth. "But we both know that you're just as into me as I am into you."

He chewed and swallowed. "Truth." He kissed me.

The moment our lips met, an image flashed through my mind. *Blood dripping... flowing... lots and lots of it...* My heart began pounding against my chest. I gasped and raised my head, stunned.

"What is it?" Derek asked. "What's wrong?"

"I'm not sure..." I frowned. I couldn't deny the fear. Suddenly, I felt like we were being watched, like we were in danger. "Could we go somewhere else, please?" I asked him.

"Of course," Derek said, looking at me with concern.

We hurriedly packed up. As we headed back to the hotel, I clung to Derek tightly.

"Everything's going to be all right now, Sofia," he assured me, kissing my forehead.

"I know," I told him. But I still couldn't shake the feeling that the cure and our marriage were in no way the end. This was only the beginning.

CHAPTER 48: VIVIENNE

The number of hunters Arron sent to "patrol" The Shade left me ill at ease. To trust them would be a fatal mistake.

I couldn't blame Derek for the choice he'd made. I had to trust that he knew what he was doing, but danger loomed over all of us, and everyone in The Shade felt it.

Ian, Anna and Kyle had been brought to hunter headquarters. We'd asked that regular reports of their status be given to us, but it had been two weeks and not a single piece of news had been shared with us. We'd followed up several times, only to be ignored.

The tension in The Shade was growing by the minute. Even the humans admitted to holding a severe mistrust towards the hunters.

"What are we up against?" I asked Aiden. We were standing on top of one of the towers of the Crimson Fortress, looking over the island, a soft evening wind blowing against our faces. "Who is this

Arron?"

Aiden shrugged. "He's the one in control. He calls all the shots as far as hunters are concerned."

"What's he like?"

"Ruthless." Aiden frowned. "I honestly don't understand why he agreed to Derek's terms. That was unlike him, but something about their conversation... They knew something. It's like they came to an understanding, Arron and Derek. I'm not sure what it is. I just know that this grace period Arron is giving us... it comes with a price."

As if the constant visions of the future weren't already bothering me enough, Aiden had to add this tidbit of knowledge, increasing my discomfort with the whole situation. "If you didn't feel right about it, why didn't you say something about it then?"

Aiden shrugged. "Derek and Sofia went through hell to be together. From the looks of things, they'll return to utter chaos once they get back here. They deserve their one month."

"You're right." I nodded. I wanted to reassure myself that we were going to be okay, that my brother knew what he was doing. Still, something was nagging at me. "Tell me, Aiden, do you really believe for one minute that the hunters would be willing to work with us?"

"Not for one minute. We all became hunters for one reason and one reason alone, Vivienne. It's because every single one of us harbors a deep hatred for vampires. I can only imagine what kind of hatred Arron has for your kind. A lifetime of that isn't easy to just forget and let go of because a cure has emerged."

I was silent as I thought through what I'd just been told. I began shaking my head.

"What is it, Vivienne? Why all of a sudden are you asking me these questions? I was expecting you to ask them soon after Derek and Sofia left. I was surprised that you didn't."

"I didn't want to ask because I wanted to first observe. Well, that and because I didn't want to deal with the reality of it all, but with the visions and the way things are being handled here in The Shade... The sense of tension and animosity... It feels like..."

"A volcano waiting to explode." Aiden squared his shoulders, standing to his full height, as he crossed his arms over his chest. It was as if he was steeling himself for something. "What visions have you been seeing, Vivienne?"

I cringed. I didn't know where to begin. Each vision was confusing, oftentimes surreal, never as clear as the visions I used to have. Still, each vision I saw had one thing in common: blood. Lots and lots of blood.

And that was why I longed for Derek's presence. I'd never felt as safe as I did when I was around him, but Xavier's challenge was still ringing in my ears—the challenge to live life for myself, on my own. That was the only thing that kept me from trying to locate my brother and his wife.

I drew a deep breath as I turned my attention toward Aiden. "I don't understand the visions, Aiden. I can't even explain them, but what I do know is that the hunters are only the beginning of our problems. Derek killed Emilia over Sofia, then they were able to find the cure. The Elder isn't just going to let that go."

"But we all know what Emilia said before she died. The Elder can't touch them as long as they remain in the light."

"There's darkness in everyone, Aiden. One dance with darkness and the Elder will capitalize on that. Besides, the Elder doesn't have to go directly for them—not yet."

"What do you mean?"

"I think he's going to attack the people who matter to them first. He's going to come for us."

Aiden's brows furrowed as he cleared his throat. He directed his eyes forward, toward the horizon. "Then let him come."

I swallowed hard, wondering if we had what it took to conquer what we were up against. "True sanctuary has been found. Now, the battle to keep everyone away from it has begun."

Epilogue: Kiev

I couldn't pry my eyes away from Sofia. She was a stunning find and I could immediately see why Derek Novak had fallen for her. There was something about Sofia that drew me to her and I couldn't help but feel a pang of jealousy as I stood beneath the shade of a cliff, watching the married couple frolicking in the waves.

You want her.

The voice came with a chilling breeze that crept from the nape of my neck to the base of my spine. A coldness enveloped me as my father made his dark presence known.

My entire body tensed. Despite the number of years I had spent serving the Elder, I'd never gotten used to his presence. I had no idea how Emilia had been able to bear it—she'd spent more time with the Elder than I ever had. Truth be told, I'd been thankful when Emilia came to the Blood Keep. She had gotten most of the

Elder's attention; thus, more of his anger.

I swallowed hard as I fixed my gaze on the redhead as she leaped into the arms of Derek Novak. "I don't think that bastard deserves her."

The Elder's taunting scoff echoed against my eardrums. It was perhaps the most terrifying thing about the Elder. When he was around, he invaded my senses—every single one. Except my sight. He was a force heard, tasted, smelled and felt, but he was never seen. I was beginning to think that he was nothing but a substance, a darkness that consumed those who allowed it.

I don't care who deserves Sofia Novak. She deserves my wrath for taking both Derek Novak and Emilia from me.

I clenched my fists at the mention of my dead sister. I had never been fond of Emilia, but her death was still enough reason to put Derek Novak through as much pain as possible. However, my master had instructed us that Derek was not to be harmed or killed. Our goal was to draw him back to the dark side.

"He's human now, Master. Why do you still want him?"

Who says I still want him? I couldn't care less about Derek Novak now. Though I must warn you, Kiev. He doesn't realize it yet, but he may be more powerful in his present state than he ever was as one of our kind. Do not underestimate him.

I paused for a moment, confused. "If we're not after Derek Novak, then who..."

We're after Sofia.

Despite my bewilderment, I was thrilled by the prospect of having Sofia under our control... *my* control. "Because she's immune?"

Not just that. Derek and Sofia Novak will have children. Once Sofia is bearing her first, it is of utmost importance that she be brought to the Blood Keep. Their children will be too much of a threat unless they are raised by us.

My stomach turned. The idea that Derek, who had succumbed so many times to darkness, could marry and even have children with Sofia, the embodiment of light, made me sick.

Do not disappoint me, Kiev. Keep those blood-red eyes of yours on them and once you are certain that she is pregnant, take her. They took my child. Now I'll take theirs.

I breathed a sigh of relief the moment the Elder's presence left. With him gone, I was able to be honest with myself regarding why I wanted Sofia.

She gave me a lingering sense of hope.

At that moment, I swore to myself that I would do everything to get Derek Novak out of the picture and make Sofia mine. Because if her light could still save the likes of Derek Novak, perhaps I wasn't too far gone.

Sofia represented the one thing that had eluded me over the past centuries: redemption.

Ready for the PENULTIMATE book in Derek and Sofia's story?

Book 6: A Gate of Night is the **penultimate** book in Derek and Sofia's series as we move toward the thrilling finale in Book 7!

It is available to purchase now!
Visit www.bellaforrest.net for more information.

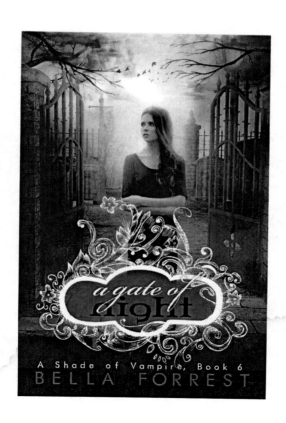

ΠOTE FROM THE AUTHOR

Dear Shaddict,

If you want to stay informed about my latest book releases, visit this website to subscribe to my new releases email list: www.forrestbooks.com

You can also check out my other novels by visiting my website: www.bellaforrest.net

And don't forget to come say hello on Facebook: www.facebook.com/AShadeOfVampire

Thank you for reading!

Love,
Bella

CPSIA information can be obtained
at www.ICGtesting.com
Printed in the USA
LVOW12s1558180716

496766LV00003B/693/P